Crazy FOR YOU

RINA GRAY

Crimson Romance

New York London Toronto Sydney New Delhi

CRIMSON
ROMANCE
Crimson Romance
An Imprint of Simon & Schuster, Inc.
1230 Avenue of the Americas
New York, NY 10020

First Crimson Romance MAY 2017

CRIMSON ROMANCE and colophon are trademarks of Simon and Schuster.

For information about special discounts for bulk purchases, please contact Simon & Schuster Special Sales at 1-866-506-1949 or business@simonandschuster.com.

The Simon & Schuster Speakers Bureau can bring authors to your live event. For more information or to book an event contact the Simon & Schuster Speakers Bureau at 1-866-248-3049 or visit our website at www.simonspeakers.com.

Cover images ©Shutterstock/wavebreakmedia

Manufactured in the United States of America

10 9 8 7 6 5 4 3 2 1

Library of Congress Cataloging-in-Publication Data has been applied for.

ISBN 978-1-5072-0622-5
ISBN 978-1-5072-0473-3 (ebook)

Chapter One

Seated on the dance studio wood floor, fists against her thighs, Charlotte Jones stretched her muscles to the limit, cooling down after the grueling class she'd finished teaching ten minutes ago.

"Charlotte, honey, we need to talk."

Charlotte looked up, not at all surprised to find Tiana and Melanie staring at her in the mirror. From her friends' expressions, she knew what they wanted to discuss. Both had been trying to get her to meet up for the past few days. Tiana, the ringleader of the soon-to-be intervention, stood legs splayed. Hands on hips, her toothpick arms and puffed-out chest were the perfect impersonation of the Man of Steel.

Charlotte took a deep breath—for patience, not from the cooldown—and studied her two friends' reflections. They were her best friends—heck, the only friends she'd made since moving to New York City after college four years ago. The friends Charlotte had met when she first moved to the city were nice, but after she'd declined invites to social events that required money, they'd stopped asking. Somehow over the next four years she became a homebody.

Mel and Tiana were a godsend. Although the two had been friends since high school, they'd happily, and sometimes without taking no for an answer, invited Charlotte out, or to stay in for girls' night. Charlotte had met Melanie through her boss, Damien. Although Mel had lived in Atlanta for a while, she'd often traveled to New York to cover sports events. It was obvious to Charlotte or anyone who'd paid attention that Melanie and Damien loved each other, but they were too afraid to risk their friendship. Thankfully, Mel had taken matters into her own hands by masterminding an operation to seduce her best friend, Damien. Around the same time, Charlotte had met Tiana when she moved to New York for a job offer. Tiana had often regaled Charlotte and Mel with funny stories about her office prank wars with her grad school nemesis, Nathan. "Hello, earth to Charlotte." Tiana cocked her head.

Melanie twirled her long, curly locks around her finger. Her usually genuine smile was absent. In its place perched a tight, cheer-captain smile.

Charlotte knew why they wanted to talk. She hadn't exactly been her normally cheerful self the past few months. Her stomach grumbled, the true culprit. Truth be told, she was *hangry*—hungry and angry. *I'll eat a few carrot sticks after "the talk."* Smiling brightly in the mirror, she hoped to convey that she was mentally stable. "Let me finish stretching. I'll meet you both in the locker room."

Melanie's tight shoulders relaxed, and her smile transformed from fake to relieved. "All right, Charlotte. See you in a few."

They left, and Charlotte finally relaxed. Instead of stretching, she stared at herself in the mirror, verifying and validating her weight-loss progress.

Jiggling an arm in the air, she flexed a bicep and then pinched the tricep. "Not bad." She smiled, finally seeing the results of seemingly endless push-ups and pull-ups.

Her hands then slid over her blue fitted tank top. Squeezing her sides, she gathered doughy, plump flesh. Strands of dark brown hair slipped from the topknot at the crown of her head to frame her oval-shaped face and caramel skin.

You're perfect just as you are, Charlotte. Don't let nobody tell you different, ya hear? Her stomach clenched, anticipating the burst of pain that hit and spread whenever she remembered that fragile, Deep South voice.

"Work in progress, Charlie," she comforted herself and blinked away tears. "Don't give up." *Besides, you have no choice.*

Rising from her seated position, she jogged to the locker room. Every second was an opportunity to burn calories. She'd read somewhere that keeping the body in an active state could turn her metabolism into a virtual furnace for burning fat. And she needed all the help she could get.

"Charlotte!" One of the moms at the center and a member of her church waved her down.

"Hey, Ms. Dana! Everything okay?"

Ms. Dana powered walked across the Astroturf. "Yes, yes. I just wanted to thank you for helping Keri with her college essays."

Charlotte waved her hand. "That's no problem. I—"

"No, Charlotte I'm serious. You came to our house, spent hours of your time. My husband and I ... we're not great at the writing thing. Keri's dad is great at math, and I'm not really great at either subject." Ms. Dana hopped from one foot to another and lowered her eyes.

Charlotte reached for Ms. Dana's hand. "We all have our talents and I'm glad I could help. All I ask is that you tell me when she gets accepted to Columbia."

"Of course." Ms. Dana smiled. "I'll see you at church, right?"

"Yes. I'm ushering this Sunday and hosting the bake sale."

"Saint Charlotte." The older woman smiled and squeezed her hand. "Always giving and volunteering. You're a good woman."

Charlotte waved off the praise. "I enjoy helping out and I've got the time."

And I have no life.

"And we appreciate all that you do. I'll see you around."

"Later!" Charlotte continued toward the locker room and then pushed opened the door. She caught her friends near a stall, whispering in hushed tones. The door slammed behind her. Their heads jerked, and eyes focused on her.

"What's up?" She walked to her locker, gearing herself up for *the talk*.

No matter what they said, she would stay the course. After her doctor had delivered the scary news that she was prediabetic and well on her way to type 2 diabetes, she'd become motivated.

All her life, she could never shake the extra pounds—not even through dance. Charlotte had discovered her love of dancing as a preteen when she'd signed up for classes at the local community center. Her mother had been so happy, and predicted Charlotte would lose the "baby fat" in no time, but it never happened.

But dance had never been about weight loss. It'd allowed her to escape to a new world, to get lost in hip hop, R&B, and jazz. Years later, she'd finally cracked the code and lost twenty-six pounds! Twenty-six whole pounds, and she wasn't stopping for anyone—even well-meaning friends. Besides, they could never understand what it was like. Compared to her petite friends, she was nearly triple their size at an eighteen. *Or am I a sixteen now?*

Melanie squinted her eyes and tilted her head. "You seem a bit out of sorts lately." Tiana nodded in agreement. Charlotte mentally rolled her eyes.

Melanie continued. "I don't know how to say this but … you need a sandwich. And not a small one on multigrain bread. Like one of those footlongs from Subway."

"Or Panera, if you're feeling fancy," Tiana added.

"A sandwich?" Charlotte shifted her gaze from one friend to another. Both were nodding frantically. "Are we having this little chat because I snapped at the Girl Scout?"

Tiana cocked her head and snorted. "You made her cry, Charlotte, which is crazy because *you* cry during Hallmark commercials and coo at every baby you see. You have to admit this is not typical Charlotte Jones behavior."

Charlotte twirled the combo into the lock, swung the door open, and removed her gym bag and purse. "Not my fault.

She was pushing Thin Mints. Anything with the word 'thin' in it should be for people who are or want to be thin. Those darn things were a hundred and sixty calories for five freaking cookies! That's practically false advertising."

Tiana put her hand over her mouth and whispered to Melanie, "She's worse than we thought."

"What's that?" Charlotte asked, although she'd clearly heard Tiana.

"You heard me. You've been so uptight lately. Hell, you need a sandwich, a drink, and a man."

The tips of Charlotte's ears burned, and heat rushed to her cheeks. She squeezed her hands into fists. "A sandwich is full of carbs and calories. Drinks are liquid calories, and a man ... is calorie-free but not drama-free. I don't need that in my life right now."

Well, there was *one* man who was worth the drama, but he didn't even know she existed. Okay, he did, but not much else. She was the living and breathing example of the Alicia Keys song "You Don't Know My Name." She snorted. Everyone knew Alicia Keys, but the last time Jake Ross saw Charlotte, he'd called her Charlene. That was back when Damien was Jake's publicist and Charlotte was Damien's assistant. The pro baseball player had met her more than a half dozen times and still didn't remember her name.

"Earth to Charlotte," Melanie yelled, snapping fingers in front of Charlotte's face.

"Sorry, Mel." Closing the locker door, she turned to face her friends. "Look, you guys are right. I have been a bit uptight. I'll work on it."

"It's not just you being uptight, honey." Melanie stepped closer and placed a hand on Charlotte's shoulder. "Ever since you went back home for your grandmother's funeral, you've been down. I get it and I know you two were close. How are you and your family holding up?"

"My family is good," Charlotte lied.

Nearly six months had passed, and she still couldn't believe her grandmother, the only soul who'd understood and loved her unconditionally, had died. Charlotte didn't talk about it—not to her family, nor her friends. And she definitely didn't want to share that a few months after Big Mama died, Charlotte learned she had the very thing that killed her grandmother. But if she lost weight and took her anti-diabetic medication, she could get her blood sugar level back to normal. *And no diabetes.*

Melanie squeezed Charlotte's shoulder. "That's good. Back to the sandwich. I know you're focused and, believe me, I understand you want to stay on track with your weight loss. You look great, by the way." She waved. "But you need to do it in a way that lets you sustain your results *and* your sanity. I don't want to lecture you, but we are here if you need us. We're happy to help."

Charlotte smiled and studied her friends' petite frames. Flat stomachs and no rolls in sight. "Sure, hon. I will." *Not.* "And to put your mind at ease, I'll be sure to eat an extra piece of chicken at your cookout this weekend. Deal?"

Tiana and Melanie smiled at her. "Deal."

• • •

"Jake, Jake! Is it true that you, Destiny Collins, and Rafaela Martin are in some sort of polygamous relationship?"

Dodging the paparazzi's questions, Jake Ross shook his head and hurried through the doors of Refurbished Dreams, the nonprofit where he volunteered. The organization helped young athletes from middle school to high school rehab injuries. If the injury was too extensive, they'd help the young people find other dreams. Damien, his old publicist, had strong-armed him into helping a young man who wasn't adjusting well. After a few weeks of volunteering, Jake had fallen in love with the kids.

"Is it true you were abducted by aliens and given the ability to throw fastballs?"

"Aliens, huh? That's a new one." *At least the last question was about baseball.*

Camera bulbs continued to flash, but thankfully the rabid paparazzi didn't follow him inside. Turning the corner, he walked toward the lobby to sign in.

He smiled when he saw his former mentee seated behind the desk. "What's going on, Dax?" The young man stood, walked around the desk, and raised his hand. They both grinned as they slapped palms, wiggled fingers, and bumped fists and then chests in an elaborate handshake routine. Every pro player had one, and Jake had created it as motivation for Dax while he rehabbed his rotator cuff.

Looking over Jake's shoulder, Dax shook his head. "I see you've brought the circus with you again."

Jake rubbed a hand over his face and sighed. "Yeah, man. Sorry about that. They know my volunteer schedule, so they hound me."

"We don't mind," a voice behind him just said. He turned around to greet his former publicist, Damien. "Press equals more exposure for Refurbished Dreams."

"Okay, guys, you ready to learn a new routine today?"

Jake's neck prickled when he heard that sultry, Southern voice. Damien's hot little media coordinator had taken it upon herself to offer dance classes after the nonprofit added a studio. She'd already amassed quite a following—and not just of people taking the class. Older brothers, fathers, hell even grandfathers stood around to watch the normally shy beauty roll, dip, and shake her hips. He hadn't noticed Charlotte before the classes. She'd worked for Damien, Jake's former publicist, and he recognized her face. During their meetings, Charlotte would always greet him at the office, hand him his coffee just the way he liked it, and in her soft voice ask if he needed anything else.

There was no invitation for more in her voice, like most single or not-so-single women he encountered. Just pure Southern hospitality. Not that he'd give her more. Good girl vibes dripped off her. Like she sung with birds, skipped around in a forest, and spoke in a secret language to her woodland creature friends.

He chuckled, remembering her back when he was a hot shot rookie. Ankles crossed, legs squeezed tight, and skirt at a respectable length below her knees. Prim and proper. Cute, but boring. *Or so I thought.* Until he saw her lead a hip-hop dance class six months ago. He stopped dead center in the middle of the gym, waiting for her to turn around. He needed to see if her face was as gorgeous as her ass that swayed to the beat. So engrossed, Jake hadn't even noticed Damien sneak up behind him until he slapped his shoulder. He leaned in and whispered, "Don't even think about touching my employee."

"C-charlene?" Jake was shocked at the revelation. *Dayum! Damien's little wallflower assistant can move like that?*

"Her name is Charlotte, fool, and she's like a little sister to me. Stay. Away." Damien growled and squeezed his shoulder, making his warning clear.

The warning was a waste of Damien's breath. Jake hadn't needed it. Despite popular belief, he didn't enjoy breaking hearts, which was why he stuck to a specific type of woman. Sweet and kind and sensitive were a no-go.

Damien, Jake, and Dax turned around to the open studio as Beyoncé's latest hit blared from the speakers.

Charlotte faced the mirror as she snaked her body into a slow figure-eight twist.

Every time he watched those hips zig and zag, that back arch, and lush ass jiggle, he promised himself that next time he would look away. No staring like a pervert with his hands down his pants in a triple-X movie theater.

The kids at the center probably thought he had a small bladder considering the number of times he rushed off after gazing at Charlotte for too long. And the promise he'd made to himself was always empty because no way in hell was he missing her performance. He was spellbound by the brown-eyed, curvy beauty.

The music sped up, and she twirled, stomped her feet, and twisted her body to the rocking beat.

Dax leaned over and put his hands on Jake's shoulder. "Damn, she's fine. And she's thick with it, too. Well, she was until she started losing all that weight." Lust dripped from his just-reached-puberty voice.

Damien whacked him upside the head.

"Oww, D!"

"Stop talking about Charlotte like that. She's a good girl."

Yeah, but you wouldn't know it by the way she moves. Jake was a bad boy, and he liked his women bad. Real bad. Mind blowing sex and things that would make Madonna blush.

Unfortunately, his bad-boy rep was the reason why his face graced the covers of gossip rags instead of sports magazines. And it was the reason why he was in jeopardy of losing a potential multi-million-dollar sponsorship deal. The media had caught him, Rafaela, and Destiny having sex in Destiny's trailer on a movie set. It had been exciting, hot, and he was thinking with his dick instead of his head. Next thing he knew, a swarm of cameras surrounded them, and now Jake Jr. had its own Tumblr site and Twitter account. Thankfully, Fiete had stuck by him, although they had removed his ads for a few months until things cooled down. They also cut a big chunk of his contract, due to a morality clause, slicing his profit to nearly half of what had been offered.

I'll get Threx to sign me on. Shaking off his thoughts, Jake shifted his attention back to Charlotte. She lifted a hand to her forehead and slowed her movements, swaying to the music. Except, this time it didn't seem like a dance. Bending over at the waist, she clutched her knees and closed her eyes.

His heartbeat tripled time. *She's about to pass out!* Jake rushed into the studio, but he wasn't able to reach her in time.

Charlotte fell, and her head cracked against the wood floor.

"Charlotte! Oh my God!" one of her students shouted.

Jake pushed concerned parents and students out of the way to get to her. "Give her space!" Gathering her into his arms, he pressed two fingers against her carotid artery and sighed at the weak, erratic beat.

"Charlotte." He gently shook her shoulders. "Open your eyes, Charlotte."

Big brown eyes fluttered open, blinked, and then squinted up at him. "You know my name," she whispered in an awed voice.

Chapter Two

The pressure on Charlotte's eyelids had to weigh two tons, and her head … good God! Had Thor swung his mighty hammer and whacked her temple?

A wave of nausea rolled from her stomach to her throat. Groaning against the pain, she closed her eyes. *Sleep.* The deep, dark abyss was a haven from the persistent pang in her skull.

"Of course I know who you are. Now wake up, Sleeping Beauty."

A grunt that sounded more like an animal and less like a lady escaped her throat. No way was she prying her eyes open, not even to stare into the hypnotic eyes of her sexy crush as he cradled her in his arms.

"Charlotte, I really need you to look at me."

A delicious tingle spread up her spine. Jake's deep, sexy voice could convince a nun to forego her oath. She slowly opened her eyes. Four gray eyes set against caramel skin blinked at her. Jake waved fingers in front of her face, but she could only focus on his eyes.

"How many?" His deep voice made her shiver.

"Four eyes. You look good with four eyes."

His laughter vibrated against her arms. She curled deeper into him, feeling warm and safe.

Strong fingers massaged her scalp. "Mmm," she purred.

"She's got a knot on the back of her head, and she's not seeing straight. Somebody call an ambulance."

"Already done," a far away and familiar voice answered. "They're on the way."

"Going back to sleep now," she said.

"Stay with me, angel."

"I'm no angel."

"Yes, you are."

She tried raising her hands, but her arms were tucked tight against his body. "Really? I don't feel a halo." She sighed. Even to her ears, she knew it was heavy on the dramatic side.

"What's wrong?" he asked.

"I don't want to die. I haven't even had an orgasm yet."

Jake's glittery gray eyes danced with laughter as the edges of her vision grew dark.

Dying in Jake's arms isn't a bad way to go.

• • •

Jake tapped his toes as he and Charlotte waited for the doctor. When the medics went to put Charlotte in the ambulance, he hadn't been able to let her go. Dammit! The woman had scared him half to death as she drifted in and out of their hilarious conversation.

The next thing he knew, he'd shoved Damien out of the way to ride with her to the emergency room. The medics wouldn't let him at first, but then he lied and said he was her boyfriend. Damien would probably give him shit about that later. *Too damn bad.*

The curtain swished open. Stethoscope wrapped around his neck, a man with dark blond hair stepped into the room, head down as he studied a chart.

"Ms. ... " The doctor raised his head and smiled. "Hey! Jake Ross! I'm a big fan."

"Thanks, man." Jake nodded and then glanced at Charlotte. "How's she doing?"

The doctor cleared his throat, and his blue eyes focused on Jake. "I know Nurse Wootson informed you that Ms. Jones is severely dehydrated, which is why we have her on the IV. We'll also need to do a CT scan to check for a concussion. Once she wakes, I'll ask her a few questions to test her cognitive skills."

"I'm awake, doc," a sweet voice whispered from the bed.

"Ms. Jones, I'm Dr. Merrick." Reaching into his coat pocket, he pulled out a small flashlight. "You gave your boyfriend quite a scare. How are you feeling?"

She scrunched that cute button nose. "Boyfriend?" She tilted her head at Jake.

The doctor raised an eyebrow.

"We're trying to keep it a secret, so we don't get harassed by the media." He forced a smile and then returned his focus on Charlotte, giving her a look that he hoped conveyed, "Play along."

"Answer Dr. Merrick, angel."

She nodded and whispered, "A little sluggish, but I'm good."

"Can you sit up?" the doctor asked. "I want to ask you a few questions, okay?"

"All right." She pulled herself up and scooted against the pillow.

"Do you have a history of fainting? Any reason to cause you to pass out today?"

"Well, I ... " She glanced past Dr. Merrick's shoulder to peek at Jake and then looked down. A blush bloomed across her cheeks before she cleared her throat. "I've been doing an intense diet and exercise routine."

Curiosity led Jake to a chair near Charlotte. His hand sought hers. She seemed embarrassed and he wanted to give her comfort.

"Can you tell me about your routine, Ms. Jones? How many calories do you consume and how long are your workouts?"

Charlotte nibbled her lips and gripped the blanket draped across her legs.

Jake squeezed her other hand. "Tell him, Charlotte. He just wants to help."

Taking a deep breath, she focused on the doctor. "I have one main meal a day, usually four hundred to five hundred calories. And then, for a snack in the afternoon, I usually eat a kale salad or cabbage soup."

Is she serious? Only six hundred calories a day? No wonder she's been dropping weight so quickly.

"Mmm." The doctor typed notes on a tablet. "And your workouts?"

"Umm … usually two, sometimes three times a day. I'm a part-time dance instructor, so I create the routines and then teach the classes. I also go to the gym and run two miles a day on the treadmill."

The doctor stopped taking notes and shook his head. "You're running yourself into the ground, Ms. Jones. It's like a car with no gas—heck, with no wheels. You don't have enough energy to sustain your lifestyle. I highly advise that you eat more food."

"I will."

"Good." Dr. Merrick turned to face Jake. "And you make sure to feed your girlfriend."

Charlotte's eyes popped, and her teeth sank into her bottom lip.

Jake nodded. She needed to work on her poker face. "Will do, Dr. Merrick." A chirp from his phone interrupted the conversation. He'd been ignoring it, worried about Charlotte. Now that she was awake, he pulled the phone from his back pocket and swiped it open. Eight missed calls from his agent, Gina, and two from his publicist, Mark.

Shit. What now?

"Excuse me. Charlotte, I'll be back in a minute. Hang tight, okay?"

"Oh-okay, Jake."

His hands started to move toward her brown cherub face. But instead of giving in to the desire to stroke her soft skin, he squeezed his hand into a fist and stood to leave.

Dr. Merrick continued to speak to Charlotte as Jake walked into the hallway.

Opening the text app, he was greeted by new messages from Melanie, Damien, and his agent Gina.

Melanie: Hi sweetie. We're all worried over here. Which hospital are you in and what is her room number? Thank you for taking care of my friend.

Damien: Answer your damn phone!

Jake shook his head and decided to respond to Melanie first. One, because her text was much more reasonable, and two, because it would piss Damien off that Jake texted his wife.

Damien was still mildly upset that Jake and Melanie had faked a relationship once to make him jealous. Of course, kissing her once hadn't helped either. But it was all in the name of love. And who was he to turn his back on helping a friend find true love?

Jake smiled as he typed.

Hey, babe. She doesn't have a room yet. We're in the ER at Montefiore. Not sure if they'll admit her overnight. She's up and alert. The doctor is with her now.

He skipped over Tiana's text because Mel was probably beside her and zeroed in on his agent's.

Gina: Your girlfriend was rushed to the hospital because she's pregnant with your baby???? Apparently you don't want the multimillion-dollar deal with Threx to go through. Call me. Now!

Damn. *What blabbermouth at the hospital lied?* Everyone at Refurbished Dreams would have kept their mouths shut.

Jake called Gina. She was a spitfire and was probably about to blow.

"What in the entire hell, Jake? Do you know how many calls and emails I've gotten in the past hour?" Her Italian accent was thick with anger.

"Gina, it's not what you think." Jake recounted the story between her groans and growls.

"Jake, you're a celebrity. You can't lie about having a girlfriend, especially when you just got dinged for having a threesome with a model and an actress. And let's not even bring up the Denise McKesson pregnancy scare."

The Denise McKesson fiasco was just over a year ago. The worst part had been disappointing his family. They'd questioned him mercilessly, asking about the C-list actress, her family, and her morals. He couldn't answer one question. Denise had been a one-night stand that wouldn't die. *Stage-one clinger.* He saw it in her dark eyes before they screwed, but his dick hadn't cared. She was hot and willing. *Big, big mistake.*

His grandmother had admonished him after he couldn't even recall when they'd hooked up to confirm the date Denise had become pregnant. After Grandma Etta hit him upside the head with her purse that could double as a carry-on bag, she'd chewed him out for hours.

But underneath her sharp words—and his mother's silence, which spoke volumes—he promised himself that he'd be more careful, like carrying his own condoms. And the most important rule: If a woman says "It's okay, I'm on birth control," run for the hills.

Jake rubbed his knuckles across his beard and sighed. He wasn't going to touch the threesome thing. That was one hundred percent true, and he had no regrets, minus the impact on his money. "Look, what I do in my sex life, whether with one or more women at a time, is my damn business," he growled. "And as far as Denise, we both know that woman was out to trap me."

"Uh-huh," Gina replied in a get-out-of-here voice. "And you made it so easy for her by screwing her seven ways to Sunday. Oh, and let's not forget the flight attendant, or the coffee shop girl. All of them ran to the tabloids just as soon as you rolled out of their beds."

Damn. I need to get these chicks to sign an NDA like that Fifty Shades *dude.*

"So I like to have sex." He shrugged. "It's natural. Doesn't mean I'm a bad guy. And I'm tired of people assuming everyone woman I screw is having my baby."

"And what have I told you, Ross? Perception is ... "

"Reality. Look, I was concerned about a ... a friend. I'm sorry this has been blown out of proportion, but we can fix this."

"We?"

"Well, I mean you and Mark. You guys work for the same agency and two heads are better than one. That's what I'm paying you for, right?"

A long-suffering sigh echoed in his ear, followed by the sound of typing. No doubt, she was clicking open her timer and charging him out the ass for overtime. "Tell me everything you know about this woman."

Walking back into the room, Jake peeped through the curtain opening. Charlotte was now standing in front of Dr. Merrick, touching her nose.

"She's ... she's sweet."

Gina coughed. "Sweet? I don't believe any woman you're dating is sweet."

"I'm not really dating her, remember? But like I said, she's nice. Goes to church and works with that organization I volunteer for a few days a month. You know, Refurbished Dreams. She does media relations, I think. She also volunteers as a dance instructor, and everybody there loves her. She's a Southern girl. I can hear it in her voice, but I can't pinpoint exactly where she's from."

"Hmmm … " Gina stopped typing. "I think I can fix this."

"That's what I'm talking about, Gina! I knew you'd come up with something."

"It's going to take some hard work and sacrifice. And of course I'll need to run this by Mark, but I'm sure he'll be on board." Her voice was animated and unsure.

"Gina, you know me. I'll do whatever it takes. I'll work hard. I don't want to lose out on this money."

The Threx shoe deal was the ticket to buying his parents and brothers their dream homes. Sure, they hadn't asked for it, but they'd all contributed to his success. He wouldn't have made it to the majors without all their sacrifices.

"I'm glad to hear that because I have an idea. I'll need to run it by Mark, but we need to send a media alert for a press conference. Hopefully we can do something later this week. There you will announce that you met a good girl—the love of your life—and you will play the devoted boyfriend."

"What in the—"

"And then," Gina continued, "you will keep *it* in your pants and stay faithful until this deal goes through. Can you handle that, Mr. Bad Boy of Baseball?"

Jake rolled his eyes at the stupid name the media had given him. "This is ridiculous. We're living in the twenty-first century. Why does it matter who I date and what I do?"

"You mean *who* you do. And it matters because you're a role model. Don't say you don't care because I know you do. Otherwise, you wouldn't volunteer all your free hours at that nonprofit or spend time spoiling your nieces and nephews during the off-season. Do you think they don't see the tabloids and articles and blogs about your flavor of the month?"

Jake leaned against the wall and banged his head.

"Caleb, Kyrie, Ava, and Danica are too young to understand—"

"No, they aren't. They may not have a phone, but they have access to tablets and computers and, hell, they can see the photos of you and your legion of women on the covers of magazines at the grocery store."

"Gina, team meeting in five," someone in the background shouted.

"I'm wrapping up now." His agent took a deep breath. "Jake, you are an excellent pitcher. You'll be one of the greats, I'm sure of it. But because of your looks and your reputation, some people may not take you seriously. You hired Mark and me because you wanted to be marketable, to turn this deal around. Help me do my job. Bite the bullet and ask little Ms. Church Lady to do you a solid. Lay on the charm if you have to, but get this done."

Jake gripped the phone tight. Damn, but he hated being told what to do. He was tired of people judging his life. He was a good person, dammit. He donated money. Volunteered his time and fucking recycled. Frankly, it wasn't anyone's business who he banged.

"Fine, Gina," shot from his lips. "I'll *ask* Charlotte if she is willing to work with me. But just as soon as the ink on the deal is dry, I'm back to being me. I'm not a one-woman man."

"Fine, Jake. Get ready to meet the press."

Chapter Three

Dr. Merrick stepped out of the curtained area as Jake returned.

"How is she, doc?"

"Ms. Jones passed the cognitive and neurological exams with flying colors. But we still need to schedule a CT scan, so we're going to keep her a few more hours."

How in the hell did I get into this mess? "Thanks for taking care of my ... of Charlotte."

The doctor clapped his back. "My pleasure. Oh, and my dad is a huge fan. Would you mind signing this?" Dr. Merrick patted his shirt and pant pocket and then pulled out a small piece of white paper.

"Sure." Jake obliged and handed the signed paper and pen back to the doctor.

"Thanks again, Jake. I'll stop by again to check on her. See you later."

Jake waved and then took a deep breath as he gripped the curtain. *Here goes nothing.* "Charlotte, it's Jake. Can I come in?"

"Come in."

He swung open the off-white screen. She was propped against a pillow, and her bed was now L-shaped.

"How are you feeling?" He returned to his seat by the bed.

She ran her hands through her long, dark tresses. "I feel like I cracked my skull open and scrambled some things around. Other than that, I'm all right." She shrugged and chuckled. "Definitely not one of my finest moments."

"Seemed like more than a moment." He leaned forward. "You're not taking care of yourself."

"I—"

"I don't understand why you're killing yourself to lose weight." He shook his head. He would never understand why women tortured themselves to look a certain way.

Her mouth dropped open, and then her eyes narrowed. Turning her head, she mumbled something under her breath.

"What was that?" he asked.

She turned her head to look at him. Her sweet face morphed into a confused frown. "I said you're one to talk. All you date are rail-thin supermodels."

"No, I—"

"Yes, you do. Your past four or five women you've been seen with more than once have been models. Oh, and one actress. Well, she was a model turned actress, so … yeah."

Irritation buzzed like mosquitos. He was tired of explaining his lifestyle and he damn sure wasn't in the mood to have the conversation again. "Apparently I had a fling with a flight attendant and barista," he said, recalling the women Gina had mentioned earlier.

"Both were aspiring models, and they snagged pretty good contracts after they name-dropped you." She cocked her head and squinted her eyes. "Don't you talk to the women you date?"

"I don't date. I fuck."

Charlotte clutched her collarbone and gasped better than a scandalized eighteenth century society lady.

You need her to agree to this, not hate you. "Look. It's not about me. It's about you. Take care of yourself. If you want to lose weight and keep it off, you need to do it the right way."

"Like you would understand."

"I do, Charlotte. I was overweight well into my teens. My parents encouraged me to play a sport, and I chose baseball. Seemed like less running, especially as a pitcher."

A lifetime ago, he was the nerdy, overweight, awkward kid hosting *Magic: The Gathering* tournaments and reading comic books. But he also remembered the looks of concern from his well-meaning parents, grandparents, aunts, and uncles about his weight ... The taunts from neighborhood kid and classmates ... The dread in the pit of his stomach when gym class involved running a timed mile, and he knew he would never finish.

The flashback jarred his confidence, pulling him back to a time when he was quite the unassuming wallflower. A time when neither the girls nor the cool kids would give him the time of day. A time when he was the fat, stuttering kid with thick, coke bottle glasses.

Jake broke through the murky surface of his mind's eye and took a deep breath. Relaxing his tense body, he pushed his chair closer to the bed. He didn't know her story, but if she'd grown up overweight, poking at her mistakes wouldn't help.

"Look, I'm sorry. I'm not trying to lecture you. I just know from experience ... this takes time. Losing weight is a process. Be kind and patient with your body, and you'll hit your goal."

Charlotte nodded. "It's okay. And thank you for, you know ... taking care of me. Why are you here, by the way? Why did Dr. Merrick call you my boyfriend?"

"I kind of lied to one of the EMTs. I wanted to make sure you were okay, and I knew they wouldn't let me stay with you if I told them the truth."

Charlotte's brown cheeks splashed pink. "Well, thanks again. I owe you one."

Jake's heart sped at the perfect opening. "Well, there is a way you can pay me back. That is, if you're willing to help me."

"Anything, Jake." Her pretty brown eyes glittered, seeming eager to please.

"Right. The thing is, when I told the EMT you were my girlfriend, someone must have spilled the beans to the media.

Now there's a rumor going on that we're an item." He swallowed, waiting for her to digest the first bit of news.

"Oh, okay." She looked down at her clasped hands. "So you want me to go on record and say we aren't together?" Her voice was tender and shaky, and it moved something in his heart.

He sighed. "The opposite, actually. I need you to tell them we're together."

"What?" Her eyes and mouth popped open.

"I need you to pretend you're my girlfriend. You see, I have this rep of being a player—"

"No kidding." Her mouth twisted into a mischievous smile.

Jake laughed. "Totally unfounded."

"Totally," she agreed.

"Yeah, well, I have a major deal on the line with Threx. Their brand is family-focused, and they're really particular about who represents them. If I screw up in the press again, then they aren't going to sign the deal ... a *multimillion*-dollar deal."

She whistled. "That's nothing to sneeze at."

"No, it's not." He shook his head. "So would you be willing to help me? I know it's an inconvenience, but I'll compensate you for your time."

Her nose scrunched. "I don't know ... " She looked down at her lap. "I don't want to be the butt of anyone's joke," she whispered.

"Joke? Why would people joke about us?"

"Take a wild guess, Jake, but I think we covered it. You just got caught with your junk out next to a model and actress. And I'm ... just me."

Is she insane? Does she not realize that every guy drools after her at the center?

"Charlotte, I know I have a rep, and it's well-earned, but ... you've got to know you're gorgeous."

She rolled her eyes. "You don't have to lie or kiss my butt to get me to agree to help you. I know I'm not butt ugly, but compared to those women ... " She sighed. "I just don't know. I don't want people to stare and judge and compare me to the others."

"Charlotte, I don't know what to say ... all I can tell you is to look in a freaking mirror. Haven't other men given you compliments?"

"Cat-calling on the street." She shrugged. "I don't date much. I'm busy between the center and my volunteer work at church."

"Well, on behalf of mankind, I apologize. You really are something else, and I'm not blowing smoke up your ass. It's just that ... " He stopped himself. Now wasn't the time to give advice or have heart-to-hearts.

"What is it?" She leaned closer as if he held the key to her lack of dates.

"You ... okay, don't get me wrong, but you give off this vibe that you want a husband, three-point-five kids, and a nice house with a white picket fence."

She jerked and leaned away. "Yeah. And?" Her tone was defensive. "Most people want that."

Jake bobbed his head. "Yeah, but you seem to want it right away. Any guy that steps to you knows that he has to have his shit together. And spoiler alert, a lot of men, especially in their twenties, don't have their shit together."

She shook her head. "Not true. I just want to date around, get to know someone, and yes, I'd like to date a guy who knows what he wants and doesn't play games." She sighed. "Is ... is that really what you thought when you met me? We barely discussed anything outside of your career."

Yes. "I plead the fifth."

"Whatever." She crossed her arms across her chest. "It's not like you know me anyway."

"You're right, I don't, and I apologize for being judgmental. But you do *seem* like a nice woman, and I could really use your help."

Charlotte nibbled her lip and sighed. "I'll help you, Jake. But I don't want your money. It makes me feel like I'm prostituting myself."

"I'm not trying to buy you, Charlotte. But dealing with the paparazzi can be tough. It's not like the nice media you deal with at Refurbished Dreams. You'll be under a microscope, and then you'll have to spend a lot of time with me to convince everyone we're together." He squeezed her hand. "C'mon, there has to be something I can do."

Charlotte shook her head, her eyes resolved. "There's nothing I need. I have a great job. Great friends. I'm not rich, but I'm comfortable. I would tell you to give money to Refurbished Dreams, but we both know you're already donating a large sum this year."

Jake sighed. He didn't like owing someone. There had to be something she wanted. *I can help her with fitness.*

"I've got it! I'll help you lose weight ... the right way."

Charlotte shook her head. "That doesn't seem like a good idea at all."

"Why not?" he quickly fired back. "Off-season is in a few months, and I've got the time. I know all about health and fitness, and I can teach you how to cook—"

"Look at me." She waved her hands over her body. "I know how to cook."

"I was going to say cook healthy and delicious meals, not boring cabbage soup and plain kale salads. Just ... just let me do this. I can guarantee you'll hit your goal." He clapped his hand on his thighs, excited about the idea. This would count as payback for her "girlfriend" time. "What is your goal weight?"

"I don't know."

"Yes, you do. I'm your trainer. You have to tell me the truth about this stuff."

She crossed her arms over her chest. "I didn't agree to you being my trainer."

"You're gonna say yes. Now, how much?"

"Fifty?" Her voice squeaked.

He scanned her body. She could stand to lose twenty-five, maybe thirty. Fifty pounds would put her in the same category as the rail-thin models she'd accused him of dating. It would be a crying shame if she lost all those luscious curves.

He nodded. He knew women well enough to know that he couldn't argue about weight loss. He'd just make damn sure to stop her at twenty-five pounds.

"All right. We'll start next Monday. I'll come by your place, take a look at your fridge, and figure out what supplies we'll need. Seems like you have the cardio thing down pat, but we'll need to add weights."

"I don't want to lift weights and get bulky."

"You won't. Trust me, if you add weights to your routine, you'll drop the weight and keep your muscles."

Charlotte nodded as if she were hyping herself up. "Fine. We have a deal. I'll be your ... your girlfriend, and you'll be my trainer. But ... I have one request."

"Anything." He cleared his throat. "I mean, you're helping me after all."

She nodded. "While we're together, I mean for pretend, of course, I want you to be faithful. I don't want you to embarrass me if you decide to have sex with another woman."

"Of course. I'd never embarrass you like that. I have a request too."

She waved her hand. "Ask."

"Let's keep this to ourselves. No telling friends or family. People mean well, but I don't want this to leak. Oh, and no falling for each other."

Charlotte snorted. "I've had my experience with a bad boy, and I'm not looking for another broken heart. So ... deal."

Was that the dude that didn't give her an orgasm? Not your business, Ross. Jake offered his hand to seal the deal.

Her small, warm hand clasped his. "Okay, then I guess we can be officially fake boyfriend and girlfriend then." Her soft voice caressed his skin.

"Charlotte!" Melanie and Damien rushed in, followed by Nathan and Tiana. The *Get Well Soon* balloon in Melanie's hand scraped the ceiling.

"Girl, you scared us half to death!" Melanie wrapped the balloon around a chair.

Tiana rushed to her other side. "We brought your phone and purse from the center."

"Thanks, Tiana." Charlotte smiled at her friend, fluffing the pillow behind her head.

"Well ... don't thank us yet," Melanie sat in the empty chair on the opposite side of Jake.

"*Someone* may have called your mom and told her what happened."

"What?" Charlotte yelled and immediately winced, grabbing her head.

Damien squared his shoulders. "Yes. I did it. As your boss, it's my responsibility to contact your next of kin in the case of an emergency. You cracking your skull against the floor is deemed as such. She wants you to call her back ASAP."

• • •

Charlotte stared at the phone screen. *Do it. Call Mama.* The last time she'd spoken to her mother... Charlotte sighed. Harsh words had been exchanged at Big Mama's funeral. When a well-wisher from their old church had dropped off a pecan pie and offered Charlotte a slice, her mother had interrupted.

"Charlotte doesn't need all that sugar." Her mother grabbed the plate from Charlotte's hands.

She handed the plate to Charlotte's sister. "Put that up for me, Prissy."

Prissy grabbed the plate and whispered to Charlotte, "Slow down, sis." She had the audacity to look concerned before she flounced away in her size zero black dress.

Irritated and embarrassed, Charlotte pulled her mother to the side. "Why did you have to do that? You took the pie away like I have some weird addiction to food."

Her mother looked confused. "I'm scared for you, baby. Big Mama just died because she couldn't control her sugar and food portions. She struggled, sweetie. And you've been eating all weekend—"

"What?" Charlotte interrupted. "No, I haven't." She had, embarrassingly so, but she was heartbroken.

"Yes, you have. Charlie, we're all upset about Big Mama, but you don't need to process your feelings through food." Her mom gave her a pitying look. "Big Mama wouldn't want that from you. She'd want you to be healthy."

"Don't you *dare* put words into Big Mama's mouth. She'd want me to be happy, and she darn sure wouldn't snatch anything from me like I'm a toddler who doesn't know how to care for themselves. I'm sick to death of you and Prissy and Daddy always getting on my back about my weight. Yes, I may be eating a bit more, but Big Mama just died!"

"Charlie, baby—"

"I'm out of here." She hurried to her room and grabbed her already packed bag.

Since the funeral, Mama and Prissy had called more than a dozen times. Prissy had sent the last message, calling her selfish and a coward. *Whatever. She's the queen of being selfish.*

Prissy was three years older, and had pretended Charlotte hadn't existed while they were in school. She'd always kicked her out of her room, calling her a pathetic nerd.

Charlotte swallowed down her bitter memories and called her mom.

Her mother answered after one ring. "Charlotte! Are you okay? Your boss told me you cracked your head wide open."

She exhaled at the exaggeration. She was sure her boss hadn't said those words. "I'm fine, Mama. Just hit my head, no concussion or anything. I'm in perfect health."

"Are you now?" Her mother's voice ended on a high pitch. "Maybe you should come home, since you're so *healthy* and all."

"Well I have work … things are busy. And plus, I have a boyfriend and—"

"A boyfriend? Vance! Charlotte has a boyfriend," her mother yelled at her father.

"Yes, Mama. Is that such a big deal?"

"You've never brought a young man home. So yes, it's a big deal. But anyway, tell us about him."

"Well … he's famous."

"F-famous?" she squeaked in an excited voice. "Who is he?"

"Jake Ross."

"That ball player?" Her voice dripped with disdain. "The man caught on camera having sex with those two women?"

"Yes, the one and only." Charlotte kept her voice light. "But he's changed. Under all that … bluster, he's a good man."

"Honey, do you think being in a relationship with someone like him is a good idea?"

"Why not?"

"I mean, is it a good match? You're not his usual type of … of woman."

Thin, gorgeous. Got it. "So you think I'm not good enough for him? Wow, thanks, Mom."

"Now wait a minute, Charlotte. I didn't mean it like that. I'd … I'd like to meet him. Get to know him to make sure. I mean you guys really don't seem to match well; you're *different*."

"Different?" Charlotte sighed. "You know what, I knew this was a bad idea. I'll talk to you later."

"Charlotte, listen to me, baby. H-he just seems like the type of man that—"

"Jake and I are together. I know that doesn't match up in your ideal world of perfection, b-but we care about each other." She usually hated to lie, but for some reason, she wanted to pretend. To pretend Jake liked the way she looked, that he'd looked across the room and saw her, and she took his breath away. That she was the woman of his dreams.

"If anyone calls to ask about Jake or me say 'no comment.' And please don't tell them about how I'm such a disappointment to you. Bye, Mama." She clicked off before her mother broke her heart again.

Chapter Four

Charlotte blinked rapidly, overwhelmed by the flashing lights and quick camera clicks. One hand was death-gripped to her chair, while the other was sandwiched between Jake's large and calloused hands.

"When did you know Charlotte was the one for you?" a reporter from a gossip column asked.

When Jake proposed they lie to the media about their relationship, she'd known it would be difficult. But this was too much. No question was too inappropriate. One reporter even insinuated Jake had just crawled out of another woman's bed earlier that morning. Charlotte had been comforted by the fact that he'd snuck into her apartment at the crack of dawn to cram on today's public hearing, aka press conference.

"I noticed Charlotte about a year ago." Squeezing her sweaty palm, he offered an encouraging smile. He continued looking at her as if she took his breath away.

Don't I wish. They'd met two years ago, but his cool eyes would always skip over her as if she were part of the furniture in Damien's office. Now, here she was lying to the entire free world that they were together. She gulped down the ball of nervousness in her throat. She hated to lie, and a small part of her wished this was real, but a larger part was relieved. Jake Ross had heartbreaker written all over him. From the way he winked and smiled at women to his unapologetic views about relationships. *I don't date. I fuck.* Yeah, fuck women's hearts over. No, she would not be yet another woman on his list. No matter how delectable he looked in his tight black Henley and distressed jeans. *Yum. No, yuck! Focus, Charlotte!*

"She previously worked for an agency that handled my publicity." Jake's voice broke into her mini-argument with herself.

"She was so cute, prim, and proper, but I ... wasn't ready to pursue her just yet. She's a forever type of girl."

A collective *aww* rose from the crowd.

"And Charlotte? How did you know Jake was the one?"

"I ... " She looked down at her sensible black leather pumps.

C'mon, girl. You guys went over this already. What was the answer? What did Mark say to do if I blanked out?

She snapped her attention back to Jake. "I mean, he's Jake Ross, and he's hard to resist."

She smiled, and he smiled back. But something was off. It wasn't genuine, not like the smile he'd gifted her in the ER.

"All right, ladies and gentlemen." Mark gripped a microphone in his hand. "No more questions. Jake and Charlotte appreciate your interest, but as you can see, Charlotte is an all-American girl raised in the South. She's not used to being in the public eye, so let's give her and Jake some privacy. If you have any questions about Jake regarding *baseball*, please feel free to contact me. Thank you."

Putting a hand on the small of Charlotte's back, Jake guided her off stage and then exhaled and cracked his neck. "You did well."

"Really?" Charlotte kept walking toward the back entrance. "You didn't seem to like my last answer. I'm sorry if I said something wrong. I just forgot what we'd practiced this morning." She took a cleansing breath. "I'm not used to all of this."

Jake stopped beside her, gently gripped her shoulders, and turned her to face him. "I know you aren't. There was no way to prepare for the flashing lights and invasive questions. I appreciate you doing me this favor."

"You're welcome, Jacob."

He let go of her shoulders and laughed. "Jacob?"

"That's your name, isn't it?"

"Yeah, that's my name, but everyone calls me Jake."

"Well, since I'm your 'girlfriend,'" she dipped her fingers in air quotes, "I get to call you something else. It's either Jacob or pookie."

Jake's deep chuckle gave her shivers. On the inside.

"No pookie."

"Love muffin? Oh, I know! Stud muffin."

Jake shook his head. "Nothing with food."

Charlotte shrugged. "Darn it. I guess honey bunches of oats is out."

"That's definitely out. We have some time. For now, just call me Jacob. I kind of like it coming from you."

He likes me calling him Jacob! Charlotte told her inner groupie to settle, but she couldn't stop the smile from spreading.

"Where to next, Jacob?"

"Let's go to your place. It's time for me to start my end of the deal."

"All right, but be gentle."

"Always."

• • •

Charlotte was nervous as she slid the key into the lock. In a few moments, Jake the Great would be stepping into her matchbox apartment. She turned her back to the door. "Before you come in, I need to tell you something."

"Are you a serial killer?"

Her head jerked back at his ridiculous question. "No, I—"

"Crazy stalker or groupie?"

That's debatable when it comes to you. "No, Jacob, that's not it."

He gently moved her away from the door and twisted the key. "Then that's all I need to know. It's okay if your apartment isn't pristine."

"Wait!"

Too late. Jake pushed the door open and stepped into her domain.

Why, oh, why didn't I move my embarrassing collection to my room?

He prowled about the one-bedroom apartment. Heat rose from her cheeks and then rolled through her body. She wanted to curl up in a tight ball like a roly-poly.

He walked over to her comic book wall of fame. *More like shame, now.* The vintage covers of famous comic book heroes, from Iron Man and Spider-Man to Wonder Woman and Catwoman, graced her wall. In a pullout Ikea cabinet, hundreds of mint condition comics were lined up on display.

Pulling out a cabinet shelf, Jake skimmed his long fingers over the covers. He hesitated for a moment and then turned. "May I?" He gestured to the bookshelf.

Charlotte nodded, her throat dry.

"I've been looking for the first cover of the Christopher Priest Black Panther run. Where did you find this?"

"On, umm, eBay." She walked beside him. "You're a Black Panther fan?"

"I'm a comic book fan. Used to collect them."

"As a kid?" He'd probably grown out of it when he hit his teens. *Unlike me.*

"No. Up until I went pro. Haven't had much time these days."

Charlotte's heart fluttered. She couldn't believe THE Jacob Ross collected comic books. Or maybe he was just saying that to make her feel better.

His wandering hands continued to peruse, stopping on a thin gold rope. He picked it up and snapped it against the floor. "Didn't realize you were so adventurous, angel."

Her cheeks broke out in flames. "It's a lasso."

The rope dangled from his hand. "I know you're from the South, but New York doesn't have a lot of livestock roaming around."

She giggled at his joke. "It's Wonder Woman's Lasso of Truth. She's my favorite."

"That's right. So, if I tie this around you," he wrapped the rope around her waist, "you have to tell me the truth, right?"

"Uh huh." She nodded, breathless from the turn of events.

Jake tilted his head down, intense eyes on her. "That a promise?"

Her heart traveled to her ears, beating loudly and recklessly. All she could manage to do was nod.

He jerked her closer, putting her body flush to his chest. "Why haven't you had an orgasm?"

The cobra-like trance he'd had over her vanished. She slow-blinked her eyes. "What?"

"I asked why you haven't had an orgasm." He was louder this time and enunciated each word. "When you bumped your head you said that you didn't want to die because you hadn't had an orgasm."

Sweet baby Jesus in a manager wrapped in a blanket on top of the hay. Just kill me now, Lord. Create a black hole, and I'll slide right in.

"I—"

"The truth, angel." Gripping the rope tighter, he pulled her even closer. "Lasso of Truth, remember?"

She waited for a few beats to see if God would perform the black-hole miracle. *No such luck.*

"Right," she whispered. "I don't know why I haven't had one. I just haven't had much opportunity."

"Are you a virgin?"

"No."

Something flashed briefly in his gray eyes. *Disappointment?*

"You sure?"

She was sure. Oh, so pitifully sure. During college, the most popular guy on campus had asked her out. They'd dated for almost a month, and he'd convinced her to take it to the next level because he *loved her.* She snorted. Yeah, right. Her naïve heart fell for it, and she gave him her virginity. A gift she'd considered sacred. And she'd tried, boy had she'd tried to relax and enjoy herself, but it hurt like hell. What had made the situation worse was that he'd been impatient, so unlike the loving and sweet man she'd gotten to know weeks before. She asked him to stop. He complied, rolled out of bed, and slammed her door shut. The next day he'd dumped her, and told her they didn't have any chemistry. Later, she'd heard the playboy and his friends had a running bet on deflowering virgins around campus. After that experience, she'd promised herself to never again fall for a man who was so callous with women's hearts.

"I've had sex only once, but it counts. Well, minus the orgasm. But the penetration part and—"

"I got it," he bit off, stepping away and taking the lasso with him. He put it back on the shelf and cleared his throat. "All right, we have a lot to do here. Do you have a notepad?"

"Sure, I need to get it from my desk. Be right back." She rushed into the bedroom, heart pounding. *What was that?*

Jake must already be feeling the effects of celibacy. That was the only reason to explain the orgasm question. Or maybe he was curious, like a social scientist observing abnormal behavior. Opening a drawer, she grabbed a blue-and-white Wonder Woman notepad and groaned. She could only imagine what he would think about her fangirl stationery.

She returned to the living room and spotted him in the kitchen, bent over with his tight ass on display as he surveyed her fridge.

After she'd checked her mouth for drool, she cleared her throat. "I've got the paper, Jacob."

He popped his head from the fridge and nodded. "Good. We need to make a list and go for a grocery run. Let's sit down. I want to get a feel of your favorite foods, to make sure you enjoy what I cook you."

"You're really going to cook for me?"

"It's not a big deal. I like cooking. I can't promise to do it every day, especially with the playoffs around the corner, but I'll prep so you don't have to do much."

"It's okay. I enjoy cooking. If you show me once or twice, I can figure it out."

"All right. Sounds like a plan. Do me a favor and write down your favorite meals, broken down by breakfast, lunch, dinner, and snacks." He pulled off a few pieces of paper from the pad. "And, on one of the pieces of paper, write down your weight."

"I don't think it's necessary to—"

"Yes, it is. I want to make sure you lose no more than a pound a week. I'll also need to take your measurements."

Measure my thighs and arms and stomach? Oh heck no!

"I don't feel comfortable with you knowing my size. Can you just tell me what I need to do? Don't worry about how many inches I lose. I'll tell you how many, but not my measurements."

"Deal on the measurements. No deal on the weight. I need to adjust your meal portion according to your size. Now, I can look and figure it out, but I value my life too much to piss you off with an incorrect guess. So," he pointed his pen at her, "do me a favor and get your ass on the scale."

"Fine," she hissed. "But if you laugh or tell anyone about this, I. Will. Kill. You!"

"Think of me as your personal trainer-slash-therapist. Everything that goes on here is confidential."

Charlotte returned from the bathroom and shoved the small slip of paper into his hand.

He looked at the weight she wrote in the tiniest script possible. He smiled and tucked the paper into his pocket. "Easy peasy, Charlotte. I'll get you to your goal in no time."

Chapter Five

"Give me two more, Charlotte."

She dropped to her knees, wiping the sweat from her brow. Jake was good on his word, and for the past few weeks, he'd been working her body and her nerves.

"You got this. Two more push-ups. I'll do them with you."

Please don't. Huffing, she lowered her body to the floor and struggled to push herself back up. Only ten minutes ago, Jake had her curl ten-pound dumbbells. Arms shaking, she lowered her chest to the floor again. But this time, she collapsed.

"Good job, Charlotte. Rest up all day tomorrow. Next up is leg day."

Rolling over onto her back, she sighed. She had a love-hate relationship with leg day. After an hour and a half of leg presses, curls, and weighted front and back squats, she could barely climb the stairs to her apartment.

But there were benefits to leg day. Sexy, sweaty benefits. Jake usually stood behind her as they faced the mirror. His intense stormy eyes focused solely on her, chest to her back, as they squatted together. The other day, she'd accidently brushed her butt against his crotch. Not that it meant anything to him. He'd simply stepped back and continued with instructions.

"Up you go." Jake offered his hand and hefted her up. "Ready to smile for the camera?"

The media ate up their "gym dates" as one of the reporters called it. When she'd told Jake about the gym date article, he laughed, and the next day brought her a Pokémon shirt that read "I Only Date Gym Leaders." Only the truly nerdy would get the message.

There was definitely more to Jake than being an extremely good-looking, millionaire athlete and it made it harder for her to stick to her plan to guard her heart.

"Sure." She smiled at him. "Just let me freshen up, and I'll be out in five."

She hurried to the locker room and changed into a light pullover sweatshirt, then pulled her lip gloss, deodorant, and body spray from her bag. No time for a shower. That gave his fans and the media too much of an opportunity to harass Jake while he waited. The media had also begun to follow her to and from work and had snapped a few pictures of her going out with Melanie and Tiana.

Lip balm in hand, she paused and stared at herself in the mirror. Just three weeks under Jake's tutelage, and she could already see results. Despite his desire for her to lose only a pound per week, the weight had dropped drastically. She'd lost twelve pounds. Her face was slimmer, and arms—previously the bane of her existence—were toned. But there was something else, something in her eyes and her spirit that couldn't be weighed or measured.

She looked away, too afraid to delve deeper. The dates, dinners, and exercising together … just temporary. They only had a relationship because of a deal. One that hinged on a billion-dollar corporation's decision to finalize the contract and sign him as their celebrity endorsement.

She didn't know how long those things could take, but every morning she woke up with a boulder in her stomach, dreading the day she would get the call that her services were no longer needed.

Shaking her head, she zipped the bag closed and hurried out of the locker room. She looked forward to cooking dinner at his place, something they'd discovered they enjoyed doing together. Afterwards, they would settle down and watch a movie. Usually a shoot-them-up action flick or superhero movie. And then fall into a debate on which character would kick the others' asses. After a few hours of hanging out, Charlotte would return home. *Alone.*

She pushed the door open and smiled when she spotted him leaning against a nearby wall. Her smiled faltered when she saw a gorgeous woman beside him. Charlotte ducked behind the corner and spied.

"You haven't called me in weeks, Jake. The twins and I are getting lonely." The woman twirled her brown twist around her fingers.

Good gracious. He really does love threesomes!

"Well you know I've been busy. I'm in a relationship now."

"Is that right?" She stepped closer and dragged her fingers down his chest. "Because you told me you weren't the relationship type."

A swarm of jelly fish stung Charlotte's insides and paralyzed her body. *He's not yours.* She repeated it to herself. Didn't help. She took a painful deep breath and stared on.

"My girlfriend is special." He took a step back from her hands. "And she doesn't like other women touching me."

That's right. Back up, lady! A grin split her face.

"Fine." The woman shrugged. "I can respect that. But when you're ready to branch out, call me. You've got my number."

"I won't. I'm happy with my girl."

The sting of jealousy continued to ease. Charlotte knew she had no right to get upset, but she was happy he was holding up his end of the bargain. She didn't dare delve into the other reasons for her relief.

After the woman walked off, Charlotte stepped around the corner and adjusted her attitude.

"There you are." Jake leaned in and hooked her waist.

Her heart sputtered like the dying engine in her dad's '78 Chevy. Even in loose basketball shorts and a fitted black tee, the man was still drool-worthy.

"I was about to go in there and find you. What are you in the mood to eat?"

"Thai lettuce wraps and a cucumber salad?"

He kissed her head. "Sounds good, babe. Let's go to my place."

• • •

"You're seriously telling me you wouldn't want another *Hulk* reboot?" Jake poured olive oil into the pan.

"No. Heck, no." Charlotte shook her pretty head. "They've tried and failed. I can't take another disappointing movie. Keep him in *The Avengers* as part of the ensemble cast but no more flying solo."

"But you gotta admit that the last guy ... " He snapped his fingers. "What's his name?"

"Mark Ruffalo."

"Yeah. He did a good job."

"He did a great job, but I'm sticking to my guns. No more *Hulk* movies. It's going to be another blockbuster disaster. They focus too much on his strength and power."

"Well, he is strong."

"So, what? There are other more powerful mutants. Look at the Omega levels like Jean Gray, Vulcan, and Iceman. They would so kick his ass. And the Hulk doesn't even have telekinesis and can't fly."

"Who needs to fly when you can travel to another continent in a single jump?" he argued. "Anyway, we're talking about the *Avengers* universe."

"Fine, fine. I think Scarlet Witch could kick his ass. And I'm not saying the Hulk isn't powerful. I'm just saying it's time for other heroes to get their due, like Black Panther. And I want to see Luke Cage on the silver screen, too. Oh!" She snapped her fingers. "And the new Iron Man. Or should I say Iron *Woman*. I love me some Robert Downey Jr., but I'm ready for Riri."

Jake was glad Hollywood was finally making black characters the stars of superheroes movies and television. "Can't argue with that. It's about damn time we are the heroes and not the sidekick."

She hopped onto the marble counter and watched him cook. She looked damn comfortable and sexy in his kitchen. Swinging her legs, she gave him a smile. "So, if you had the choice to have one power, one ability, what would you choose?"

"Omnipresence."

"Omnipresence?" She snorted. "Why? So you can have multiple wives and girlfriends in different dimensions?"

"Ouch, angel." He shook his head and lowered the burner heat. "That would require me to be either a cheater or a polygamist. My powers would be too badass to be used to juggle women."

"Why omnipresence then?"

"You're able to be present in all places at all times. If you're everywhere at once, it's impossible to die."

"And boring." Charlotte rolled her eyes.

"Right letter, wrong word. *Badass*. Not boring."

"You've gotta have a weakness."

"Okay, what's your power?"

"Hmm. It's a tie between being telepathic, a healer, and invisibility. Actually, I wouldn't mind controlling the elements like Storm, too."

"Choose one. You made the rules."

"Healer, I guess."

"Why healing?"

Ticking her head down, she stopped swinging her legs. "So I can save those I love."

"That's a pretty good power."

"I know, right?" She smiled and looked away.

The camaraderie had faded. In its place now sat unease, or was it sadness that had caused her shoulders to droop and her eyes to well with unshed tears?

The conversation was obviously over when she slid off the counter and walked out of the kitchen. She was trying to pull away, but he wouldn't let her.

"Pass me the peanut sauce." Jake pointed to the cabinet with one hand as he sautéed chicken with the other.

"Got it." She flashed him a shy smile and reached for the sauce. Soft, pert breasts brushed his arms. A zap of electricity heated his body, and his heart punched through his chest. After turning the stove on low, he shifted to face her.

She licked her lips. Jake's eyes zeroed in on the target, her mouth. Crowding her space, he leaned down, cupped the back of her head, and descended until he crushed his lips against her softness. *So damn sweet.* A forbidden fruit he was all too happy to sample. And he did, lick by delicious lick until they were both breathless.

The bottle slipped from her hands and toppled on the floor. Charlotte jumped away and touched her bruised lips. Lips he'd thoroughly kissed, if her pink-tinged cheeks were any indication.

She cleared her throat. "I d-don't think … we shouldn't have done that."

Sucking in his breath, he stilled as if concrete blocks weighted down his shoes. He could damn near taste the confusion permeating the air. Fighting his instincts to dominate and claim, he slowed his breathing. Not that it did any damn good. If it were possible, he would still his heartbeat, still the adrenaline that surged through his body, and still the blood that rushed through his veins. He yearned to hold onto the warmth and intimacy she'd offered.

The loss of her warmth made him shiver. And dammit, he was tired of being cold.

His shy trainee picked up the bottle and put it on the counter before backing out of the kitchen.

Pulling in a deep breath, he uselessly attempted to calm the rush of blood funneling to his other head. *If I keep this up, I'm gonna have a permanent zipper imprint.*

"Come back in here. We made out. Sometimes we'll have to do that for the camera. No big deal." He shrugged.

"S-so. That was pretend? Like practice?"

"Yep," he lied and it tasted like soot on his tongue.

She nodded. "That makes sense, I guess. As long as it's pretend. I don't want there to be any confusion." Her voice sounded off-pitch, weird. Like she was convincing herself of something. He wasn't the only liar in the room.

"We're on the same page."

Quiet as a church mouse, she returned and leaned against the opposite end of the counter.

Focusing on cooking, he tapped the spatula against the wok and then poured Sriracha over the chicken. *She's putting distance between us. Not a bad idea.* He needed to keep his head in the game. Get the deal and, after a few respectable weeks—two weeks, tops—end their fake relationship. Jake had held up his end of the bargain. She'd lost weight and looked damn good too. No doubt she would easily find a real boyfriend to replace him. *Someone worthy of her.* His stomach churned.

Mark would no doubt spin some bullshit about them respecting each other, but being better off as friends. Then he'd need to cool his heels for a month and, after his time was up, console himself in the arms of a beautiful woman.

Damn. He couldn't even get himself excited at the prospect.

A sweet sigh interrupted his thoughts. One that had him imagining silken sheets and soft skin and luscious thighs wrapped around his waist.

"What's up?" He didn't turn around. He didn't want to tempt himself with the cute pout that she would, no doubt, have on her face.

"Are we watching *Jessica Jones* tonight?"

"Is that actually a question? Fire up Netflix. I'll plate our food."

"Okay," her soft and eager voice answered.

After fixing their plates, he hurried into the living room. Typically, he would set the formal dining room as his mother and grandmother had drilled into his head. But after Charlotte had introduced him to the action-packed show, they'd become hooked on watching it during dinner.

She squirmed, seated as far as possible on the other end of the couch. Spooked like a horse in a barnyard fire, she smoothed her hands over her Lycra-clad legs, nibbling her plump bottom lip and darting her attention from the jazz art on the wall to the blank TV screen.

"I'm starting to develop a complex."

Charlotte's attention darted back to him. "What do you mean?" She grabbed the plate he proffered and placed it on the table.

"Why do you always sit on the far end of the couch?"

She shrugged, stared at her lap, and then resumed rubbing the shiny material around her delectable thighs.

"Wow, angel. I haven't felt this rejected since I was twelve years old and my next door neighbor stood me up for the Valentine's Day dance." He sat in the middle seat, next to her.

Charlotte's head jerked. "Someone was dumb enough to stand you up?"

"Yeah, I told you I wasn't always the ladies' man that you know and love today."

"So when did you turn into a ladies' man?" Her eyes gleamed with interest. *Yes!* She hadn't scooted further away.

"Right after middle school. I started running the summer before my freshman year. I wanted to make the varsity baseball team and knew I needed to get into shape to do it. I was also blessed with a growth spurt that summer and begged my dad to get me contacts. All of a sudden, I'm the "It" guy in high school. All the guys wanted to be my friends, all the girls wanted to screw … " He cleared his throat. "I mean, *date* me."

Charlotte rolled her eyes. "You don't have to censor yourself around me, Jacob."

"I know. But you're a lady, and you deserve respect." He dipped his wrap into the sauce.

"How did it make you feel?"

He lifted his finger for time to chew and swallow. "How did what make me feel?"

Grabbing her plate, she tucked a leg under the other. "How did going from being a … a… "

"I think the word you're searching for is 'reject'."

"No, never." She shook her head vehemently. "I mean, how did it feel to become popular, practically overnight?"

Jake remembered the jocks suddenly giving him pats on the back in the hallways, and the girls sneaking letters into his locker, giving him sly looks and whispering all the things they'd do for him, *to him*. "It was … weird. Overwhelming at first. I tried to keep my old friends from middle school, but they didn't seem to want to hang out with me anymore. I don't blame them. I became friends with the guys who would pick us last in gym class. Well, with the exception of baseball for me. The guys that would crack jokes or pretend we didn't exist. So, I guess I didn't like it at first."

"And the girls?"

"That was overwhelming, too. I had no idea what I was doing, and I was way over my head. But then cockiness and hormones took over, and I quickly got over my fear."

"Fear? Of what?"

"Of people finding out who I really am. Just an anime, video game, math-loving geek whose idea of a good time is dressing up as my favorite character at Comic-Con."

He plucked another piece of lettuce from the plate and piled on chicken. "And then … well, people saw the outside and assumed the kind of guy I was. Hell, even teachers didn't take me seriously. If I turned in a paper that was stellar, they assumed someone else had completed the assignment. I guess I just became what everyone believed I was. But you know that ad campaign that I did for Nathan and Tiana's company? The one about the many faces of Jake Ross?"

"Yeah, I remember. I was at one of the shoots, shadowing Tiana and Nathan. Was all that stuff about you being a nerd true? I loved the concept but assumed it was scripted."

"Yeah. You and a million other people. I loved those commercials. I was proud because, for the first time in over a decade, I was actually myself."

Scooting closer, she rubbed his thigh. "I'm sorry."

"For what? You didn't do anything."

"Yes, I did. I'm no better than your classmates. I made assumptions about who you are and I … " She squeezed her eyes shut and licked her lips. Her eyelids fluttered open, and big, brown, earnest eyes filled with determination. But on the edges, a hint of apprehension lingered. "You're … you know that you're a good-looking guy. But until we started hanging out, I just saw the surface. You're so much more than the shell God gave you. I wish people could see how beautiful you truly are."

Clasping her cheek, he zeroed in on those gorgeous lips. He wanted to bite and suck. *Fuck it. I'm going for it.*

Bzzzz!

His cell phone vibrated on the table. Charlotte jumped away, mumbling something about Jessica Jones. He looked down at his screen and saw a text from his brother D'Mario.

Ma and Grandma Etta have been complaining about not meeting your new girlfriend. Expect a call from them soon. Probably tonight.

Damn. He didn't need his family getting involved with anything right now. He hated to lie to them, but no way was he going to try to explain to his eighty-seven-year-old grandmother that he and

Charlotte were in a fake relationship because he wanted to get a multimillion-dollar deal. Even if it meant buying his parents and siblings a house. Grandma Etta would demand he pick out a thin branch or, as she called it, a switch from outside and let her swat him across his ass.

He texted thanks to his brother and focused back on Charlotte, who was once again seated on the far end of the couch. "That complex I mentioned earlier? It's getting worse. Why don't you want to sit beside me?"

Her eyes were wary. "Because I think we've done enough practicing for tonight." She sagged her shoulders. "And I probably stink. I did a quick wash off in the locker room, but not a full shower."

"Why not?"

"Because I didn't want you to wait for me. I know how you get antsy about someone harassing you for an autograph."

Damn, she's sweet. All of his ex-hookups would've loved the exposure. "You're worth the wait. You know what? You could take a shower here." He could feel himself getting hard, imagining her soapy and wet.

"No, no." She shook her head. "It wouldn't be proper."

"Proper?" Moving in closer, he gripped her waist and whispered, "Take off the halo and have a little fun with me."

The look in her eyes wasn't the brush-off he expected. No, it was something else entirely that dared him to move his grip lower and then squeeze and spank the tight, round object of his obsession.

Hunger, longing, and passion burned in those big brown eyes. A flash of pink teased him when she licked her lips—another thing that haunted his dreams. A shaky hand slid up his chest. His heartbeat ramped up and sped under her touch. *This time, I won't pretend this is for practice.*

The *Star Trek* theme blasted from his phone, rattling the side table.

Dammit!

The hand that had so lovingly stroked his chest now pushed him away. "You should get that."

Reaching over without looking, he pressed the button to silence the cock-blocking device. "So you'll bring your stuff over to shower?" He needed a small victory, a consolation prize after the loss of her lush body flush against his.

She tucked a loose bang behind her ear. "Okay. Next time I'll bring my shower stuff and some extra clothes."

He wanted to chuck his phone out the window but instead grabbed the cell from the table. Thirty more seconds, and he could've had her on her back, pulling him close and not pushing him away. He looked down at the screen and saw "Mom" on the missed call list. *Damn, she's starting already.*

He sighed. "That was my mom, which brings me to our next order of business. First, eat your food before it gets cold." He nodded to her plate on the table. "Second, we need to talk about my family."

"We do?" Her hands froze midway through rolling the piece of lettuce.

"Yes, we do. Go ahead and eat." He waited until she finished the wrap. "My brother just gave me the heads up that my mom and grandmother want to meet you. I think it would be best if we flew down to Alabama instead of them coming to New York. Less risk of paparazzi, and I can see my nieces and nephews."

"But don't you want us to be in front of the media? You know, for the sponsorship deal?"

"Yes, but I'd rather not have my family around the media. The kids still aren't used to it. We can take a few photos, and have Mark send a few pics out to the press."

Charlotte nodded. "That could work."

"So does that mean you'll come with me?"

"I-I guess. Where would I stay? What part of Alabama are you from?"

"Eat." He waved to her plate again.

She rolled her eyes and complied.

"We'll stay at my parents' house. My grandmother lives there as well. It's more eyes, but you'll have your own room, and I'll be on the couch since my mother and father won't let us sleep together until we're married. I mean ... n-not that it's going to happen." *I'm not turning in my player card anytime soon.*

Charlotte nodded as she bit into another wrap. "Right," she whispered.

"Oh, and I'm from Mobile."

"Are you serious?" Her voice garbled a bit from the lettuce wrap in her mouth.

He laughed. "Chew and swallow, Charlotte. I can't hear you."

"First, you force me to eat. Now, you force me to speak." She huffed. "I'm from Pensacola, Florida. We're practically neighbors."

"That's cool. We can swing by and visit your folks, too."

Grabbing her water, she gulped it down. "Yeah, I'll see ... if ... they're ... around ... "

Is she hiding something? He didn't like that. But instead of giving her the third degree, he let it lie. "So are you okay with the plan? We could leave on Friday evening and return on Sunday."

"Sure, sure."

He was suddenly excited at the prospect of Charlotte meeting his family. They would love her. He could see his grandmother sharing family recipes and his mom going shopping with her. Charlotte would most likely spoil his nieces and nephews, and they would adore her, too.

Slow down, Ross. She's not your girl. This time, he did the moving away. Maybe having some space between them wasn't a bad thing. He was the bad boy of baseball. He loved women and they loved him. He wasn't ready for anything serious.

Chapter Six

Charlotte was in love ... with Jake's family. The moment they'd entered his parents' four-bedroom, ranch-style home, everyone had been welcoming and gracious. From the way his family teased him, she almost forgot he was a millionaire baseball player.

Grandma Etta, her favorite family member at the moment—she switched favorite family members every ten minutes—was hilarious.

The eighty-seven-year-old woman was the first person to rush out to greet them. The walking cane seemed to hinder rather than assist her descending the three front-porch steps. Smiling, Jake had opened his arms for her to rush into, but his smile quickly disappeared when Grandma Etta had given Charlotte a hug first. The matriarch kissed her cheek and not-so-quietly whispered, "Thank God for you. I thought JR was gonna come home with one of those fast-looking models."

He ran a hand over his face and sighed. "Like I've told you time and time again, just because they're models doesn't mean they're fast."

Grandma Etta jerked back her head and, somehow, the curls that formed a white halo around her head didn't move an inch. "Ha! You hear that, Theresa?" she yelled into the house. "The last one didn't have a stitch of clothes on. Lord, I thought she was gonna catch *old and new*-monia."

Now, Charlotte, Jake, his dad, and his grandmother sat around the kitchen table while Jake's mother Theresa stirred a pot of gumbo and fried corn bread.

Gerald, Jake's father, plopped two cups with ice in front of her. "We need you to settle an argument, Ms. Charlotte." He turned around and grabbed two glass pitchers from the granite countertops. "Mama Etta and I have a long-standing competition on who has the best sweet tea."

Oh, no.

Jake, seated next to her, squeezed her shoulders. "Sorry, angel. Both sets of my grandparents grew up together and have been in competition for decades. Since my dad is the next generation, he feels it's up to him to uphold the Ross family feud."

Gerald poured tea into both glasses and then waved his hand toward the drinks. "Go ahead. Don't be shy."

Charlotte averted her gaze from the drinks to Jake. "Do something!" she hissed under her breath.

His deep laugh reverberated in her belly. The sexy sound would've usually given her a quiver elsewhere, but her attention was occupied by the Hatfield and McCoy Tea Feud. "C'mon, Dad. We just got here," Jake half-heartedly argued.

Hands folded over her chest, Mama Etta reclined in her chair and nodded toward the drinks. "You're not diabetic, now, are you, sweetie?"

The pace of her heartbeat sped. *Do they know?* "Ummm … w-why do you ask?"

"Wouldn't want Gerald to send somebody else into a diabetic coma."

"Oh, goodness," Charlotte whispered under her breath. She didn't want to be outed for her prediabetes by overly sweet tea. She hadn't told anyone about her condition and had no plans to do so. She didn't want anyone to feel sorry for her or treat her differently, especially since she'd planned to get better. *I'll sneak off and check my blood sugar after we eat.*

Gerald stroked his snow-white goatee. "You didn't mistake the salt for the sugar again, did ya, Mama Etta? We wouldn't want to repeat the mix-up you had back in ninety-nine when you spiked Sheila's blood pressure."

Jake patted and squeezed her thigh. She looked down at her jumping knee, then jerked her head back to him. She stopped her nervous tic and gave him a smile. Well, she tried to, but the effort was more like a kid being forced to smile on school picture day.

"Oh, Lord." Theresa shook her salt-and-pepper curls, thumped the wooden spoon against the pot, and then pointed it like a weapon at the dueling duo. "Why can't we ever have a nice family dinner? I thought I told both of you to not harass Charlotte. Lord knows JR has never, *ever* brought a nice girl home, and here you both go, trying to scare her off." She shook her head again and returned to stirring the pot, mumbling under her breath.

"Now don't pitch a hissy fit, baby," Grandma Etta's soft and sure voice responded. "If she can handle all those nosy reporters, she can handle judging a sweet tea contest."

Theresa is officially my favorite family member. Charlotte narrowed her gaze at Jake. No thanks to her fake boyfriend, whose body shook with silent laughter.

"Go on, now." Gerald waved at the tea again. "We promise we won't have any hard feelings."

"O-okay." *Darn it!* She picked up the glass to her right and lifted it to her mouth. After hesitating for a few seconds, she gulped down some courage followed by the cold, brown beverage. She smacked her lips. "Very good. I love the fresh-squeezed lemon, and there's a nice balance of sugar."

Jake full-out laughed this time. "Who knew you were so good at this?"

She shrugged. "I'm from the South, too. You know we take our sweet tea very seriously."

Gerald wiggled his brows and smiled. "Son, did I tell you how much I approve of your lady?" His dad turned to the fridge and returned with a glass of milk. "Take a few seconds and cleanse your palate. Then try the next one."

Jake lifted an eyebrow. "Since when did you add milk to the competition?"

Gerald shrugged and sat beside him. "Learned it from the Food Channel your mother always has on. I don't want people to mix my work of art with Mama Etta's backwoods tea."

Charlotte choked on the milk she'd been drinking.

"Now don't make me get up and conk you over the head with my cane, Gerald."

He lifted his hands in the air in surrender. "Don't get yourself all worked up, Mama Etta. Save that energy for the disappointment you'll have when you lose."

Lifting her cane, she pushed Jake's chest back. "Move, JR. Let me at your daddy."

Charlotte quickly lifted the glass of tea and swallowed. "Mmm!" she yelled. "This one is good." She smacked her lips again, trying to get a feel of the flavors. "This one has a nice lemon-lime taste. Oh, and I detect a hint of orange, too. Very nice. Both are really, really good!"

Jake's dad leaned in closer. "But which one is *the best*?"

Everyone went silent. Even Theresa stopped her ministrations over the stove and looked at Charlotte expectantly.

"I ... umm ... " She looked to Jake for help. His eyes pointed down. She followed his silent direction, and she saw his finger form the number one.

She took a deep breath. *One it is.*

"Well, after much deliberation, I think the best tea is—"

"Unka Jake!"

Two pigtails whipped past Charlotte and jumped into Jake's lap.

"Hey, Ava baby. How's my beautiful niece doing?"

Thank God! Charlotte's shoulders sagged, and she wiped the sweat that had formed over her brow.

She caught Theresa laughing at her antics. Jake's mom smiled and winked.

The little girl tugged on his T-shirt. "I so happy you here, Unka Jake!"

The sight of Unka Jake in a fitted tee, looking at his niece adoringly, was too much for Charlotte's ovaries.

Three other little people ran into the kitchen and crowded them. Another little girl, around the age of six or seven, waved at Charlotte. "Are you Uncle Jake's girlllllfriend?"

Charlotte couldn't bring herself to lie out loud, especially to a child, so she smiled and changed the subject. "What's your name?"

"Danica." The little girl rocked on her heels, her hands clasped behind her back. "Everybody calls me Dani 'cept Uncle Jake." She grinned, her missing front teeth on full display. "Uncle Jake says beautiful girls shouldn't be called by a boy's name."

Charlotte leaned down to whisper. "My name's Charlotte, but my family calls me Charlie."

"I bet Uncle Jake doesn't call you Charlie."

She mentally reviewed the last few weeks: lots of angels and a few Charlottes, but never Charlie.

Huh. That's weird. "No, he hasn't."

"That's cause you're beautiful, too!" She crooked her finger with chipped sparkly pink polish. "I like you," she whispered.

"I like you, too," Charlotte whispered back. Little Danica just replaced Theresa as her favorite family member. *She's good for my ego.*

"Why don't you give Uncle Jake a hug?" Jake interrupted their conversation.

"Dinner's ready. Everyone grab a bowl and go to the formal dining room," Theresa yelled over the chattering family.

"Guests first." Offering his arm, Gerald guided Charlotte to the front of the forming line. "Besides, once you get settled, you can finally tell us who won."

Her stomach dropped. "Yes. Umm, I'd be happy to."

She silently freaked at the spread. Between the sweet tea, cornbread, gumbo, and chocolate cake, her diet was toast. *Not to mention my blood sugar level.*

"It's all right." Jake wrapped his arms around her waist and kissed her neck. "Just watch your portion size, and let's call this a cheat meal."

She sighed and leaned against him. "How did you know what I was thinking?"

Stepping back, he grabbed a bowl and scooped up a nice portion of gumbo and then a piece of cornbread before handing the bowl to her. "I dunno. I guess I'm just attuned to you."

She had fallen in love with Jake's family. A dozen butterflies fluttered in her chest. Maybe, just maybe, she was falling a little in love with Jake, too.

• • •

Just as Jake expected, Charlotte had everyone—from his brothers and their wives to his parents and Grandma Etta, to the two sets of aunts and uncles that had stopped by to visit—wrapped around her pretty finger.

Even his youngest nephew Kyrie, who rarely went to anyone outside of the family, was mesmerized. The toddler, now seated on Charlotte's lap, even tried to hit him with his toy truck when Jake leaned in to hug Charlotte.

He loved spending time with his family, but for once, he wanted to hole up somewhere quiet, snuggle on the couch with his girlfriend, and watch Netflix. Or "Netflix and chill," as his mentee would say. Not that he and Charlotte were chilling—a.k.a. hooking up. But he'd settle for a kiss, or two, or two hundred from her.

"All right, fam. Charlotte and I need to turn in. It's been a long day."

"What?" his Uncle Gus shouted. "The flight from New York is only a few hours."

"More like four and half hours, Uncle Gus, but who's counting."

"The night is still young. You're young, and so is your lady." Uncle Gus patted his back pocket and pulled out an unopened deck of cards. "Besides, I need to whip your behind in a few rounds of spades."

His mom clapped her hands. "Sounds good. The young folks versus the wise folks."

They really are trying to run my girlfriend—I mean Charlotte—off.

"I don't think that's a good idea, Ma."

"Why not?" She cocked her hips and swung her head in Charlotte's direction. "Charlie baby, don't you want to play spades with us? You aren't tired, are you?" Her voice and smile were both sweet, but the woman was a card shark. No matter how much she liked you, she didn't mind beating the brakes off someone in a game of spades. Even Grandma Etta and his dad were afraid.

"No, no. I'm not tired. I'd love to play."

Jake shook his head. "Angel, you don't know what you're getting into. Last time we all played, Dad slept on the couch, and Uncle Gus threatened to cut Uncle Fred." He pointed to one of his brothers. "D'Mario was written out of Grandma Etta's will."

"Oh, hush now, JR. I called the lawyer and wrote 'im back in. You're gonna make Charlotte think we're crazy."

"Yeah, hush, JR," his mother parroted. "Charlie, we aren't crazy, just passionate."

Charlotte's eyes were wide as she looked around the room, and she clutched Kyrie tighter in her arms. "I, uh, it's fine. We can play as long as everyone tosses their switchblades into the middle of the room."

Uncle Gus threw back his head, slapped his thigh, and laughed. "I like this one. And it wasn't a switchblade, it was a butter knife." He pointed his stout finger to Jake's dad. "JR always did have a wild imagination."

Sure I did. "Well, butter knife or not," he turned and pointed to everyone in the room, "do not scare off my girl, or you'll have to answer to me."

"Fine, fine. Don't get your jockstrap in a twist," Grandma Etta yelled from across the room.

• • •

To Jake's knowledge, there were two times when Charlotte took off the halo: One, when she danced, and two, when she played spades. The woman was kicking ass and taking names. *And here I thought I was protecting her.*

During the second game, Charlotte had dropped him and partnered with his mom. He wasn't the best spades player. As a child, he'd prefer trading Pokémon cards with his friends rather than play with his rowdy family.

When he'd feigned outrage, she shrugged and said, "Sorry, but your mom has the Kobe Bryant killer instinct."

He was surprised at his mother, too. She only ever partnered with Dad or Grandma Etta.

Charlotte fanned out the cards in her hand, threw him a sexy smirk, and then slapped a card on the table.

Jumping from her seat, his mother screamed. "Ha! We set you. Five-time champs! Charlie is my new spades partner."

"Now wait a minute, baby," his dad pouted from the couch.

"Only when she's in town." His mom batted her lashes. "You know I love you, Gerald, but she's the best."

Uncle Gus stood and gave Charlotte a hug. "You have my respect, Charlie. I thought you were going to be as bad as your boyfriend."

"I have other talents," Jake replied, used to his family's ribbing.

"We've got to get the kids to bed." His brother Rich stood as well. "We'll see you guys tomorrow at the cookout."

"Cookout?"

"Yeah. Ma didn't tell you?"

Jake shook his head as he watched his mom do a victory dance around the room. "No, she didn't. Let me guess ... she invited everyone and their mamas."

"Yup. She's told everyone at church and the neighbors that you finally settled down with a nice girl."

Jake shuddered, imagining the things his mother had said to her church friends. They probably high-fived each other for their prayers finally being answered. He gave his brother a hug. "Thanks for the heads-up. Let me kiss my nieces and nephews goodbye, and I'll see you all tomorrow."

Chapter Seven

Guests trickled in for the cookout. As Jake had predicted, everyone from his Little League coach to the pastor of their church was here. Church folk being one-half of the guests did not stop his childhood friend Shawn from regaling Charlotte with stories from their youth.

"So there Jake was, naked as the day he was born, crawling out of his girlfriend's bedroom window. Located on the second floor, mind you."

Charlotte giggled into her cup of his father's sweet tea. She'd finally confessed to him earlier that his dad's family recipe was her favorite, although he'd advised her that, if asked, to say Grandma Etta's tea was the best. Dad would get over the contest. Grandma Etta would not. His grandma still held a grudge with her second cousin when she said Dolly Parton's "I Will Always Love You" was better than the Whitney Houston remake.

Charlotte took another sip. "Wait. How did you see Jake shimmying down from the bedroom window?"

Jake shook his head. "More like climbing out the window. Like 007."

"Yeah, right. Let me tell you the true story, Charlotte." Shawn took a bite of his shrimp and then said, "I was outside in the car, parked on the curb with his girl's cousin, who was visiting from out of town. We wanted some privacy." He wiggled his eyebrows.

Nodding, Charlotte leaned into his friend and whispered, "I can only imagine two horny teenage boys trying to get laid."

"So anyway, where was I?" Shawn asked.

Charlotte hugged her torso and smiled dreamily. "Jacob ... butt-naked ... crawling out of a window."

She seems to be enjoying the thought of me naked. Jake winked, and she dropped her head-in-the-clouds expression and replaced it with a hand-caught-in-the-cookie-jar one.

Shawn snapped his fingers. "Right. So, me and the girl's cousin were having a reeeal good time. That is until we were interrupted by a bunch of yelling I couldn't make out at first. But what I did hear was 'I'm gonna shoot your ... '" Looking around, he hesitated and whispered the rest. "'You-know-what off.' Next thing I know, Jake sprinted toward the car screaming like a little girl and yelled, 'Go, go, go!' He ordered her cousin to get out and yelled at me to drive."

Shawn and Charlotte were clutching their stomachs and laughing.

Jake cleared his throat, which did nothing to interrupt their cackling. "I'm sure my girlfriend doesn't want to hear about my youthful escapades." *And what happened to the bro code?* Mildly annoyed, Jake tilted his head and gave Shawn what he hoped conveyed, "Shut the hell up!"

His friend's eyes stretched, and he lifted his hands in the air. "Ah, man. Sorry about that. My bad." Turning to Charlotte, he gave her a hug. "I hope I didn't say anything to make you uncomfortable."

He's still hugging her. Something foreign and ugly tugged at Jake's insides. His friend needed to take a step back—waaaaay back—from Charlotte.

"Oh, no!" She tilted her head up to his six-foot-five friend. "Noooo. Not at all. In fact, please feel free to share more stories about Jacob." She threw a grin in Jake's direction. "And here I thought you were a sweet and innocent boy who traded Pokémon cards."

"He did that, too." Shawn rubbed her shoulder. "Then he discovered boobs."

Charlotte broke into another fit of laughter.

Between the shoulder rub and boobs comment, Jake saw red. Despite his inner turmoil, he calmly moved Charlotte away from his devilish friend by tucking her into his side. "Let's grab something to drink. I'm thirsty."

She gave him a dazzling smile. "Okay, sweetheart. I wouldn't mind a glass of water." His heart stumbled at the endearment. He usually wasn't a guy who liked it when women called him pet names. It reeked of familiarity, and he was all for the one-night, no-more-than-a-one-week fling. But when Charlotte whispered *sweetheart*, it made him want to stand on top of a mountain, beat his chest, and maybe flip a few birds in his cocky-ass friend's direction.

Jake bent over and lightly kissed her temple. "Later, Shawn," he said without turning around.

Walking a few feet away, he finally relaxed. "We probably need to break away soon and go visit your folks."

Her bright smile immediately disappeared. "Wouldn't it be rude if we left the event that's celebrating you?"

"Nah." He scanned the crowd, taking in the picnic tables and platters upon platters of food. "I haven't seen my mom since it started. Trust me when I tell you I won't be missed. Now ... they may miss you." Guiding her to the orange cooler, he filled a cup with water. "But you already met my mother's prayer circle. They're the ones who prayed every Wednesday after Bible study that I would find a good, God-fearing girl."

He took a sip.

"I thought you were joking when you first told me that, but they really were concerned about you."

"Yeah, and every time I come down to visit my folks, my mom tries to get me to join the prayer circle. I told them to pray for the Yankees to win the World Series, not for a woman they deem appropriate."

Her head drooped, and she stared at the grass.

"What's wrong?"

Her eyes fluttered to his. The confusion and confliction swirling in those brown depths pierced his chest. "They think I'm some … some sweet girl you fell in love with, but that's far from the truth," she whispered. "And what's worse, I'm a liar." She waved a hand between them. "We're liars. God didn't answer their prayers."

Jake lifted her trembling hand and guided her to the side of the house for privacy. "Hey now." He tipped her chin so her eyes focused on his. "You aren't a liar. You're a good person who's doing me a favor. You didn't ask for money like most people do. Hell, I had to all but force you to accept help for personal training. And unlike the women I've been with in the past, you don't use or abuse my fame. You see me, the person, not the cash cow, the world-famous pitcher, the millionaire player. I like that … no, I love that about you, Charlotte." He moved his hands to cup her face. "No matter what happens, we've found something special … friendship. I'd like to think that we'll remain close after this, right?"

"I … sure. We can be friends … I guess." She didn't seem to like the idea.

Fire burned through his stomach. This entire time he'd assumed that she'd enjoyed his company. Maybe she was just being polite. "You don't want us to stay in touch?"

"I … of course, I do, Jacob, but it doesn't seem feasible."

"And why the hell not?"

She nibbled her bottom lip. "Maybe, if you were just an ordinary man, we could be friends. But the media hounds you. And when you start dating your models again, the media hounds are going to wonder why I'm still hanging around. Then I'll seem like a pathetic loser who isn't over you. Which isn't true of course because we aren't together and we don't like each other like that," she rambled on.

Stepping back, he ran his fingers over his close-cut hair. "I don't give a damn what the media thinks."

"And the women?"

"They'll adjust. We're friends. They'll just have to accept that."

Charlotte wrapped her arms around her torso. "Maybe so, but to them, we'll technically be exes. No one wants her boyfriend to hang out with an ex-girlfriend."

"I'm telling you, they'll be fine. If they don't understand or accept our friendship, then they can leave."

"All right then ... what about me?"

Damn, she's argumentative today. "What about you?"

"W-well what happens when I get a boyfriend? I can't rightly tell him we fooled the world for a sports endorsement deal to go through. So, what then?"

I'll pummel him into the ground for even thinking he can take you away from me.

He didn't like the turn of the conversation, didn't like the way it made him feel when she shared her plans to be with another man. The desire to stake his claim nearly bowled him over. But he wouldn't. *He couldn't.* She deserved more than a guy who ran through women. She deserved a guy who would get up on Sunday mornings and go to church, not a party animal who was too busy shooing women out of his apartment on Sunday mornings. No, she deserved a nice, solid, church-bred boyfriend. *And I hope he bores her to death.*

"We're skipping too far ahead. We'll cross that bridge when we get there. For now, let's make our rounds, say goodbye, and then visit your folks."

• • •

Charlotte stared at the ranch-style homes in the older neighborhood. She sighed and lightly thumped her head against the passenger-side car window. Squeezing her eyes shut, she tried and failed to block out the houses and the memories that rushed through her mind: Homemade pies and family gatherings ... bike races around the neighborhood ... her precious comic book collection.

Her childhood hadn't been terrible, but it wasn't warm and loving like the one Jacob had. Neighborhood kids would sometimes tease about her weight, but no more than they did about the kid down the street with the big ears or her next door neighbor, Lonny, who had a crooked nose.

No, her childhood scars were unknowingly inflicted by those who loved her. What would her parents say when they saw her? She'd rushed out of the house and straight to the airport after Big Mama's funeral.

A hole the size of Texas burned her chest. She could almost hear Big Mama's sweet voice, smell her flowery scent, and feel her loving hug. Her grandmother was the only one who'd truly understood her, who truly accepted her. Big Mama didn't make her weigh in once a month, didn't make her steamed veggies and boiled chicken without seasoning, and rabbit-sized portions, while the rest of the family ate more because they had better metabolisms, according to Charlotte's mother. No, Big Mama would often go head-to-head with her mother, telling her to "Leave my baby alone. She's perfect." Now she was gone. *Forever.*

"We're here, Charlotte."

Jake clicked off the navigation system. "Are you all right? You don't seem that excited to see your folks. Aren't you all close?"

She sighed. They didn't have enough time to discuss her weird family dynamics. "It's fine. They love me, and I love them, but they … my parents, especially my dad, didn't … *don't* understand me."

Jake's eyes glittered. "Was he mean to you?" His cool voice clipped on the word *mean.*

"No, no. Like I said, my family loves me, but they just don't get me. I was the blerd before the phrase was coined."

He laughed. "Blerd? You mean black nerd?"

"Yeah. As a child, I was into things they just weren't. Add that to the fact that I've always been chubby, unlike my mom, dad, sister, and brother, and … there you go. Middle-child syndrome at its best." She tried to laugh off the pain. But from the look on Jake's face, he wasn't buying it.

Unbuckling their seat belts, he leaned in. "Let's make a deal. We go in, be polite, and stay for all of an hour. I can fake our having to leave early. Maybe a headache or something, and we're out of there."

"I like that idea." She grinned.

"Okay, we need a signal."

Had he leaned in closer? His woodsy cologne teased her senses. "Like … Ca-caw!" Charlotte mimicked a bird.

"I'm thinking something a little less obvious."

"Okay, then … if we're leaving, that means something bad happened or I just want to get out of there. So maybe we can say something a villain would say."

"What about … kneel before Zod?"

"Yes! The *Superman* villain, General Zod. I like it. But instead of saying the whole thing, let's just say 'Oh my Zod.'"

Stroking her cheek, he grinned. His minty breath tempted her to sample a taste of his full lips.

"We've got a plan. You know I have your back, right? No matter what."

"Yes. I know. And I have yours, too."

Chapter Eight

"Charlie baby! It's so good to see you." Charlotte's mother, Vera, wrapped her slim arms around her daughter's waist. "And look at you." She stepped back, scrutinizing Charlotte like a drill sergeant inspecting a recruit. "You've lost a lot of weight. I hope you aren't doing one of those fad diets." Her voice was stern. "How many pounds have you lost?"

Charlotte smoothed the non-existent wrinkles from her shirt. "Um … I don't know, Mama. I don't focus on the scale." Charlotte didn't want to get into a weight loss discussion with her mom.

Vera shifted her attention toward Jake. "Nice to finally meet you. I would say I've heard so much about you, but this young lady," she pointed to Charlotte, "hasn't told me much."

"Sorry, Mama. It's been a whirlwind."

"Yes, I heard that from the sound bites on *Entertainment Tonight*." Her mother shook her head. "Where are my manners? Come in, come in."

Charlotte stepped into the living room that had previously been a garage. She slipped her ballet flats off at the door and turned to Jake. "Take off your shoes."

Smirking, he shuffled his black and green Nikes off on the tile floor and then placed them on the shoe rack.

A bubble of amusement rose in her chest. She, Charlotte Gayle Jones, just told Jacob Ross, hottie millionaire baseball player, to take off his shoes in her childhood home.

"C'mon, Charlie, everyone's here to see you and your new beau. Even Priscilla and David."

Ughhh. Not Perfect Priss.

She was so not looking forward to her siblings' nosy questions. They could be worse than their parents.

Her feet sank into the fluffy dark brown carpet. A warm, calloused hand slipped into hers, startling her.

Jake winked and gave her hand an encouraging squeeze. *Jake the Great was now Jake the Protector.*

She gave him a reassuring smile and followed her mother. Passing the galley kitchen and rounding the corner, she found her brother, sister, and father seated around the walnut dining-room table.

Letting go of her hand, Jake immediately strode toward her father. "Mr. Jones." He extended his hand.

Her father gave him a tight smile, stood, and shook his hand. "Nice to finally meet you, young man. Call me Vance."

"Nice to meet you too." Jake offered his greetings to Perfect Priss and her brother David.

Her mother clapped her hands. "Charlie told us you all were coming from a cookout, so I didn't go all out." She waved her hands at the spread of hummus, carrots, pita bread, and tomato and cucumber salad. "But I did whip up a few snacks for us to nibble. Are you two hungry?"

"No, Mama. I'm full."

"Okay. Jake, honey, what about you? Can I get you food or anything to drink? We have water, tea, lemonade, and diet cola."

"I'm fine. Thank you, Mrs. Jones."

She waved him off. "Mrs. Jones makes me feel old. Call me Vera." She pointed to the empty seat at the foot of the table. "Have a seat, honey."

Charlotte's heart thumped loudly as she stared at the empty chair. Pressure compressed her chest. She couldn't breathe, but she had to get it out. "No, that's … " She gulped a breath. "Big Mama's chair."

Her mother furrowed her brow. "Charlie, honey … she's … she's gone. We only have six chairs."

"How about I grab another one from the kitchen?" Jake offered. His voice sounded so far away, but she could see her grandmother as clear as day, smiling that secret smile that she did only for Charlotte and sneaking a piece of chocolate under the table when her mother dumped steamed veggies and tasteless chicken in front of her.

"Charlie?" she heard her sister call out, voice laced with concern.

"S-sorry. I'll get the chair from the kitchen. Be right back." She rushed from the room before anyone could stop her.

Whispered voices filtered in. Most likely her mother was explaining her erratic behavior. Big Mama had died just six months ago, and they were already trying to erase her memory. Charlotte wouldn't have it. No, she would scoot her chair right next to Big Mama's seat. If she breathed deeply enough, maybe she could even smell her grandmother's rose oil fragrance.

"I'm back everyone," she announced before reentering the room.

Giving her a tight smile, Jake sat to the right of Big Mama's chair. Charlotte sat to the left. A bit crowded, but she didn't care.

Her family and Jake settled into conversation, mostly about the baseball season. David asked what he thought about the trades rumors of a few of Jake's teammates. Her parents asked how he'd liked growing up in Alabama. After a few minutes, Charlotte's shoulders began to relax, and she settled into her chair. Maybe her family wasn't so bad after all.

And with him by her side, she didn't feel so awkward or so different or so alone. Jake was a natural charmer and a perfect match for her family. Everyone was fit and in shape, and he could talk about everything from the latest Tyler Perry movie to football and politics. Big Mama would've loved him at first sight.

"So … " Priscilla chirped from across the table. "How did you two *really* meet?"

Her brother David snorted. "Like you don't know. You and Mom are practically inhaling those tabloids."

"Hush, David," her mother admonished. "Everyone knows those things are full of junk." Jake chuckled.

"No worries. Charlotte and I met about two years ago. Her boss Damien used to be my publicist before he switched jobs to work at the nonprofit. We reconnected because I'm a regular volunteer there and I see your daughter at the center all the time. We got to know each other better and realized we enjoy the same things and … well … you know your daughter best. What's not to love?"

"Mmm hmm," her sister muttered. "Our Charlie *is* unique. She used to drive Mama crazy with her comics and video game obsessions. I'm sure she's much different from the women you usually date." Her sister dropped the teasing look when she peered over at Charlotte. "I mean no harm. I just want to make sure you both get along."

Charlotte's hands shook with anger. No, with disappointment. Always the same with Prissy. Charlotte's tear ducts had dried and she was all cried out. Still, the tickle in her nose and the pressure behind her eyes were muscle memory, and it egged her on to run away and cry. Memories from years upon years of being the square peg, middle child that didn't quite fit in with her round hole, perfect family.

"Right," Charlotte bit out, her voice laced with bitterness. "Because Jake the Great would never look twice at someone like me."

Her father cleared his throat. "I think what your sister means is that we want to make sure you're the right fit for each other. Jake, you seem to like sports and the outdoors and our Charlotte is a homebody. And, no offense, son, but from what the media says, you are a bit of a player."

Jake exhaled and turned to Priscilla. "I enjoy comic books and games, too. We actually grew up quite similarly, which is why she and I connected. I get to be the real me with your sister, not the person people think I am. And even if we were opposites, that wouldn't matter." He nodded to her father. "Vance, I appreciate your concern for Charlotte, but I would never step out on your daughter. She's a wonderful woman, and I'm lucky to have her in my life."

Oh, God. Here we go. Charlotte reached for the square white plate placed neatly on the corner of the table and then piled on a lump of hummus and a few slices of pita bread.

Her mother gave the same concerned look she'd perfected over the last twenty-six years. "Oh, Charlie, honey. I thought you said you were full from the barbeque? Let's just drop the subject. You know," she looked at Jake and whispered, "Charlotte is a stress eater."

Charlotte dropped the plate. The ceramic square made a sharp crack against the table. She jumped from her seat. "Zod!"

"What's that, honey?" her mother asked.

"Zod, Zod, Zod, Zod, Zod!"

"Sit down, Charlie," her father commanded.

She shook her head. No, she wouldn't sit down. Jake stood, grabbed her hand, and nodded. Thank goodness he supported her.

Jake cleared his throat. "I have an early day tomorrow. Charlotte and I need to leave. Now."

"Leave?" Her mother stood and wrung her hands. "But you just got here, and we haven't seen you since ... since Big Mama passed."

"I guess she's too good to come see us after running off to the big city with her celebrity boyfriend." Priscilla's catty voice bit Charlotte like a persistent mosquito.

She ripped her hand from Jake's. Congo drums pounded in her chest, and fire shot through her veins. They didn't get it. After all these years, they still didn't get it.

"I haven't been back because I'm trying to build up my self-esteem. The only person who understood and loved me for *me* was Big Mama."

"What?" her sister yelled.

"What are you talking about? We love you." Her mother's brows knitted and her brown eyes sparkled with tears.

"You think you do, but you don't. You've always made me feel different. *Charlie, why don't you play sports or be a cheerleader like Prissy? You aren't losing weight from dance classes. Charlie, why are you always holed up in your room with your head in the clouds? Charlie, you have such a pretty face. You'd be a knockout if you lost some weight.*" Her voice broke off on the end.

"I ... I didn't mean it like that." Her mother massaged a temple. "We just wanted you to be active."

"No, you wanted me to be a perfect Barbie like you and Priscilla. You sent me to fat camp. Then you told Ms. Nancy, who gossiped to everyone in the neighborhood!"

Her father pounded his fist on the table. "That's enough, young lady. You will not yell at your mother in our home!"

"No. It's not enough. I'm not enough. I've never fit in with this family. You all have always made me feel bad about my weight. No one but Big Mama—"

"Big Mama," her mother cut in, "God rest her soul, died from diabetes. And your grandfather, God rest his soul, died from a stroke. Your father's brother is also a diabetic and has high blood pressure. Now maybe ... *maybe* I went about things the wrong way. But I have always loved you, you've got to know that. I just wanted to make sure you were healthy."

Charlotte looked around the room. Her mother wiped tears from her eyes. Priscilla, for once, was quiet. Contemplative. David was, as usual, quiet with his arms folded across his chest. Her father avoided her eyes, staring at the grandfather clock in the corner of the room.

"Let's go, angel." Jake grabbed her hand, grabbed their shoes, and dragged her out of the house. He clicked the key fob. The chirp from the car barely registered. "In you go." He guided her into the passenger seat, buckled her seat belt, and then walked to the driver's side.

Movement from the blinds in the front window caught her attention. She couldn't make out who it was. Most likely Priss or her mother.

"So ... I'm thinking Zod was a bad choice."

Charlotte turned to face him, tossed her head back, and laughed. Could be from the hilarity of his random statement or the exhilaration from finally telling her family the truth. Either way, she knew she would be okay.

"I'm sorry about your grandmother."

"Thanks," she whispered. "She was a good woman."

He gripped the steering wheel and stared straight ahead. "I want you to know that everything that went down in there ... you can talk to me. About anything."

Charlotte sighed. "Sorry for all the drama. I know you didn't sign up for my family issues."

"Speaking of issues ... " He drummed his fingers on the wheel.

"Yeah?" Her heart thundered.

"The diabetes thing ... seems like it runs in your family. Are you okay?"

"Am I okay? Doesn't it look like I'm okay?" She playfully nudged his shoulder and gave him a plastic smile. His question had thrown her for a loop. She'd forgotten her mom had given Jake the rundown of their unhealthy family tree.

He didn't move, didn't smile. Jake used his lecturer voice, the one he used for the kids at the center. "What I'm asking is are you diabetic?"

Her foot frenetically tapped against the door. "Umm ... no. No I'm not diabetic." *Technically.*

He smiled and then leaned over to kiss her cheek. "I'm relieved. Uncle Gus is diabetic and I know he's had it rough. I'm glad you're taking the steps to be healthy."

Throat closed, Charlotte fiddled with the seat belt and gave him a tight smile. She didn't want to say anything more to pile on to the sky-high stack of lies.

"All right. Let's get you home. We'll be back to New York in twelve hours. We can binge watch a few episodes of *Daredevil*, and I'll even throw in a foot rub."

"Really?"

"Really. Anything for you."

Chapter Nine

Charlotte upped the treadmill speed from a brisk warm-up to a full-out sprint. Long and steady breathing turned to short and frequent spurts, but the familiar burn in her lungs didn't deter her focus.

This type of pain she could manage. With more practice and conditioning, the aches and soreness would fade. The trip south to her childhood home had taught her that even after twenty-six years of being conditioned to her parents' disappointment, the pain would never disappear.

She resolved to avoid painful situations. Avoid her parents. Avoid her siblings. Avoid Jake. Just thinking about her fake boyfriend squeezed her overtaxed lungs.

Jake represented all the things she couldn't have but so desperately wanted. She'd lied to everyone—her family, friends, the entire world about their relationship. But she wouldn't lie to herself anymore. She had fallen head-over-heels in love with him. Unfortunately, he was biding his time. *Time*, her Big Mama used to say, *heals all wounds*. Charlotte was banking on that. It would take a lot of time, but her plan, as cowardly as it was, seemed to be working. *Guard your heart.*

She hadn't seen Jake in nearly a week. Dodging his calls, she worked out at the Refurbished Dreams gym when she knew he wasn't on the schedule to volunteer.

"Now I'm really starting to get a complex."

She nearly tripped over the sexy voice that haunted her dreams. *He's here? Someone must've told him.* Lowering the speed on the treadmill's dashboard, she slowed her pace and turned to face him. "Hey. What are you doing here?"

"What am I … " Quicksilver eyes narrowed as he blew out a breath. "A better question is why are you avoiding me?"

"I-I'm not avoiding you. I've just been busy with work." She had a strong urge to turn around to verify if her pants had caught on fire. Instead, she averted her eyes and reached for a towel to pat herself dry.

Yanking the emergency stop cord on the treadmill, he towered over the machine.

"Hey!" she protested. "I have ten minutes left."

"You and I are gonna have a conversation. We can have it now, at your job, where everyone can overhear, or we can take a quick walk to your place. Your choice."

She rolled her eyes, tempted to call his bluff. No way was he going to risk blowing his precious reputation by having a "lovers' spat" in public.

Hopping on the side of the treadmill, he leaned close to her ear and whispered, "Do not tempt me. I've called you and texted you, and you've been M.I.A. I don't know what's in your head, but we're going to work through it."

She jerked her head back. "Don't worry. I won't sabotage your chances at getting your millions and into the warm beds of countless women." She swallowed as if forcing down a spoonful of castor oil. Her words were bitter, ugly, and cruel. *I'm turning into a coward and a shrew. I need to apologize.*

Before she could, his eyes changed lightning quick from mildly pissed to supremely angry. "Not gonna ask again," he growled. "Do you wanna have it out right now?"

Her eyes scanned the room. They were getting stares from mentees, parents, and other volunteers. No. This wasn't the place. She didn't want him to invade her home with his sexiness, but she'd rather have a private conversation outside her place of employment.

"Let me get my bag from the locker room, and I'll meet you outside."

● ● ●

Jake stood behind Charlotte while she rooted through her purse for her apartment key. The woman was driving him batshit crazy. In all his adult life, he'd never had to track down a woman. After day four—yes, he'd counted—he'd called Damien. Charlotte's boss was no help at all and seemed to take glee in giving Jake vague answers.

Finally, he texted his mentee, Dax, to be on the lookout. The following day, Dax snapped a picture of Charlotte's ass with a message that read, *She's here and looking good.* Jake made a mental note to himself to smack the back of Dax's head at the first opportunity. He was a good kid, but he was also the type to share that pic with friends.

Unlocking the door, Charlotte dropped her gym bag near the entry and rushed to the kitchen. Swinging open the refrigerator door, she pulled out a bottled water and took a deep gulp. "You want one?"

He shook his head. No, he wanted to get to the bottom of why she was avoiding him. He had a theory it had something to do with the confrontation with her parents. They'd bonded that weekend. He was sure of it.

"No. I'd like for you to sit and discuss what's going on."

"I'd rather stand."

"Fine." He sat down on her loveseat. "Stand if you want, just tell me what's up."

She shrugged. The off-shoulder t-shirt slouched even further down her arm. "Like I said, I've been busy."

"Right. What have you been so busy doing?"

"Working with the media for my job and my dance classes, writing guest posts and articles to generate publicity for the center, and hanging with friends. You know, I do have a life outside of our agreement."

Acid corroded his insides. "You know this is more than an agreement. I thought after everything that happened with our families last week that—"

Gripping the bottle, she shook her head. "No, I don't want to talk about it."

"Your parents," he continued over her protest. "I get it. They want you to fit into a mold that isn't you. But I saw the tears in your mother's eyes ... the guilt lingering in your father's. They love you."

Charlotte tossed the empty bottle into the recycling bin. "No, they don't. The only person in the world who loved me was buried six feet under six months ago."

"You can't believe that."

"I do!" She pointed to the door. "If you keep bringing them up, you can leave. We can talk about anything else but them."

He stood and slowly walked toward her. Chest heaving, she backed herself against the refrigerator.

Nowhere to hide. Closing the distance, he slapped his palms on the top of the freezer, boxing her in. Her scent intoxicated him, and he nearly lost his focus. The throbbing vein in her neck was tempting the hell out of him, begging him to lick, nibble, and mark her. "Don't you want me—I mean, us to be friends?"

Expelling a breath, she pushed against his chest.

He backed away and scanned her face. Lips quivering, she lowered her chin and stared at the floor. Damn, he'd hurt her. He didn't know how or why, but her pain blended into his own. "Why are you upset?"

"Sure. Whatever." She squeezed her eyes shut. "We're friends." She spat the words out like a curse.

"You don't want us to be friends?"

Eyes still closed, she remained silent. Damn, this entire time he thought there was something special. He'd never spent so much time with a woman without trying to get into her pants. Sure, he wanted in Charlotte's pants more than he wanted to win the World Series, but she was a forever girl. And as much as he'd like to be, he wasn't a forever man. He couldn't go there with her. Not now, maybe never.

He needed to focus on getting the deal, securing his nieces' and nephews' futures, and buying his parents and siblings their dream homes. Pay them back, somehow, for the countless hours they spent coaching him, going to games, and supporting his dream.

"So, you don't enjoy our time together?"

She shook her head.

"Fine, Charlotte. Just say the words, and I'm outta here. I can get the damn Threx deal some other way, and I'll never darken your doorstep again."

"That's not the problem, Jake. I want you here. I enjoy your company too much. I love your family, and I loved that you had my back at my parents' house. I … " She ducked from under his arms and rushed toward the living room.

He turned to follow her.

Shaking her head, she waved her hands. "This whole thing is so confusing. I don't know where reality begins and fantasy ends. This past month, us spending every day together, I've gotten to know you. You're a great man, and now you're my best friend. But the foundation of whatever we are started on a lie. And I can't tell what's the truth and what isn't."

He grabbed the back of his neck, sighing in relief. "Truth or dare."

Her bright eyes shimmered. "What? Now isn't the time for games."

He pushed off the fridge, marched to the comic book cabinet, and whipped out the Lasso of Truth.

Her eyes widened, and she backed away.

He drew closer and, like a determined cowboy, he looped and locked her in. Her chest heaved against his stomach. "I'll give you a choice again. Truth," he tightened the lasso against her lush ass, "or dare."

"Truth."

Damn, he wanted a dare. Dare him to take her on the couch, to relieve the throbbing ache pressing against his jeans. Dare him to taste every inch of her delectable body.

"Are we friends?"

She nodded.

"Now, your turn. Ask me a question. Any question, and I'll tell you the God's honest truth." *Ask me what I want.*

She pushed away, forcing him to drop the lasso. "H-how do you … "

"How do I what?" He softened his tone, hoping to encourage her to ask the question she clearly needed him to answer.

"Do you like me … umm … as a friend, I mean."

He stepped into her space again. This time, he pulled her into a hug. "The truth is, you're my best friend. You know more than even my homeboy Shawn and my brothers know. Truth is, I'm finding the boy I lost in high school. Truth is, I'm my best self when I'm with you. I've never been as close to another woman as I have with you. I like … " He stopped himself. Damn, he felt like he was in the hot seat at an intervention with Dr. Phil. But he'd placed himself there. "I like who I am when I'm with you."

Her shoulders relaxed. "I'm sorry for acting like a brat. You've been nothing but forthcoming and kind. And I'm … I'm just way into my feelings right now. Friends again?" *Friends.* Damn, he was starting to hate the word, but it would have to do. He couldn't give her more. More meant he would eventually break her heart when he'd developed a taste for other women. "Yes, friends."

She shyly smiled at him.

"Okay, friend," he said. "I'm starving. Can we grab something to eat?"

"How about I freshen up and we can stay in? I was going to bake some fish and whip up a salad."

"Sounds good, angel. But before you shower, can I use your restroom?"

"Of course." She jerked her thumb toward the hallway. "It's around the corner. You can't miss it."

He stared at her. Standing there in her workout clothes, she looked so damn fine in her tight black shirt and even tighter black pants. His hands itched to explore her curves like a sculptor admiring a fine piece of art. "What is it?" She gave him a small smile.

That small smile caused a large explosion of something he wasn't quite ready to name in his chest. "Nothing." He shook his head. "This way," he jerked his head toward the bathroom, "right?"

Real smooth, Ross.

"Right." She snorted and then turned around to open the fridge.

Don't look at her ass. He looked at her ass. A damn fine ass.

His dick swelled. Now he would be using the bathroom for an entirely different reason.

Turning around and walking toward the bathroom, he ran through his stats from last season. Thankfully, numbers did the trick on his slugger. He did his business, then reached for the eucalyptus mint soap and washed his hands. A small white device propped in front of a hand mirror caught his attention. After toweling his hands dry, he picked up the contraption that reminded him of a mini walkie-talkie his friends had used as preteens and pressed the OK button. A flashing icon that looked like a blood drop appeared.

Jake's blood went cold. He knew what it was but had to be sure. Opening her medicine cabinet, he found a small black kit that looked about the size to store the device. He then spotted a stack of white strips.

Red hot energy coursed through his body. The fainting spell … her family having a history of diabetes. *She told me she wasn't diabetic.* "Friends my ass." He wanted to smash the monitor to smithereens. Instead, he marched into the kitchen.

Charlotte hummed as she seasoned two pieces of salmon.

He waved the device in front of her face. "Why didn't you tell me?"

She lifted her head, and her eyes widened when she saw the monitor. "I … " She crossed her arms. "Why were you digging in my medicine cabinet?"

"It was near your sink, out for anyone to see."

She shook her head, averted her eyes to the sink, and washed her hands. "It's nothing, and I—"

"No, Charlotte. It's something. I'm your friend, or so you say." He pointed to his chest and moved closer. "And I'm your trainer. It was imperative that you tell me about you being diabetic. Hell, I could've recommended you eat something that would've been bad for your health."

"I don't have diabetes!" She jerked her hands up in a defense. "I have *prediabetes.* My gynecologist actually found out, and then I went to a general practitioner. But I'm doing well. My levels are going down, thanks to you."

"Why didn't you tell me? Why didn't you trust me?"

Licking her lips, she looked down at her feet. "It's not that I don't trust you. I just … you know Big Mama died from diabetes. And to be honest, we've had so many people in our family who lived with it that it didn't hit me until she died from complications.

And now … I don't want you or my family or my friends to treat me differently, and you would've if you'd known. So, I haven't told anyone." She squeezed her eyes and her fists. "I'm going to beat this. And trust me, after passing out and bumping my head, I knew I had to do this the right way. And you've taught me a lot. I'm not going to put my life in danger any longer."

He flinched at the word *danger*. He couldn't imagine a world without Charlotte in it. And she was right. She would win. *They* would win. She wouldn't be alone in this. Not ever again.

She nibbled her lips and rubbed her elbows as if warding off cold temperatures.

Releasing his grip around the monitor, he placed it on the counter and then opened his arms.

"Come here."

She rushed to him, wrapping her arms around his waist.

He kissed the top of her head. "We're in this together. I've got you."

"Okay, Jacob."

"And don't lie to me again." He didn't try to hide the gruffness in his voice. She needed to know that what she'd done, even lying by omission, was risky. Not to mention that he didn't like the fact that his angel felt it was okay to hide things from him.

"I won't. Not ever again. And I'm sorry."

"It's okay." He whispered against her head. His voice was calm, but his mind still raced, dizzy from the turn of events. He squeezed tighter and realized he didn't want to let her go. Not physically and not emotionally. This no longer was about a deal or helping out a friend. The thought of losing her twisted his insides. Charlotte meant something to him, and life was too damn short not to explore those feelings.

"Friends again?" she whispered.

Hell fucking no.

He was about to tell her as much when a buzz interrupted the moment, and she stepped away from his arms. Grabbing the phone from his pocket, he saw a text from his agent. "Damn. Gina wants us to go to some charity event this Thursday. Can you make it?"

"Sure." She gave him a shy smile. "It'll be fun."

He smiled back. She had no idea, but he planned to wine and dine her. Then she wouldn't have a doubt in her mind where they stood with each other.

Chapter Ten

Charlotte smoothed her fire-engine red chiffon gown as she stared into the full-length mirror. She had to admit that the stylist Jake hired for her was a genius. The halter top emphasized her full and pert breasts, and the skirt flared right below her hips, covering and highlighting all the right places. She twirled to check out her backside. *Not bad, Ms. Jones.*

She felt a bit like Cinderella but bolder, wiser, and—dare she say—sexier. Surprisingly, she was excited to attend the celebrity-studded event to raise money to build schools in Africa.

A phone ringing cut short her perusal. Grabbing her cell, she swiped the screen without looking. She knew it was probably Jake.

"Hey," his deep voice rumbled, causing all kinds of chaos to her heart. "I'm downstairs. Are you ready?"

"Yes. I'll be down soon."

"No. I'm coming upstairs to get you."

"Ummm … okay, I guess. I mean, I can just walk downstairs."

"Charlotte, I've been imagining what you'd be wearing all day, and I'll be damned if I get a half-assed experience of you hopping into the limo. We have time. Unlock the door *after* you confirm that it's me."

Charlotte rolled her eyes. The man was unnaturally preoccupied with her safety. She lived in an okay neighborhood, and her neighbors were friendly.

"All right, Jacob."

"That's my girl. See you soon."

Charlotte slipped her phone into a satin clutch and gave herself one last look. *You've got this.* Rushing to the bathroom, she put on the finishing touches—another swipe of clear deodorant, another dab of gloss, and a quick spritz of perfume.

The door buzzer made her to hurry through her touch-up. "Coming, coming!" She hustled through the living room and flung open the door.

"What did I tell you about … " But the anger wrinkling his brows and flattening his lips disappeared. In its place burned a smoldering, let-me-change-my-panties gaze. The path of his heated stare started north at the curls piled atop her head, then slowly took in the necklace the stylist had found, and finally landed south to the fitted red dress.

"Daaaammnn, angel. I see you took off the halo tonight."

I'll take off more if you let me. Instead, Charlotte smiled. "And you look pretty darn good yourself." Which was not an empty compliment. The man was Fine with a capital F and sure to turn heads on the red carpet. He wore a classic, European-style tux with satin lapels, black shirt, and a black bowtie. She wanted to unwrap him. *With my teeth.*

The only color that stood out was the stark gray of his eyes.

"Let's get the hell out of here before that dress becomes an area rug."

"My dress on the floor? Why would I do that?"

"*You* wouldn't be doing anything. The pleasure would be all mine."

For once, she didn't shy away from his bold comment. "We can stay in and snuggle on the couch." She stepped closer. "But," she reached for his bowtie, "you have to keep this on."

"Woman," he grumbled, "Are you trying to kill me?"

She shrugged, liking, no … loving the turn in their conversation. "I dunno. Maybe."

"I would love nothing more than to stay in with you. But I'm a big donor and have a speech to give tonight. Once I've said my bit, we can leave. Does that work?"

Everything sounded good to her. But she had to know, no ... *needed* to know it wouldn't be another night of hanging out with a friend. "What are your plans when we get back?"

"Don't you worry, angel. I have a lot of plans for you. Exhausting plans. Naughty plans. Plans I don't want to say out loud, or I will take you over there." He pointed to the couch. "And you'll know the real reason behind my name Jake the Great."

"So ... so you wouldn't say this to just any woman, right?" She licked her lips. "You wouldn't just say that to a *friend*?"

"Yes, we're friends. But we can be more than friends if you'll let me."

Should I? The man had his own Tumblr account with shots of his body parts. He once took two women to the ESPY Awards. "You aren't the relationship type. What changed?"

He scrubbed his hand over his face. "I don't know, maybe the diabetes scare. The way you were with my family. We have fun together and when the deal gets inked I don't want this to end. I have to admit, I haven't been in a monogamous relationship before, but it's worth a shot."

"Worth a shot?" She folded her arms across her chest. "This isn't some experiment when you test the limits of you being faithful. I'm not willing to be a try-to-keep-it-in-your-pants phase in your life."

Jake groaned and tilted his head to look at the ceiling. "Good grief, you're a tough cookie to crack."

"I like you, Jacob. But I like *me*, more."

He lowered his head, his eyes met hers. "I like you more, too." He gave her a look so hot, she was tempted to lock herself in the bathroom and turn the shower on cold. "I want to give this a real chance."

"No more fake relationship?"

"We are very much real." He smiled, much like a predator who finally claimed its prey. "Maybe tonight can be our first."

The satin clutch slipped from her fingers. Wild horses galloped in her chest. "First what?" she whispered.

"Date." He smiled, his grin devilish and eyes dancing with humor. "What did you think I meant?"

She scrambled for her purse on the floor. "What you said." She wouldn't give him the satisfaction of knowing her mind was in the gutter. A place she was familiar with a lot these days, thanks to Jake. "What time is your speech?"

"Eight thirty." Grabbing her hand, he tugged her into the hallway. "I'll see if I can push it up."

"Good." She grinned and nearly slipped out of her shoes. *Like Cinderella again, except this girl doesn't have a curfew.* Yes, she was definitely feeling up her prince. Tonight.

• • •

Jake was bored out of his ever-loving mind. He didn't regret giving and volunteering his time, but he hated rubbing elbows with other famous people and eating overpriced, bland food at these charity galas.

He had to admit that tonight's event didn't seem as pretentious as most. Other than the red carpet at the entry, the venue and decorations were minimal and welcoming. Instead of valuable paintings and sculptures in the lobby, life-sized pictures of children who benefited from the program were displayed. Next to each was a black-and-gold plaque explaining the child's story.

No time to spend with Charlotte as he'd been ushered into the gold-and-white-decorated ballroom by the event coordinator soon after arriving.

The stick-thin woman with frizzy golden hair tapped her headset and nodded. "Yes, I'm speaking to him now." She refocused her sharp, hazel eyes on him. "I was told you wanted to push up the speech, and I think we'll be able to accommodate."

"Thank you," he replied.

Giving him a tight smile, she perused the schedule on her clipboard.

He dutifully nodded his head as she read over the plan and talking points, taking note of the food station on the left side of the room. He focused back on the conversation and realized she was going over his speech. Again.

Jeez. Do they think I'm an idiot?

Clapping his hands together, he smiled. "I've got it, Sasha. I need to get back to my date."

His shy date was probably somewhere alone in the corner, overthinking what she should eat and drink. Or getting hit on by a celebrity. The woman was temptation in the flesh, and she didn't even know it. He rushed back into the lobby, scouring the area for his lady in red.

He shook his head, mentally kicking himself again for not taking Charlotte up on her offer to stay in. He was surprised she took the initiative, and it was damn sexy. He didn't know what it was, but his Charlotte was getting more confident, and he loved a confident woman. Catching a glimpse of crimson, he finally found her.

Lightly clasping her throat, she tossed her head back. A group of mostly men and a few women surrounded her: a couple of donors from Refurbished Dreams, one of the foundation's board members, and a football player that made Jake seem like a boy scout. Donald fucking Grayson. The cocky football player had once tried to start a feud with him over a model they'd both dated. Jake hadn't put up much of a fight over her, but he'd knock out a few teeth over Charlotte.

Determined to get his girl, he quickened his pace. Well, he tried but was pulled aside by a teammate. Reggie had a heart of gold but was too damn talkative. Before the man could corner him into an hour-long conversation, Jake stretched his hand for a shake. "Hey man, let's catch up later. I need to grab my woman." He jerked his head toward the group.

Reggie looked at Charlotte and then gave Jake a shit-eating grin. "No worries, man. It looks like Donald Grayson is trying to step to your girl."

The retired player was getting a little too familiar. If Grayson rubbed her shoulder one more damn time, he'd be leaving in a full body cast compliments of Jake the Great. Never mind he was an all-star defensive linebacker. *I can take him.*

"Caviar, Mr. Ross? Mr. Lopez?" a young man in a white coat and black pants asked.

"No," they both answered, Jake a little more rudely.

He pushed past the crowd and got stopped again. This time by a five-foot-eleven underwear model. Rafaela.

"Jake Ross." She rolled the R. He used to think that was sexy. Now he was unamused. Turning around, he focused on her sepia brown eyes, lined with determination and deception. Damn it! Rafaela was up to something. *Nuh-uh. Not going there.*

"Jake, you naughty, naughty man. You've been avoiding me."

"Yes, I have." *Let's cut through the bullshit.* "I'm in a committed relationship now. I texted that to you over a month ago."

Her eyes narrowed. "Well, I … I have much to discuss with you. Something important that you wouldn't want your delicate little flower to know about."

He leaned in closer. "Let me get a few things straight with you. I am not that guy. I'm not going to fall into your trap. And you know what trap I mean." He lowered his gaze to the juncture between her legs. "We had a good time, but now the good times are over. I'm with an amazing woman, and I don't need you to fuck this up for me. Find another boy toy. I'm not the one."

"Hmm … Is that so, Mr. Jake the Great? Well, you certainly weren't saying that last week when I took care of your needs because your little flower couldn't."

A gasp from behind him sent chills across his spine. *Double damn.* Rafaela had timed it just right.

He turned around. "Angel." Her hurt expression burned through him. Those large brown eyes brimmed with tears, and her cupid bow's mouth trembled. "This is not what it looks or sounds like."

"I knew it. I knew it. It was too good to be true. It always is," Charlotte whispered.

"No!" He grabbed an elbow, and hustled her into a corner. "It's not too good to be true. This is real. I'm real. Don't believe the lies of someone you don't know." He leaned in and whispered, "You know me. Believe in me."

A few nearby conversations went quiet, but he didn't care. He needed to get through the layers upon layers of insecurity. What happened to the confident woman he'd escorted from her apartment? She was somewhere in there, and she had to know that his past conquests didn't compare to her.

Sighing, she leaned into his chest. "We'll keep our plans to leave after the speech, right?"

The knot of tension in his chest unraveled. "Yes. Give me fifteen, twenty minutes tops, and we'll blow this joint."

"Okay. Go on. I'll be fine."

"Are you sure?"

"Don't worry. Do your thing, and we can get on with it later." Her tone was fatalistic, as if she hadn't believed a word he'd said.

At least she's willing to listen.

"We'll work it out." He leaned in to kiss her forehead, and she flinched.

Damn.

• • •

Charlotte paced her apartment floor as Jake recounted the run-in with his ex. She wanted to believe him. She really, truly wanted to believe him, but a little voice inside her head wouldn't let her get past it. If only she could've seen his reaction to what Rafaela had said and not his back. All Charlotte saw was the smug and confident smirk on the beautiful model's face.

"Don't let her ruin this for us." He sat, legs spread on her sofa. "We were finally on the same page."

"I want to believe you, but I—"

"Then do it. Stop with this insecure bullshit!"

She stopped her pacing, gripping the phone in her hand. "Insecure?"

"Yes. Insecure. Since we've been together—yes, fake together, but together—I have been nothing but faithful and attentive to you."

Anger bubbled and boiled, but it wasn't fluid and fiery. She was frozen in place. For once, she wanted to smack someone. "I am not insecure, and I didn't say I didn't believe you. But I want to be smart about it, too. I can't tell you how many friends I've had to comfort because they put their trust in a guy that lied or cheated. We've been hanging out for all of a month. I'm not going to kiss your … your ass and give you a humanitarian award. You already got one tonight."

He shook his head. "You don't believe me. Otherwise, we wouldn't be having this conversation. What happened to us being best friends? What happened to us knowing so much about each other?"

"Look, Jake. Whatever happened between you and that model, I know you are a decent guy. But you don't exactly have a sterling rep with the ladies. How I am supposed to believe out of all the women you've been with you suddenly see something in me?" She

pointed to her chest. "Something that makes you want to do …
whatever it is we were going to do."

Twin buzzes from their phones caught their attention. Charlotte
glanced at the screen.

Gina: What the hell happened tonight? Tell me you aren't back with
Rafaela???

She sighed. Jake's agent had sent a group text. A link to an
article was attached.

"Is Jake Ross back at it again? Scorned lover maintains she and Jake
were together last week."

Thumb touching the screen, she was tempted to click the link.
Jake scrubbed a hand over his face. "So what is it, Charlotte?"
His voice was hoarse and tired. "Are you going to believe Rafaela,
a woman who I barely remember spending time with, and a stupid
article from a gossip blog, or me?"

Sighing, she pressed the link and scrolled. Her breath caught
when she saw Jake and Rafaela, coffee in hand and smiling together.
Queasiness invaded her. Clutching her phone like a lifeline, she
staggered to a wall for support. She'd had this feeling once before:
in college and after four too many margaritas. The sick and gross
feeling would only disappear with the soberness of time or a few
dozen dry heaves in the toilet.

"What's it going to be?"

"I need to think, Jake." Her voice was soft. *Can he could hear
my sad attempt to speak over the hot, painful lump in my throat?*
"Please, give me time to process."

"Your answer is yes or no. Right here and now. You trust me,
or you don't."

"You aren't going to force me into a decision. I need to think."

"No, you need to sulk and hide. Just like you did when we came back from Alabama. Just like you're doing with your family."

"Jake, I'm telling you to please give me a day. Maybe two."

"So no is your answer." He stood and walked towards the door. "Do me a favor, Charlotte … "

Damn, she never hated her name more than this moment.

"When you're all alone in your apartment—reading your comics because you're too afraid of the world to live—think about why you love superheroes so much and why Wonder Woman is your favorite."

He cracked open the door.

She was suffocating. She couldn't breathe. Every word was a lash to her battered soul.

"Wait, Jacob." She lifted a hand. "Wait."

Gripping the door frame, he turned. "Yes?"

"What about our … the deal?"

"Fuck the deal." Storming into the hallway, he slammed the door shut.

She slid onto the floor, tilting her head against the wall. The framed poster of Wonder Woman taunted her, especially the words.

"And remember that, in a world of ordinary mortals, you are a Wonder Woman."

Tears welled, and Wonder Woman became a mixture of blues and reds and whites.

Chapter Eleven

A gentleman and group of British ladies dressed in nineteenth-century corsets and bonnets kept Charlotte company.

Too bad they were actors on TV in *Jane Eyre*.

She squirted spray cheese into her mouth and then tossed in a cracker. Putting cheese on a cracker was too much work. "He's a big fat liar, Jane. They all lie."

She angled the can again for another dose of cheesy goodness. A knock on the front door diverted her aim from her mouth to her cheek. Picking up the remote, she quickly muted the film, hoping the unexpected company would leave. Hopefully they hadn't heard the movie.

"I know you're in there because you just turned off your television!" The endearing yet unwelcome female voice yelling from the other side of the door confirmed her fears.

Melanie.

"C'mon!" She knocked again. "I know you're in there."

Charlotte dashed to the kitchen to grab a napkin. She wiped her cheek, then tugged an oversized shirt over her leggings.

"Who is it?" Charlotte teased.

"Your two favorite people in the whole wide world," Melanie's overly chirpy voice replied.

And she brought her enforcer, Tiana. Charlotte sighed. Damien had noticed she wasn't her usual self and told his wife. *Great.*

"I wasn't expecting company."

"We don't care!" Tiana responded in the same sing-songy voice. "Now open up."

"Fine." She unhooked the chain and twisted the lock open.

Stepping back, she let her uninvited guests into her apartment. Tiana and Melanie rushed past her, each with a grocery bag in hand, and went straight to the kitchen.

"Make yourself at home."

"Sarcasm doesn't become you," Melanie said, sliding the bag onto the counter.

Charlotte massaged her forehead. "Sorry I'm such a grump. I guess Damien told you I wasn't in the best mood."

"Yeah, he figured it was something between you and Jake. So, he harassed Jake, and I'm here to harass you. BTW, we saw some of that coverage between Jake and that model."

Rushing into the kitchen, Charlotte slammed her palms on the high-top counter. "He what?"

"Correction," Melanie said, smiling. "*We* harassed Jake. And now, imagine our surprise when we found out that our sweet little friend was the one to break it off."

Charlotte rolled her eyes. "Yeah, so sorry I didn't believe he wasn't secretly hooking up with a freaking supermodel."

Tiana shook her head. "No, she's a regular model. Nothing super about her. And anyway, we aren't here to choose sides, right, Mel?"

"Yeah, yeah." She grumbled as she pulled out bottles. "Tonight, we are in woman solidarity. Tiana is going to whip up her world-famous nachos. You can do a salad version since you're all healthy now."

"I can eat the nacho version." Charlotte glanced at the nearly empty cheese can on the living room table. *I've been eating everything that wasn't nailed down anyway. Prediabetes be damned. Can they see the four-point-five pounds I've gained?*

"Good!" Melanie clapped her hands together. "And, of course, we have booze! Lots and lots of booze. Your fave ... margaritas." She waved at the sweet-and-sour mix, orange juice, and tequila. "We also have wine and ginny Ts."

"Ginny who?" Charlotte asked.

Tiana rolled her eyes and opened up the ground turkey packet. "Gin and tonic."

"Now you get to choose the theme for tonight. Either Men Suck, RomCom, or straight-up romance, action, or a scary movie."

Flopping onto the recliner, Charlotte crossed her ankles. "No drama?"

"Nah," Mel replied, grabbing a few cocktail glasses from the cabinet. "We didn't want to send you over the edge. So, what will it be?"

"I was watching *Jane Eyre* until you two barged your way in."

Melanie nodded and said, "I could so do *Jane Eyre*." Tiana, at the same time, shuddered and said, "Hell, no."

Melanie rolled her eyes at Tiana. "I bet if Jane were dressed like a freaking elf you'd like it. Weirdo."

Her *Lord of the Rings* obsessed friend shrugged. "Elves are awesome and magical. What's not to love?"

While her friends argued over movie preferences, Charlotte mentally reviewed her choices. Oddly enough, action movies reminded her of Jake, and she wasn't in the mood for men bashing. She still wasn't sure Jake had fake cheated on her yet. She wouldn't mind a straight-up romance.

"What kind of romance movies do you have?" she cut into their argument.

"How about *Love Jones*?" Tiana suggested.

"Hell yes!" Charlotte scooted up from her slouch position.

"I was hoping you would say that," Tiana yelled from the kitchen. "I am so ready for some brother to the night," she said, referencing the movie's main character.

"And right now I am the blues in your left thigh," Melanie quoted as she walked over to give Charlotte her margarita.

Charlotte took the drink and saluted Melanie. "Trying to become the funk in your right."

"Is that all right?" they finished in unison.

Charlotte laughed, finally embracing the impromptu girls' night. She took a deep gulp. *Whew!* Melanie did not play with the tequila. Even the OJ and the sweet-and-sour mix didn't mask it. *Fine by me.*

"Go ahead and start the movie, Charlotte." Tiana pointed to the DVD.

Charlotte picked up the movie from the counter, put it in the player, and pressed play. Soon after, Tiana finished the nachos and cheese dip and joined them.

Between the drinks, quality friend time, and lusting after Larenz Tate—who had nothing on Jacob Ross—Charlotte was feeling better.

After the movie ended, the women gabbed about their men. Well, rather, Tiana and Melanie did. Despite her sore feelings, Charlotte enjoyed the behind-the-scenes scoops on how her friends had fallen in love.

"So let me get this right," Charlotte pointed a chip at Tiana, "you're on a sex strike until Nathan agrees to go to New Zealand for your honeymoon?"

"Yes." Tiana nodded. "I want to do a set tour for *Lord of the Rings.*"

Melanie rolled her eyes. "Girl, you know you aren't gonna last more than seventy-two hours, tops. And let's be real, you're just trying to punish him for being a diva about the wedding."

Sipping a Cosmo, Tiana shrugged. "Maybe I am. I cannot wait to get married. The man is impossible. I kid you not ... he wants freaking doves released when I walk down the aisle."

"He isn't serious." Charlotte laughed and then stopped when she read her friend's serious expression.

"Oh, and he wants trumpets for when he and his dad, his best man, walk down the aisle. Freaking trumpets! Who does that?"

"Apparently Nathan," Melanie answered. "Thank goodness D didn't need all that stuff."

"That's because I graciously planned your wedding. You're welcome by the way."

"Gracias," Melanie replied without missing a beat.

Tiana chuckled. "Not to mention Damien was so happy that he supposedly won you over from your fake relationship with Jake that he hustled your ass down the aisle."

"True that." Melanie sipped without a care in the world.

Curiosity pricked at Charlotte. She'd always wanted to know the full story behind the fake relationship.

"What was that all about? How did you get Jake to agree?"

"It was his idea. He saw how hung up—"

"Obsessed," Tiana interrupted.

"Whatever. Anyway, like I was saying, Jake, being the wonderful friend that he was, suggested we make D jealous."

Fake relationships. He's good at those. Charlotte fidgeted. "When you guys were together, how did he ... I mean ... did he treat you like a *real* girlfriend?"

Mel shook her head. "No. We barely spoke. We just did the charity gig, and that was it. He was attentive but not like he is with you. Charlotte ... " She leaned in closer. "He likes you. A lot. He always has."

"Has he?" Charlotte asked. *I don't believe that.* Her thoughts must've been written on her face because her friend nodded her head.

"Yes, he has. Before you two hooked up, he always came in earlier than his volunteer time to stare at you during your dance classes."

"How do you know? You aren't there half the time."

"But your boss is. As a matter of fact, Damien was going to speak to Jake about staring at your ass. His words, not mine." She leaned back into her chair. "Said something about setting a bad example with the young men. Although they were looking at you well before Jake Ross."

Her heart trilled. *Jake looked at me? No, he stared at me.* Suppressing a smile, she shook her head before it floated right back to the clouds again. "Be still my beating heart." Her voice reeked sarcasm, although she was secretly pleased.

"I know we aren't supposed to talk about Jake." Melanie watched as Tiana made a cutting signal at her throat. "But I have to say ... he is a good man. If he said he wasn't with the model, then he wasn't. As a member of the media, some of us aren't as thorough with fact-checking. And if you look at that picture of them together—"

"Enough, Mel." Tiana gripped her glass. "We agreed. No Jake talk."

"No, you *told* me not to say anything," she snapped back. "And I didn't agree. Now let me finish because this is important. In the picture, Jake had a full beard, and this was supposedly last week. Did he grow out his beard?"

Charlotte's heart thudded in her chest. Shoot. She couldn't remember. She'd avoided him the week after their trip to Alabama. *Jake is right. I am a coward.* She shrugged. "Honestly, I don't know. I didn't see him that week. I was, umm, busy."

Melanie's face fell. "Oh, well. I thought we could close the case tonight. I was so sure you would know." *Wow! She looks like someone told her Santa doesn't exist.*

Placing her glass on a coaster, Tiana sighed. "Actually ... I saw him that week. It was a week before your charity gig, right?"

"Yes."

"Yeah, well, as you know, he works with Nathan for the Fiete sports car campaign. We filmed another concept that week, and he was definitely scruff-free. Saw him most of the week, actually."

"Oh, thank God!" Melanie hopped from her seat. "You see, Charlotte. He's innocent. Stupid celebrity stalkers and stupid *she wishes she were super, but a basic-ass model.*"

Charlotte was elated. He was telling the truth. *He really, really was.*

"Shoot. Now I have to figure out how to apologize. I didn't outright accuse Jake, but I made it seem like I didn't believe him."

"Because you didn't." Melanie wagged her finger.

"I don't blame her," Tiana argued. "He doesn't have the best reputation, and they've only been dating for what? A month." She shrugged. "I'm sure he'll understand."

Yeah. You weren't there to see the disappointment, hurt, and anger in his eyes. How he managed to convey all those feelings in his striking eyes she'd never know, but it slammed deep in her stomach.

"I don't know, guys. He was pretty upset."

Melanie tapped a finger over her lips, and Tiana grabbed her throat and hummed.

"Is sex on the table?" Melanie asked, her voice drop-dead serious.

Charlotte narrowed her eyes. "Sex is not on the table," she lied. It was definitely on the table. She just wasn't sure Jake would be open to seduction after she all but accused him of being a liar.

"All right, don't get your panties in a twist. And don't knock it until you've tried it." Melanie mumbled the last part.

"Just tell the truth and apologize. If he likes you enough, he'll forgive you. I suspect he will." That was Tiana, always the straightforward type.

Sex or tell the truth. As much as Charlotte loved her friends, they were so unhelpful.

Chapter Twelve

Any person that's decent owns up to their mistakes.

Big Mama's wise words echoed in Charlotte's head as she marched from the subway station to Jake's place. Her cute, but in no way practical, red knee-length boots clicked against the sidewalk.

She was trying to own up to her mistakes, but he'd been giving her the cold shoulder. She'd been wrong—dead wrong—about judging him like the media and tabloid readers. She hadn't believed in him. *And that had to hurt.*

After girls' night, she threw out the unhealthy snacks she'd acquired during their breakup. She wouldn't rely on food to make her happy, and she wouldn't allow her insecurities to stop her from living. *Time to be brave.*

Thunder rumbled above her head. The gray clouds that had hovered all week were finally cashing in. Rain drops trickled from the sky.

She quickened her pace. Today wasn't the best day to make the three-block trek to his place. *One more to go.*

"You can do this, girl. Ask for his forgiveness and see if he wants to try again. If he doesn't…" *Then bring on the canned cheese.* "No!"

An old woman walking beside Charlotte jumped and then hurried away.

She tried to shut down the rest of her negative thoughts, but they kept coming. *Friends.* Friends would be the purple ribbon of participation in a relay race. She didn't want that with Jacob. She wanted more. A lot more. She wanted him. Every complicated nook and cranny. Even the face that he showed her but hid from the rest of the world. Every night he haunted her dreams. Touching her, taunting her. Challenging her to take his hands and have the wildest ride of her life.

Icy raindrops raised goose bumps on her skin. Cursing her luck, she grappled her black trench coat around her body and hurried. *Just another minute.* The rain was getting stronger, and she was sure her hair wouldn't survive the trip.

Arriving in front of his condo, she rushed into the building and slammed into a mountain of muscle.

Gasping, she stumbled backward, bumping into the glass door.

"Jake … I … what are you doing here?" *What are you doing here? He lives here, you nitwit!*

He removed headphones from his ears. By the looks of it, he was going for a run … in the rain.

"Charlotte. Why are you here?"

Clutching her coat, she breathed deep. "Can we talk?"

He stared for what seemed like an hour before finally nodding. "Let's go upstairs."

She followed him to the elevator bays. *You can do this. Apologize. Feel him out. If he isn't feeling it, go to Plan B.* Seconds later, they stood in front of his penthouse. He opened the door and waved her in. Clutching her jacket, she hesitated.

Once she walked into his super-swanky condo, her life would change. An army of butterflies invaded her stomach, and the chicken noodle soup she'd eaten for lunch threatened to appear on his hardwood floor.

He lifted a brow, waving again.

You can do this. She stepped inside.

He followed her in, closing the door behind them. "Water?" His voice was clipped, formal, void of his warm and sensual tone.

"No." *This is going to go really, really bad.* "Do you mind if we sit down?"

"I'd rather stand, Charlotte. I have plans, so if you don't mind …"

Her stomach dropped. Damn, he didn't want to hear what she had to say.

"I was wrong." She stuffed her hands in her coat pockets. "You were right. I have insecurities. A lot of them. And I burdened you with them. I just couldn't reconcile that you, Jake Ross, could want plain ol' Charlotte Jones."

His gray eyes lost the dullness. A flare of anger brightened his eyes. She'd rather have those eyes laughing, mischievous, or eating her alive. But anger was something, better than the blank mask he wore when she arrived in the lobby.

"When have I ever said you were plain? Hell, when has anyone said that to you?"

She shook her head. "You haven't, no. Since we've been fake-dating, no one has said it outright. But I read it in the eyes of women we pass when we're together. They silently question *what makes her so special?* Why choose her over me? I saw it in every person, man or woman, who smirked when they saw us. Like it was only a matter of time before you dumped me. And the internet …" She shivered. "Do not get me started about those comments."

Flexing his hands, Jake paced. "It's all in your head. But a part of me gets it, I do. The thing that pissed me off is that you believed what everyone else said. I thought we had an understanding. I thought you understood me." He stopped and banged an open hand against his chest. "The real me."

"We do have something special, but it's hard to trust others when you don't accept yourself." She moved in closer. This time, *she* invaded his space. "I was wrong. So very wrong. I want to be honest with you." She licked her lips. "Can I be honest with you?'

He nodded his head.

Pulling the gold Lasso of Truth from her pocket, she wrapped it around her neck. "Here goes … I'm not perfect. I love sweets. I have a love-hate relationship with the gym. My thighs touch when I walk. My arms shake a little when I wave. I'll never have a six pack like Janet Jackson, but I like to pretend one day I will. My butt has a little more jiggle than most. But I've realized that, despite all my flaws, I am fearfully and wonderfully made because He," she pointed to the sky, "made me. And God loves me, just as I am. And for once in my life, I love me. I'm confident. And part of the reason why is because of you."

She removed the rope from her neck. "I need you to be honest with me, too. You tried, but I didn't listen. I'm sorry for that, but I'm ready now." She walked until she stood directly in front of him. Building her courage, she wrapped the lasso around his neck. "Your turn."

Her eyes searched his face, hoping to see *something*. A drumroll started in her heart, getting louder and more powerful. Cymbals crashed and clanged in her chest, waiting for the coda. *Please say something. Please, please say something.*

With a fierce and determined look in his eyes, he gripped the lasso. "I don't need this damn rope."

A mass of nerves and pain rose in her throat, and she swayed from the impact. "Y-You don't?"

"Actually, I could use it." Removing the rope from his neck, he wrapped it around her wrist. "Yeah, that'll work. And I have just enough to hook you to my headboard."

"H-headboard?"

"You're mine now, angel."

• • •

Jake tracked Charlotte's movement. Hands shaking, she gripped the belt of her trench coat and rolled back her shoulders like a swimmer preparing for a deep dive before slowly nodding.

Man, I hope that means yes.

Slowly, she unbuckled the jacket, and a flash of red and gold and blue filled his vision.

The coat fell onto the floor, revealing the sexiest outfit he'd ever seen. Charlotte, his angel, was clad in a tight red and gold corset and tiny blue panties with white stars. *My Wonder Woman.*

Stepping over her jacket with bright-red fuck-me boots, she then walked backward to his room. How she managed to convey sexy and innocent at the same time he'd never know, but the outfit was like a red flag being waved at a bull.

"Damn, woman. Are you trying to give me a heart attack?"

Shaking her head, she licked her lips. "No I … I just want to make love to you."

Charging toward her, he closed the distance and grabbed the back of her neck. "No turning back. You're mine. Say you're mine."

"I'm. Yours."

Tilting her head back, he devoured those soft lips. His heart quadrupled in his chest as he sampled her sweet honey. A moan vibrated in his mouth and warmed his chest. Scooping her into his arms, he hurried into his master bedroom, tossed her on the bed, and yanked his shirt off. With hands at his waist to pull down his jogging pants and boxer briefs, his movements slowed when he took her in. "Today we're going to tick off a goal on your bucket list."

"Bucket list?" She scrunched her nose. "I never told you my list."

He lowered his voice. "Orgasm."

She sucked in a breath. "Oh. I haven't had that."

"Yet," he growled.

Surrounded by the black and gold bedspread, Charlotte's long legs pressed together at the knees. Smooth brown skin, curves for days … no, for weeks. A tendril of hair fell over one eye. His hands itched to grab the curl and wrap it around his fist as he buried himself inside her soft folds. *Plain ol' Charlotte Jones.* Her voice echoed in his head, shooting lava through his veins. Did she realize that she was his teenaged fantasy come true? *I'll show her.*

After stripping down, he sank his knees on the bed and towered over her body.

She crossed her hands over her chest. A vein throbbed in her neck. "What are you thinking?"

"Whether I want the boots on or off."

Her eyes sparked with mischief. "I was hoping I could keep them on."

A woman after my own heart. "We're gonna have so much fun together." He reclined on his heels and reached to pull her panties past her boots. Wrapping her shapely calves around his waist, he pressed himself against her. He wanted to slide in, balls deep, but he needed to protect her.

"I've got it," Charlotte whispered. His head jerked up to her face in time to see her pull a gold foil packet from her corset.

The blood that coursed through his veins rushed to his cock. "Put it on me." His voice was strained.

"Are you sure?" She wrinkled her brow. "I don't have a lot of experience with all of this."

"Very sure, baby. Slide it on and pinch the tip."

Her fingers shook as she tore open the foil packet. He groaned when her soft hands grabbed hold and slid the rubber from tip to base. Rising to his knees, he took in her corset. "I'm gonna rip it."

"No!" Charlotte raised a hand and leaned forward. "It has a zipper in the back." Soon, brown, taut peaks spilled from the top.

He palmed the brown mounds. She sucked in a shaky breath. Lowering his mouth, he took a soft bare breast and flicked his tongue. Gasping, she threw her head back.

"Jake! Please!"

He maneuvered them so that she was on top and he on his back. "Ride me, angel."

She looked down at herself, then worried eyes flitted to his. She sucked in her stomach. "I ... "

"No."

"What?"

"Whatever it is that you're going to say, I don't want to hear it." He slapped her ass. "You're gorgeous, and you're mine. Now fuck me."

"Be serious, Jake. I'm not like those models you dated. *Chosen Magazine* wrote that—"

He lifted her from his thighs, turned her over, and swiftly entered into her silky folds. "I don't give a damn what the media says." He pulled out and slammed again. She gasped and arched her back. He wanted to tunnel his way through to the core of her but held himself back. "And I don't give a damn what internet trolls who probably still live with their mamas say." He pulled out again, but this time hovered just above her entrance, staring straight into her soul. "Trust me. Trust the man who craves you. The man who's had a fucking hard-on since the day I saw you swinging your hips in front of the mirror at the dance studio. Believe the man who nearly came in his pants when you revealed your sexy Wonder Woman outfit that no one is allowed to see but *me*. Those other women aren't ... no woman is in the same galaxy as you."

Thrusting into her again, he rode her like a man on a mission. Demanding and out of control, he stretched her to the limit, and her limber legs accommodated. He surged into her again and locked their bodies together, shouting her name as her tight muscles squeezed and grasped and spurred him on like a bucking bronco. The leather on her boots rubbed against his sides, its grainy texture a rough pressure that pushed him closer to the edge.

Lowering his head again, he sucked and lapped her breast until her fingers dug into his skin. Sharp nails skimmed his chest, and her thumbs brushed his nipples. He sucked in a shocked breath.

"You like it?" she moaned into his ears.

"I love everything you do to me, baby."

He shifted and thrust deep, determined to wring her from every twisted thought she had about her body. He wanted her spent and exhausted so that they could shut out the outside world. So that she could never think of being with anyone else but him. With one last deep thrust, he let go of the physical world and emptied his soul inside her.

"Jake, I ... " She closed her eyes and held her breath.

"Breathe, angel."

Her lashes fluttered open, surprise reflected in her dark brown eyes. "I-I'm coming!" she gasped.

Holding himself up on his forearms, he stared down at the doubt and fear in her eyes. Something else was there, hidden just beneath the surface. More than lust and desire. *Love.* Damn, she loved him. He liked that she loved him—the real him, not the celebrity persona. Charlotte wasn't going anywhere. She was his for the taking.

He wanted her confession, although he wasn't ready to make his own. He knew it was selfish, but he didn't give a damn.

"How do you feel?"

"You were amazing, Jake."

His heart twisted. He didn't want amazing. He wanted her to say the words.

"Not the sex. How do you feel about me, about us?"

"I love ... " She closed her eyes. "I love how you make me feel. I haven't felt this way before. I feel beautiful when I'm with you."

"You're beautiful, whether you're with me or without me."

He shook his head. The stubborn woman knew how she felt but wasn't ready to share. No matter. He loved a challenge. And he would enjoy fucking the confession from her soft lips.

Chapter Thirteen

"I need birth control. Lots and lots and lots of birth control."

"All right, Charlotte." Dr. Moira, her gynecologist, said with a smirk on her face. "I know you have a new beau in your life, and I appreciate your enthusiasm, but you only have to take one pill a day."

"Got it. Fill me up, doc."

"Do you know what type of birth control you want to take? There are a lot of options. And since you're prediabetic, we need to monitor your blood glucose levels for the next few months. We've gotta make sure the hormones don't impact you negatively."

Dr. Moira swiveled in her chair to face the wall of pamphlets. She pulled a few trifolds while discussing various birth control options. Meanwhile, Charlotte fantasized about her boyfriend.

I, Charlotte Jones, have a boyfriend.

She smiled, reminiscing about the past few weeks. The man was insatiable. She couldn't figure out the driving force behind his intensity. She couldn't figure out why this beautiful and talented man had a single-minded focus on her pleasure. Even now, she could taste his warm skin, feel his slightly roughened fingers tracing sexy patterns on her skin, and imagine him deep inside her. He flooded her senses. When she stared into his entrancing eyes, she could see his fevered desire to be the sole owner of her pleasure. He was on a mission to possess her. A mission she didn't want to end.

Dr. Moira cleared her throat. "All right, I can see this is all going over your head. Do you want to wait before you decide?"

Shaking her head to clear out her tawdry thoughts, Charlotte focused on the gynecologist. Dr. Moira's sea green eyes sparkled behind her glasses.

"I'll just go with the pills for now." She didn't want to start right way. *And hopefully I won't gain weight from the birth control again.* A few years ago, she'd gained fifteen pounds when she'd taken the birth control shot to alleviate cramps.

"Okay. I'll write you a prescription." She turned around to return the pamphlets. "Another thing, have you experienced any pain during intercourse?"

"Pain? No, not at all." Charlotte shook her head. "Sex has been magnificent. Magical, even."

Her doctor nodded. "Glad to hear it. Like I said, let's monitor your glucose. We'll set an appointment for a follow-up a month from now, but be sure to stay on top of checking your levels."

Charlotte nodded. "Will do."

"That's what I like to hear. Now lie back, and let's finish up this exam. Don't forget to set an appointment with Lisa before you leave."

"Got it."

"And Charlotte?"

"Yes?"

The doctor patted Charlotte's shoulder. "I'm happy for you, and as your doctor, I want you to be safe. I'd advise before you have sex without condoms that you both get tested for STIs."

Charlotte blushed. "Dr. Moira, I—"

"I'm not saying this because of Mr. Ross's reputation, and yes, I saw you both in a magazine while I was in line at a grocery store."

Charlotte was shocked by her doctor's admission.

"I would've told you this if he was any Joe Schmo. I care about your health, and I want you to be smart. Can you do that for me?"

Charlotte grabbed the doctor's hand. "It's already been done. Jake wanted me to feel safe, and he got tested a few days ago."

Her doctor released a breath and unwrapped her stethoscope from around her neck. "Good. Now let's get started."

After the examination, Charlotte removed the hospital gown and shrugged on her wool sweater and black leggings. She glanced at the clock, noted the time, and tsked. She was going to be late for a meeting with Jake and Gina. The agent had called them with vague promises of good news and that she'd wanted them to meet at her office.

Hopefully it won't last too long. She couldn't wait to share her good news with Jake. The man had been complaining about condoms, wanting nothing between the two of them.

Grabbing her phone, she pressed the car service app. No time for the train today.

• • •

Charlotte stepped into the lobby of Greer and McGregor Sports Agency and shrugged off her wool mittens.

Following directions from the friendly receptionist, Charlotte quickly arrived at Gina's office. Jake's deep, sensual laughter greeted her. She paused at the door, debating on whether to walk in or knock first.

"You're killing me, Gina."

Female laughter joined his. "God save me from hotshot football players. I almost kneed him in the nuts."

Charlotte's good manners forced her to gently knock before stepping in. "Hi, everyone."

The agent's smile dropped from her face as she motioned Charlotte forward. In the few times she'd been around Gina, Charlotte had rarely seen the agent smile. But the way Gina had been smiling at Jake made Charlotte's heart squeeze. *Have they dated? Good grief, I hope not.*

Jake stood and gave her a hug. "Hey, angel." He stepped back to give her a quick kiss.

Gina's stern face morphed into an outright frown.

"Hey, Jacob." Charlotte glanced over his shoulder. "Sorry I'm late, Gina. I had an appointment I couldn't cancel."

"No worries. I had Jake come in a bit earlier to go over a few business items. Have a seat, please." Her eyes glittered with warmth again.

A breath rushed from Charlotte's lungs. *Did I imagine something that wasn't there?*

"All right, you two *love birds*." Gina's tone held a sharp, sarcastic strike at the end. "I have some good news for you. Well, especially you, Jakey."

"Gina, what did I tell you about calling me Jakey?"

"Oh, settle down now." Gina clapped her hands together. "For the past few weeks, you guys have done a damn good job together. Both of you deserve Oscars. Between the gym dates, steamy late-night dinners, and volunteering with the kids, you have the media eating out of your hands."

Jake sighed, and Charlotte rolled her eyes. She still wasn't used to the invasion of privacy, which felt even worse now that they were actually in a relationship.

"Oh and that picture of you two outside of Charlotte's apartment in the rain. *Magnifico!*" Her Italian accent became more pronounced.

Charlotte's cheeks warmed at the memory of what happened *after* they rushed upstairs to her apartment. "I hadn't seen that one yet."

"Anyway, all of that to say," Gina pulled out a thick stack of papers from a drawer, "Threx has offered you a deal. Read it and weep, Jakey!"

Jake snatched the papers from Gina's hands and flipped through the contract. "What in the … they're offering more? A lot more. Almost double."

Smiling, Charlotte squeezed his knee. "Congrats, honey."

Jake stood and then lifted her into his arms. "Seventy million dollars," he whispered into her ears. "I can't believe it."

"Oh shit!" Charlotte rarely cursed, but this was an oh-shit moment. She giggled and grabbed his face. "You did this. Now you can make those updates to your parents' home. Or buy them a new one."

"If Dad will let me."

"Oh, he'll let you. I'll make sure of it. And you can help your brother with the down payment to his new home, too."

"Won't take much convincing with D'Mario."

Charlotte snorted. "You should build the kids a tree house in the back. I remember Danica telling me she wanted a real-life dollhouse. And then save and invest the rest. But of course, you already know that."

Jake's wide grin flip-flopped her heart.

"I couldn't have done this without you," he whispered. "I can't believe how lucky I am. I got the deal and the girl."

Gina cleared her throat. "Umm, hello? My "pretend you're in love" strategy actually worked. Am I not the woman or what?"

Jake placed Charlotte back on the ground. "Come in for this hug, too, Gina."

The agent rose. "Just this once, Jakey." She stepped into Jake's arms and gave him a squeeze.

"Now … " Gina waved for them to sit down. Leaning against her desk, she crossed her shapely legs. "Mark is in the office and wants you to swing by after this meeting to discuss the timeline for your breakup. I think a few weeks, five to six tops, and then you can go back to your playboy ways. Well, a modified version. Threx has a morality clause." Gina smirked.

Charlotte's stomach dropped.

Jake grabbed her hand. "Oh, there won't be a breakup plan, Gina. We're together. Officially together."

The agent's eyebrow raised, and she tilted her head. "Hmm. Since … since when?"

"It's been a few weeks."

"And I'm just finding out because … "

"Now don't get in a tizzy, Gina. It's not a big deal. We wanted to see where this goes, and it's going *extremely* well." He lifted Charlotte's hand and kissed it.

The agent stood, shook her head, and returned to her desk chair. "I hope you two know what you're doing. Jake, are you sure you can be faithful?"

Embarrassment flooded Charlotte's cheeks. "Jake is a good man. You shouldn't judge him for his past."

"I don't mean to be disrespectful, but Jake has never been able to hold down a relationship." Gina focused her shrewd, brown eyes on him. "I need you to try to keep it in your pants."

Jake clenched his jaw. "I can't promise you that, Gina. You see, I'll be far too busy getting in my girl's pants."

He stood, still holding Charlotte's hand. "Thanks for the help with the deal, but we've got it from here. I'll sync up with Mark later."

"Jake, I'm sorry. I didn't—"

He waved a hand. "It's fine, Gina. I'll talk to you later." He looked down at Charlotte. "Let's go celebrate."

• • •

Jake wouldn't let his agent's cavalier words mess up this day. He was on top of the world, and with his angel at his side, he could accomplish anything.

"Slow down, Jacob," Charlotte huffed beside him as they rushed down the sidewalk. "Where are we going anyway?"

He slowed his pace and looked down at his girlfriend. "How about Diago's?"

"No." She shook her head. The tassel on top of her wool cap bounced. "I'm not dressed for a nice restaurant. Let's go home. I'll cook us something delicious."

"You've cooked three days in a row. Besides, we should relax and let someone else do it."

"You know what I haven't done yet?"

"No, what?" He scanned the area for nearby restaurants.

"I haven't cooked for you in my Wonder Woman costume."

He stopped walking and pulled her to the side. "With the boots?"

"Of course." She scoffed as if he'd insulted her.

He rushed her to the edge of the curb. "Taxi!"

Chapter Fourteen

"Should I whip us up some brunch?" Jake asked as they arrived at his apartment after church service.

They'd developed an easy routine and in a few weeks, the season would be over. Although Charlotte wanted Jake's team to succeed, it looked like the team wouldn't be getting far in the playoffs with one of their major players getting injured.

When Jake was in town, they worked out, hung out with friends, caught a movie, and cooked dinner together. She'd even turned him into a Sunday church-goer.

Charlotte shrugged her purse off her shoulder and removed her green heels. "What's on the menu?"

"Whole wheat blueberry pancakes with grits and egg whites."

"Hmmm. How about applesauce pancakes since it's only seventy-five calories, lose the grits and egg whites, and substitute with fruit slices."

Jake sighed. The woman was going crazy since she hadn't lost weight in a few weeks. She'd already lost twenty-five pounds and wanted to lose the full fifty, but Jake had convinced her to compromise and only lose ten more pounds. "I thought I was the health nut here. Don't go crazy cutting calories. Honestly, you don't need to lose any more weight."

"Says the former model-dater."

"Former is the keyword." He was a changed man. *And this changed man likes hips, curves, and a fat ass.*

She placed her hands on her seductive hips. "Well, I disagree. And I weighed myself the other day. I gained a pound."

"I thought we agreed to only weigh on Sundays. Secondly, you know how weight fluctuates."

Leaning against the wall, she crossed her arms. "I'm so close to my goal, Jake. I'm just ten pounds away and don't want to screw up."

He walked over and boxed her in. "How about this? Applesauce pancakes, lose the grits, but keep the egg whites."

"But Jake, I—"

"You need the protein. Now, Sundays are usually a rest day. But since I'm such a good guy, I'll allow you to do a very special workout. One guaranteed to burn lots of calories or your money back."

"Really?" She stretched her doe eyes. "What's the workout like?"

"I call it the Jake Ross extreme workout." He grabbed her hips and lifted her into the air before peppering kisses on her neck. "You spend all day in the bedroom." He squeezed her ass. "Fifteen minutes of warm-up where I stretch your legs and eat you."

She sucked in a breath.

"Sixty minutes of intense cardio in different positions: cowgirl, the hot seat, waterfall—"

"S-sold. I'm sure I won't need my money back." She grinned. "Let's go work out."

• • •

"Everyone did great," Charlotte addressed her dance class students. "We're going to finish up the routine next week, so be sure to be here."

Claps erupted from the Refurbished Dreams studio. She gave a quick bow. "See y'all next week."

"Bye, Ms. Jones." One of her youngest students smiled and waved.

Tiana and Melanie walked up as the crowd thinned out.

"I swear you're trying to kill us!" Melanie stretched her arms and arched her back.

"Yes, these routines are not getting easier!" Tiana leaned against the mirrored wall.

"I'm not gonna lie." Charlotte turned off the speakers. "That routine was killer, even for me. Sometimes I get a little dizzy myself." A flare of pain spiked in her chest. "Do any of you have a Tylenol? My head is killing me and, now I'm starting to feel it in my chest."

"I have some in my locker." Tiana looked her over and frowned. "Are you okay? You mentioned a few days ago that you had chest pain and were tired. Still?"

"Nah, just having a few rough days. And I started birth control a month ago—that probably has something to do with it. But don't worry. I have a doctor's appointment this Friday." She'd had an appointment two weeks ago and found out her blood pressure was a bit higher, which probably alarmed Dr. Moira. This appointment would determine if she needed to switch up the pills because this one made her feel lightheaded.

"Oh, okay. Just wanted to check. We can't have another episode of you fainting on us."

"No, I'm eating the right amount of calories, thanks to my trainer." Charlotte grinned.

"I'm guessing all is well in lovers' paradise?" Melanie plopped on the wood floor and stretched her legs.

"If it were any more perfect, I would pop. He's seriously the best boyfriend ever. I can't wait until the season ends in a few weeks."

"That's right." Tiana nodded. "How are you handling him on the road?"

Charlotte shrugged, checking her Fitbit results. "I'm fine. Baseball is Jake's passion, and I would never stand in his way. We make the most of our time when we're together."

Melanie clapped her hands together. "I knew you two were meant for each other."

"Like you and Damien." Charlotte pointed at Tiana. "And Nathan and Tiana. Speaking of which, how's the wedding planning coming?"

Tiana gave the thumbs up. "I think we're finally on the same page. Releasing doves are finally off the table, but he's going to get his frat brother's son to herald me in." She rolled her eyes. "I guess can live with that. Now we have to figure out the music for the first dance."

"Well, you have plenty of time, unlike me." Melanie feigned a shudder. "The rumors are finally starting to die down that we had a rush wedding because I was knocked up. I had to rush order smelling salts for my mother, who swore I was pregnant."

Charlotte shook her head and laughed. Damien only gave Melanie a few months to plan the wedding. When Charlotte asked why he was in a rush, he'd told her he didn't want to waste any more time—they'd already wasted over a decade pretending to be just friends.

"My mom would've done the same thing, and my father would've demanded a shotgun wedding." Her heart ached at the thought of her parents. She still hadn't spoken to her family since the Zod debacle.

Jake had encouraged her to reach out, but she'd refused. She didn't want to open herself up to hurt again. But maybe he was right. Not speaking to them certainly hadn't eased her pain. *Maybe I'll give Mom a call this weekend.*

• • •

Charlotte smiled at the receptionist at the OB/GYN and checked into the office. After signing in, she settled into the hard plastic chair and pulled out her phone. A message from Jake lit her screen.

She giggled at the picture he sent: an Aquaman meme.

Last night, Jake had decided to surprise her and dressed up as a superhero. Of course, his definition of dress up was ordering a toy trident and plastic seahorses online, and his costume consisted of Jake completely naked in his hot tub. Her laughter fled when she remembered him taking her from behind. The stubble from his beard rubbing against her shoulder sent delicious tingles down her spine.

"Charlotte Jones?" A tall, dark-skinned woman in purple scrubs smiled when Charlotte waved her hand.

"Please follow me." The tech led her into a small room and took Charlotte's blood pressure and weight. When she stepped on the scale, Charlotte squeezed her eyes shut. She didn't want to see if she'd gained any more weight.

After taking her vitals, the tech gave her a small container. "We'll need a urine sample. Once you're done, you can wait in Dr. Moira's office. Third door to the right."

"Will do. Thanks."

After following instructions, Charlotte waited half an hour for the doctor to arrive.

"Hello, Ms. Jones."

Dr. Moira gave her a tight smile and settled in a chair. Clearing her throat, she adjusted her wireframe glasses.

"Well … " Dr. Moira took a deep breath. "Lots and lots of birth control didn't work. Or, you may have jumped the gun and started having unprotected sex before the medication fully activated. What I'm trying to say is … you're pregnant."

Charlotte's stomach dropped to mush on the floor. "What!" Her hands shot to her stomach. "H-how?" She rubbed her tongue against the roof of her mouth to jolt away the numbness. "How far along?" Her fingers trembled against her belly. *What are my parents going to think? How will Jake react?*

"Approximately six weeks; you're due end of May. I know the pregnancy is a shock, but that's not what I'm concerned about. I took a look at your tests, and your blood pressure is through the roof. You were doing well with your prediabetes, and maybe if you'd waited another six months, you'd be okay. But you aren't, and I'm afraid the pregnancy will be high-risk." Dr. Moira took a breath and ran through the list of health issues. "Normally this is the part where I tell you congratulations, but I know this is a shock, and more importantly this is a health risk. I have to ask … do you want to consider having an—"

"No!" Charlotte cut her off. "I w-want the baby."

Dr. Moira nodded. "Okay. Now you have to be careful and make sure to monitor your blood pressure as well as be in good blood glucose control during this pregnancy."

Charlotte sucked in a breath, overwhelmed by the news. "You said high-risk pregnancy. I know I'm at risk, but … is the baby's life at risk?" She grabbed her stomach, already protective of her unborn child.

Dr. Moira adjusted her glasses, her green eyes dull behind the lenses. "Yes. The baby is at risk."

Chapter Fifteen

Charlotte placed her hand over her belly. Two days since Dr. Moira had dropped the medical bomb, and Jake still hadn't heard the news.

Thankfully, he'd planned a guys' trip with a few of his buddies, and she now had forty-eight hours to figure out how to tell the man she loved—but wasn't quite sure how he felt about her—that she was having his baby.

Oh, and the little thing that this pregnancy is high-risk. She gripped the windowsill and took in the fantastic view from Jake's condo. He'd asked her to housesit, but she knew he'd really wanted her to stay at his place because the building had better security to protect her from the media bloodhounds.

Pushing off the window, she turned and walked toward his bedroom. *How could this happen?* She knew darn well how it happened. Sex and lots of it. Dr. Moira said Charlotte had probably already ovulated when she started the pill. Now, instead of popping birth control pills, she was popping prenatal vitamins.

She shuddered, recalling her adventure to purchase the vitamins. Like a criminal on the lam, she'd slipped on a nondescript hoodie and a Red Sox cap. *Who would suspect the girlfriend of the star pitcher of the Yankees to wear a rival's hat?* With that logic, she'd left the condo and hurried toward the nearest train stop. She boarded and rode it all the way to Harlem.

An elderly woman had crooked her finger and then patted the seat beside her. The woman had a sweet smile, like Big Mama, and instantly reminded Charlotte of front porches, sweet tea, and knitting afghans on late summer nights. Charlotte settled into the warm gooey emotion and the counterfeit Big Mama until the old biddy snatched off the hat. Twisting the cap in her veiny, pale hands, she mumbled something about "damn Red Sox fans." Then the not-so-feeble old lady tossed the hat to the other end of the train. A few people had even cheered.

After the biggest part of her disguise was revealed and a few fans recognized her, she swapped trains and returned to Jake's condo, deciding to order the pesky vitamins online. Her imagination sped through the colorful headlines that would be created if the media found out about the pregnancy. A chill skimmed her skin. She had no desire to be known as Jake's baby mama. *I'm not Denise.*

A little-known actress Jake once dated, Denise had pretended she was pregnant with his baby. His name got dragged through the mud, and people crucified the actress. Charlotte winced, remembering the unkind words. Getting emails early in the AM about the latest blog posts or news article or clip about the duo had not been fun.

She grabbed a tee and changed, then dropped her tired body on the bed, determined to figure out the best way to tell Jake the news. *Should I just tell him? Rip it off like a Band-Aid?* She buried her face in a soft pillow and screamed.

Some girls dream of their wedding day with lots of lace and white, bawling mothers, and teary-eyed fathers. Charlotte had never dreamed of that. She fantasized about the *ever after*. The babies. The cute way she'd tell her husband they were pregnant with tiny little shoes and a cute picture with a message. She sighed. But now here she was dumped in the *ever after* without experiencing the *happily* part.

And is Jake happy? A rush of emotions crawled up her throat. Although he seemed to be enjoying monogamy, the former playboy had never been in a relationship. *He's going to feel trapped.*

The grilled chicken sandwich from lunch turned to lead. Heavy, so heavy. Her stomach bottomed out. Hollow. No, not hollow. *There's a baby in there. Our baby.* According to the widget she downloaded, the baby was the size of a lentil bean. *Baby Bean.*

She wrapped her hand around her middle. A strength she'd never known infused her body. Telling Jake was the least of her worries. She needed to focus on the baby's health.

A ringing phone yanked Charlotte out of her mini-epiphany. *Mama* flashed across her screen.

Clearing her tear-clogged throat, she swiped the screen. "Hey, Mama." She tried to modulate her voice to bright and light.

"Charlie baby, you answered!" Her mother's voice shook with emotion.

Surprised by the tenderness, Charlotte's breath caught in her chest. And on the heels of her astonishment, guilt wrapped itself like a steel band across her chest. She'd gone two months without speaking to her family.

"Sorry, Mama. I just ... needed some time."

"I understand, baby. Your father and I have been talking, and we're really sorry. And I ... we were hoping you could come home sometime. Maybe in a few months during the holidays, Christmas or New Year's?"

"I-If you can't take time off we can come visit. I've always wanted to celebrate Christmas or New Year's in New York. I hear it's beautiful."

Tears welled. "It is, Mom." She wiped tears from her cheek. "It's so beautiful, and I would love it if you could come. I just need to let Jake know. My apartment is kind of small, so we'll have to book a hotel room for you and Dad."

A sigh of relief rattled into her ear. "Prissy and Davy want to come, too, if that's all right?"

Biting her lip to clamp down on the sigh that attempted to escape, Charlotte searched for the politically correct thing to say. Plain and simple, she loved her sister, but didn't like her. But family relations weren't plain and simple. They were exhausting and complicated. Charlotte didn't much mind David, but Prissy would be sure to send her blood pressure skyrocketing. *Maybe Dr. Moira could write me an excuse?* She squelched the unkind thoughts.

Her mother must've taken her silence as hesitation because she rushed on. "I know you and Prissy don't get on, and I understand. But give her a chance. She's sorry, too, and she'd like to make up for her bad behavior to you and your beau. *Entertainment Tonight* said you guys are still going strong. And you looked real nice in the red gown you wore to the charity event."

The band of guilt tightened around her chest. Her mother had kept tabs on her via entertainment shows. Could be the hormones or could be the moment, but a bucket of tears rushed forward. She hiccupped, took a quick, shallow gasp of air, and then continued crying.

"Charlotte! Baby, tell me what's wrong?"

"E-everything, Mama. Everything!"

"Honey, I need you to take deep breaths." Her mother's tone was soothing, and it made Charlotte homesick for the very first time. She did as her mother instructed and calmed her breathing as she focused on a fond memory. When she was younger, maybe seven or eight, her mother would stroke Charlotte's hair and cook her homemade soup whenever she was sad or sick. Her breathing settled into long, measured breaths.

"Tell me what's wrong, baby."

"I can't say, Mom. Not until I speak to Jake."

"I know we are still working on our relationship, but I'm your mother and I love you. I hope you know that whenever you're ready, you can count on me."

Does she mean it? Can I count on her? Jake deserved to know first, but he wouldn't be home for days, and she desperately needed advice.

Gripping the phone, she squeezed her eyes shut. "Okay, Mama. This is going to sound like a lot but here goes: I'm pregnant." The breath she held after her confession burned her lungs. Despite being a grown woman of twenty-six years, she felt like a teenager confessing a blunder.

"Oh." Her mother inhaled, reminding Charlotte to exhale. "You're pregnant ... pregnant. When are you due?"

"End of May," she squeaked. Charlotte imagined her mother fumbling to keep a straight face or maybe screaming silently while holding the phone away.

"My baby is having a baby. My first grandchild."

What? Mom's happy? "There's more."

"You're having twins?"

"No. No twins. I, well, I never told you, never told anyone but Jake that is, but ... I had a checkup a while ago and found out I was prediabetic. I was doing well with the weight loss and everything, but not so outstanding that I was out of the woods. Long story short, it's going to be a difficult pregnancy."

"Diabetes!"

"Prediabetes. There's a difference. If I eat well and exercise, I can get better."

"And the pregnancy ... what do you mean *difficult?* Like bed rest?"

"It depends on how things go, but Dr. Moira wants me checked out regularly and to take it easy. I should be all right, but I'm not sure about ... about the baby. There's a chance that he or she won't ... "

She couldn't finish. She couldn't say that Baby Bean could die.

A shadow flitted in her periphery. A tall shadow, stiff and stern and, from its crossed arms and shaking form, furious. Her brain finally caught up to the fact the shadow was cast by a man. *Jake!*

Her eyes lifted from the hardwood floor to met his dark, dreary eyes, like a looming gray cloud before the perfect storm.

Something twisted and twirled in her stomach. *Nerves … not Baby Bean.*

"I've gotta go, Mama."

"What? No! I'm coming up there to take care of you. We'll figure this out together."

"No, Mom, I'm fine." She lowered her voice, taking in Jake's ravaged expression. "Jake's here."

"Did you tell him?"

"No. Not yet."

Her mother's voice dropped to a whisper. "Did he hear?"

"Think so."

"Call me as soon as you can, okay?"

"Yes. Bye."

Hands trembling, she lowered the phone. "What did you hear?"

Veins protruded from his clenched fist and forearms. "Please tell me this is a joke."

Her heart pounded so loudly that she could barely make out his words. She shook her head and licked her dry lips. "I'm afraid not."

"Did you do it … " He shook his head and braced his arm against the doorframe. "Did you do this on purpose?"

She scrambled to her feet. "Maybe I didn't hear you correctly but did you just accuse me of getting pregnant on purpose? Are you insinuating I'm trying to trap you?"

"You've always had a crush on me—"

"Yeah. And? I had a silly little crush on you. It doesn't mean that I would purposely do that to you. My God!"

"You told me the birth control was safe after a week. And hell, you used to work with Damien to cover my publicity." He shook his head. "You know I've been through this before."

"I said *about a week*. We waited for two. Shit happens, Jake. And yes, I remember the scandal. But the truth was revealed through a paternity test. Of course, if that's what you need, I can do that for you."

"Are you sure you're pregnant?"

Nodding, she clutched her stomach. "I'm sure." The pounding in her ears grew louder. She took in the toppled over carry-on bag near his feet. "Why are you here?"

He clenched his jaw and swallowed, his Adam's apple bobbing up and down. "I wanted to surprise you. I missed you."

His quiet admission softened her heart. She moved closer to him. "I missed you, too." She reached for his cheek. "I—"

He flinched away. Nostrils flaring, he grimaced as if he'd downed something hot and bitter. "I need some time, Charlotte."

"And I need you! We," she pointed to her stomach, "need you."

His face morphed into shock from her outburst.

All her emotions—fear and pain and anger and sorrow—tumbled over and over like an out of control NASCAR auto. "Don't make me do this alone. Please, Jake." Fear and hysteria in her voice scared her. Pacing, she grabbed the ends of her hair and tugged. She hated herself for being so emotional, but she was afraid. Afraid for the life of Baby Bean, whom she already loved. Afraid that something could happen to her and she wouldn't have a chance to see her child grow up. Afraid the man who held the keys to her heart and soul didn't return her feelings.

His eyes, normally vibrant and dancing, were impassive. No intensity, no warmth, just empty and soulless.

She stopped pacing and squeezed her eyes shut. She viciously sank her teeth into her lips, hoping the physical pain would distract her from her quickly degenerating heart.

"I-I didn't trap you. I have dreams, too, you know." She slid to the floor. "Maybe not as grand as yours." She pulled her knees into her chest, focused on the floor, and rocked herself for comfort. "I'm not a liar, and I'm not a cheat. You know that." Her anger spiked. She lifted her eyes to meet his. "And you know me."

Then, rising to her feet, she smoothed out the wrinkles in her simple cotton dress and moved closer to Jake, now backing into the corner like a trapped animal.

She raised her hands in surrender. "I'm not waiting for you to make up your mind about my character, Jake. I have Baby Bean to worry about. Bean, who may not grow to full-term because of my … my defect." Lowering her hands, she injected steel into her spine. "I'm making decisions, and the first thing I'm going to do is whatever it takes to safely deliver *our* child into the world."

"And what about you?"

"What about me?"

"A high-risk pregnancy means you're most likely at risk. Maybe you shouldn't have this baby—"

"No." Her voice strangled, jarred by what he was suggesting.

"But you—"

"I am not aborting my baby. I'll be fine. There'll be some pain, but I can do this."

"How do you know? Can you guarantee your safety?"

She wiped her eyes with the back of her hands, shocked at the direction of their conversation. "Nothing in life is guaranteed. We can't live forever."

The dark clouds in Jake's eyes rolled away as lightening appeared. He swung his hand into the dresser. Expensive cologne toppled and crashed on the floor. "Dammit, Charlotte!"

She jumped.

"Damn this and damn you!"

"Damn me? I didn't get *myself* pregnant!"

"No, but you're making all the decisions. Hell, you even told your mother—your *estranged* mother—that you were pregnant before coming to me. You had an appointment with the doctor and sat on the info for who knows how long. And now you're deciding that you're having this baby, despite the risk to the baby and yourself. You're putting yourself," he waved his hands between them, "putting us, through undue emotional and physical stress. You first need to get your prediabetes under control. Then, when you're ready, you can try to have a baby.

You can try. Not us, just me. He doesn't want Bean. He doesn't want me. "Yes. I've made the decision." Grabbing her purse, she rushed out of the room.

He followed.

At the door, she turned to face him. "I had to make a decision because deep down I knew I couldn't depend on you. You let things happen to you, and you never take a stand. You didn't take a stand in high school when the popular kids who always terrorized you suddenly became your friends. You left your old friends behind. You didn't take a stand when the popular girls, who dissed you, all of a sudden wanted to get into your pants. And you didn't take a stand when you were forced to have this farce of a relationship with me, and I know now, it's a farce." She spat out her poisonous words. "So yes, I made the decision to keep Bean without you because I knew how you would react."

He averted his face as if she'd slapped him. *Good. I want him to hurt. I want him to bleed.* Grabbing ahold of her newfound strength, she yanked the door open. "If you don't step up and step up soon, *our* baby will be *my* baby."

Chapter Sixteen

He was going to be a father. *Dad.* Jake played with different name variations as he threw another ball into the mesh netting. *Me. A dad.* He grabbed another ball from the bucket. Sweat beaded on his forehead and scalp as gripped the stitching.

Charlotte marching out of his condo days ago meant one thing: She was one-hundred percent serious. If he didn't get his act together soon, she'd be out of his life. He fired the ball into the pitchback.

He finally had his shit together.

The first day had been hell. He'd ping-ponged between missing her and not trusting her. After Denise had lied to the world and attempted to throw him under the bus, he had major trust issues with women who claimed he was their baby's father. Even sweet and kind ones like Charlotte.

Jake grabbed another baseball. Today, without Charlotte's warm and shy smiles, he finally realized he'd fucked up. She was sweet and genuine, through and through. She worried what his parents would think if they ever found out about the fake relationship. She was the church member everyone called when someone was sick or shut in or when an elderly person needed someone to run errands.

These days, she crowded his thoughts more than baseball. He needed to make amends, but didn't know how.

His shoulder throbbed after hours of throwing. *I've gotta apologize. I need to see her.* He tossed one last ball and then looked at the clock. *Pitiful. Sixty-nine miles per hour.* Gathering the loose balls in the pitching cage, he returned the full bucket to the front and got ready to grovel.

. . .

"C'mon Baby Bean. Mama is trying to be healthy." Charlotte groaned and rubbed her stomach. The chicken salad she'd finished eating didn't want to settle in her stomach. Nothing settled her stomach but stupid ginger ale—which, ironically, she hated—and saltine crackers.

The door buzzer sounded. Rolling her eyes, she let out a long, exaggerated exhale that would give a melodramatic preteen a run for her money. *I'm not in the mood for unwanted company.* Even if it were probably Melanie or Tiana.

She'd told them about the pregnancy and Jake's reaction. Melanie had been shocked and upset by his accusations and threatened to castrate him with a rusted spoon. The look in her friend's bright brown eyes made Charlotte wince. Normally, cool-headed Tiana could calm down her hyper friend. But she, too, had gotten in on the I-hate-Jake-Ross bandwagon and threatened to lop off his head like the female dancing spider.

Charlotte felt marginally better that her friends could double as contract killers, but she made them promise to keep it to themselves and away from their significant others, especially her nosy, but well-meaning boss, Damien. Melanie and Tiana had rallied around her and stayed over late last night until she'd fallen asleep. Today, she just wanted to mope and watch Netflix. *Netflix and mope.* She wasn't up for any 'you'll-be-a-great-mom' speech.

The buzzer sounded again. *End of my pity party.* She stood and quietly crept to the door. "Who is it?" She didn't have a peephole to screen visitors.

"It's Jake."

Fudgesicles!

Her heart dropped, rolled, and plopped on the floor. She hadn't expected *him*. Not after the nasty words he'd spewed so effortlessly. She didn't think she could take another did-you-get-pregnant-on-purpose session.

"Ummm ... Charlotte's not here. She's ... s-she's out."

Damn this is bad. She sounded like the wolf from *Little Red Riding Hood* impersonating the recently digested grandma. Under any other circumstance, she would giggle. But this was Jacob Ross, and she'd already tossed him the panties like a groupie at an Usher concert.

I need to be clear, focused, and strong. No room for error with Jake and her heart. He needed to be gone. *By any means necessary.*

"Charlotte ... " His voice was commanding and unamused.

She quivered and then cursed. "What do you want, Jake?" She leaned against the door for strength.

"I want to talk."

"About?"

"You. Me. Bean. I need to explain some things. And ... and ... I ... I owe you an apology."

Damn right you do. "Fine." Untwisting the knob, she then unlatched the top lock and opened the door.

He looked good—damn good in his scruffy, I-don't-give-a-damn wardrobe. An old beat-up cap sat low on his head, and a plain gray tee stretched against his chest. His solemn eyes scanned her appearance before stopping at her face. Then he stepped closer. She didn't move.

I will not let him back me into a corner anymore.

His eyes flashed a mixture of frustration and remorse.

Yanking her short robe closed, she lowered her eyes. She would not be pulled into his soulful stares nor swayed by his good looks.

"Yes, Jake?" Turning on a heel, she walked to the kitchen to pour herself that ginger ale.

"Angel, I'm sorry."

The fizz settled in her drink. "What are you sorry for?"

"How I reacted. I know you would never cheat on me. I know the baby is mine, but I ... all I could think about was the Denise fiasco last year and how disappointed my family had been. Even the kids got wind of it and asked if I was bringing home a baby cousin."

A twinge of sympathy panged in her chest. Just a twinge, like the size of a microorganism. His behavior had been unconscionable. Horrible and downright cruel.

Putting her drink down, she folded her arms across her chest. "I'm sorry you had to go through that. Truly, I am. I was on the PR team when that happened and, trust me, I still have nightmares about how people dragged you and Denise through the mud. I would never willingly put you in that position again. However, it doesn't excuse what you said to me."

Please tell me this is a joke ... did you do this on purpose? Her eyes burned and her nose tingled at the humiliating and heartbreaking memory.

"You're right. It's no excuse. And I'm sorry. So damn sorry. I was a selfish bastard. At first, all I could think about was how I wasn't ready. About the danger and my career and dreams and what if—"

"Thank you for the apology. But if you don't mind, I need you to leave ... now."

"What?" He blinked, confusion marring that perfect face.

"Naptime. Bean and I are tired." *Of your excuses.* "So ... you need to go."

He jerked his head back. "I need to ... " He didn't finish his sentence, so she finished it for him.

"Go. Yes."

Steely eyes locked on her frame. His eyes were no longer remorseful but determined. Scary determined. Like he was digging in, kicking up his cleats, and prepared to strike out his opponent. *Me.*

Nostrils flared, he shook his head. "No."

"No?"

"Negative."

"You can't make me take you back, Jake." Too bad a tremble, not a firm tone, supported her bold statement.

"Maybe I can't. I've been told 'no' a lot in my life, and it never stopped me before. People told me I couldn't get a full ride to college. They told me I wouldn't make it to the pros, and when I did, they told me I'd never become an all-star."

Her eyes drifted to the muscular forearms that sat across his chest. She could visualize the people who doubted them. She could imagine Jake's drive, the obsession that rode him to prove them wrong. To succeed. She licked her lips, swallowed hard, and stepped back. Just a little. She still wasn't losing ground.

"So, go ahead," he continued. "Underestimate me. But I'm not going anywhere because I'm in this with you, all the way, and right now I'm playing the most important game of my life."

The deep, sensual promise in his voice, the resolve in his magnificent eyes, and the set of his chiseled jaw broadcasted that he was playing zero games when it came to winning her over.

She tried to rile up her fire, the one that had burned widely after Jake's rejection. She fed off the memories to stoke the embers back to life. "I can't go back there with you again. It hurts too much, and I'm done playing this … this game."

"You're right. This is not a game. This is much more important. Me, you, Bean." Walking closer, he put his palm against her stomach. She flinched and clenched from the contact. His eyes scorched her, and she was on fire. Not of her own making, but from Jake. Flames of desire, ravenous and unrelenting, burned in her veins. Yes, she was on fire, and, unbelievingly, wet for him, too.

"You can't," she whispered.

"I will," he proclaimed loudly. "I will take care of you. I will take care of Bean. I will treat you like a queen." The intensity of his eyes and his words sucked the oxygen from her lungs.

She struggled to breathe. Taking a deep breath, she backed away. "A queen needs her king."

"I'm him, angel. And if someone else tries to wear my crown or sit on my throne, I'm crushing him. You know why?"

She shook her head.

"Because you're my first thought in the morning and the last at night. I couldn't even relax on my guys' trip because I wanted to be near you. Hear your voice. Taste you. And my heart ... baby ... I'm not a sappy man, and I've never been in love before and I don't know if I am, but I can't eat and sleep and ... my pitching game is shit without you. I have no joy without you. I don't want to be without you and," he touched her stomach, "I don't want to be without Bean. We're a family now." His voice shook with emotion.

Tears swelled and spilled down her cheeks. "Are you sure, very sure, this is what you want? Me and Bean?"

"Very sure, angel." He grinned, much like she imagined a Spartan enjoying the sweet victory of a battle won. "And what's up with the name Bean?"

She sniffled and smiled. "Yeah, I kinda gave our baby a nickname. I looked online and saw that he or she is the size of a bean right about now."

His gray eyes sparkled. "What happens when the baby grows to say ... the size of a cantaloupe?

"By then, we should know the sex. Maybe we'll have a name." Charlotte shrugged and lowered her eyes to his hand on her stomach.

"Well then, the working name is Baby Bean."

"So ... " She licked her lips and lifted her eyes to meet his. "We're doing this? Are we really raising a child together? As a couple?"

"Angel, I'd have to be a dumbass to let you go." Pulling her into a hug, he kissed her forehead. "I'm an asshole but not a dumbass."

"There's a difference?" She relaxed enough to joke.

"Definitely. And I'm sorry for being an asshole. You didn't deserve that."

Charlotte nodded and leaned away from his arms. "I forgive you, Jake. I know you're new to being in a relationship, and this news is a surprise for us both. But just put yourself in my shoes and know that being in a relationship and having a baby is just as overwhelming for me, too. And I'm certainly not ready for the media to tear into us."

Jake nodded. "As far as I'm concerned, you and Baby Bean are my world, and I don't give a damn what anyone else thinks. But for now, and the safety of you and the baby, let's try to keep a lid on this for a while before we announce this to the world." He tugged her hand. "I just want it to be our news. Well, our news and your family for now." He sighed, stroking her cheek. "Wish you would've told me first, angel."

"I'm sorry. I was a wreck, and Mama called, and she was so sweet and understanding, and I—"

"I get it, baby. I do. But we're a team now. I'm going to be the one to take care of you. And I want the number to your doctor. I'm coming to all of your appointments."

"You can't come to all of them. You'll be on the road in the spring. Baby Bean will be debuting in early August." *Or earlier.* No, she didn't want to think about earlier.

"Damn. We'll figure it out." He lowered his head to her stomach and placed his strong hands on either side. "Don't come out while I'm on the road." Then he looked up at her. "Same goes for you. Make sure he stays in there safe and sound until I return."

Charlotte giggled. "We will endeavor not to disappoint you."

The weight of the world lifted from her shoulders. This was all she could've hoped for. Well, minus the bended knee and ring. But she couldn't fault him for avoiding the subject of marriage since they'd only been dating for a few months. But a part of her, the old-fashioned part, wanted to do this right. She loved Jake and Bean. She hadn't wanted to freak him out, but he'd been spot on during their conversation at the hospital. She wanted to be married with three-point-five kids in the suburbs.

But life rarely turned out the way she'd wanted it. For now, she would focus on the safe delivery of *their* baby.

• • •

"Charlotte is what?" Gina screeched, gripping the paperweight ornament on her desk. From the fire burning in her eyes, Jake could tell she was close to chucking it at his head.

"She's pregnant, Gina. Like I've already said for the third time." Jake had already met with his publicist the day before, but Gina hadn't been able to sync up with them. He sighed, not at all in the mood for Gina's over the top reaction.

"How in the … " She stood from her desk and paced the floor. Closing her eyes, she massaged her temples. "How could you be so irresponsible, Jake? You've had sex with hundreds of women—"

"Jeez, not that many." He waved his hands. "I'm no Wilt Chamberlain."

"Oh, you're a close second." She snorted and crossed her arms. "Now you go and get the supposed good girl pregnant? I thought she was all into Jesus or something?"

"Watch what you say about Charlotte." He raised a finger in warning. "She's a good woman."

"Two words." Gina formed a peace sign with her fingers. "Morality. Clause. It doesn't matter if Charlotte is a *good woman* or not. Threx is a family brand and is not going to be happy now that you have a baby mama."

He gripped the arms to the chair. "Do your ears need a cleaning? You will not disrespect her. She is the mother of my child, not just some damn baby mama. Now let's focus on the facts. We're having a child, and we're happy. But it's a high-risk pregnancy, and we don't need to add stress or be hounded by the media. Like I told Mark, we're happy about this, so there's nothing to spin."

Gina stopped her pacing. "High-risk pregnancy?" she whispered.

For the past month, Charlotte had been putting up a good front about her health and the baby, but he could see the strain lines around her mouth, the deep grooves that wrinkled her forehead, and the short intake of breath as she waited out a dizzy spell.

They'd agreed to stop the intense gym sessions, much to Charlotte's dismay, and opted to take nice long walks together. The media had noticed their change in schedule and started questioning what was going on. Mom and Dad had taken it better than expected but were now pressuring them to get married. With family in the know and the media sniffing around, he wanted Gina and Mark to help manage the situation. Soon, the entire world would find out.

"Yes. Charlotte has prediabetes, so we have to make sure we keep an eye on her blood pressure. Thank goodness we've been able to have Dr. Moira examine her at the center. The media has been snoopy lately, and Charlotte swears someone has been following her for the last several days."

Gina's face pinched at the news. Clenching and unclenching a fist, his agent counted to ten and returned to her seat. "Okay." She shook her head as if waking from a nightmare. "We can fix this." She took a deep breath. You, me, and Charlotte will meet with Threx."

"I don't want Charlotte to be—"

"I understand, Jake. I do. But she needs to be at that meeting. We need to convince them that this pregnancy is a good thing."

"This *is* a good thing."

"Right. We can say that you are a family man. Show them how excited you are. How you're a good guy that's ready to settle down." She nodded her head as if convincing herself. "I'll call the brand director and set up an appointment. I won't tell him the news over the phone. I think it's best that we go to their office and have a conversation." She leaned back. "You are so gonna pay out the ass for this overtime."

Jake noticed the bags under her eyes. *She really needs some rest.* "Sorry if I'm working you too hard. You should get some rest. Maybe take a vacation."

"Yeah, and then I'll get a call on my cell with the news that you're having quintuplets." Shuddering, she typed something on her laptop. "No thanks. I'll just wait until after the baby is born."

• • •

Charlotte scanned her closet for something to wear. "What conveys that I'm just an average, normal girl who's definitely not a gold digger?"

Her eyes stopped on the green and black tunic that her sister had surprisingly shipped from some ritzy boutique in Alabama. She fingered the material. "I can pair this with leggings and boots. A cute scarf, maybe?"

"You'll look good in anything you wear. Stop overthinking it." Jake's strong arms gently wrapped around her middle. Although the bump was barely visible and looked more like the results from a junk food weekend, he still touched her stomach and spoke to Baby Bean.

"I know, I know. But I just … I don't want to screw this up for you." She leaned against him. "I already messed things up by overestimating the birth control."

"I'm sorry but did you force me to touch and taste that sweet body of yours?"

She turned to face him. "No, but I came to your place in a trench coat. Kinda hard for any guy to say no to that. And sure, we didn't get pregnant then but it was the start of things."

"Hey!" His eyes darkened, and he cupped her cheek with both hands. "It's not your fault. We created the beautiful bean that's growing inside you together. I'm honored to have a child with you."

Smiling, she lifted on her toes to give him a kiss. "You're a good man, Jacob Ross." She kissed him again, deeply this time, and a burst of Columbian coffee and a hint of French vanilla creamer exploded on her taste buds. A glutton for his kisses, she stroked his tongue, and they kissed each other as if it were their last day on earth. Grabbing his shirt, she lowered her feet flat on the ground. "You're also a dangerous man."

"I'm *your* dangerous man. And you're *my* dangerous woman." His eyes flashed with possession. "Go and get changed before I'm tempted to have my second breakfast."

• • •

"Con … gratulations?" John Marshall, VP of Sponsorships, stared at a Jake and Charlotte from across the conference table. Skepticism covered his voice.

Charlotte, Jake, and Gina sat on one side of the table while the VP and brand director sat opposite.

The sandy-haired exec ran his fingers through his short, wavy hair. "I thought we had an understanding about our family brand? You're acting as a role model to kids who want to wear your shoes." He quickly flashed a look at Charlotte and then back at Jake. "Are you sure that—"

"Very sure." Jake's voice was firm and serious, and her heart sped up. For once, she felt a part of a team. Together, they were a force to be reckoned with.

Jake reached for her hand and gently tugged the pen away. She hadn't realized the ink had popped and stained her fingers. *Well, he's the force on the team. I'm the benchwarmer.* No longer. Charlotte needed to be strong for Jake and Bean. She would fight to keep his endorsement.

She cleared her throat to grab everyone's attention. "I assure you, gentlemen, this was a surprise—albeit a happy one—for both of us. I mean, look at me." She did a Vanna White impression. "I'm not exactly a seductress." She lifted her hand in the air and with the other pointed at the stain. "I'm so darn nervous about this meeting that I broke the pen you gave me. S-sorry about that, by the way." She placed the broken pen on the table.

"But this isn't about me. It's about Jake. He's still the stand-up guy you chose to endorse your shoes and athletic wear. He's the guy that talks to his nieces and nephews on the phone because they want him to do the grumpy-bear voice and no one does it like their Uncle Jake. He's the guy that volunteers with the youth to make sure they stay off the streets. He's the big brother to up-and-coming athletes that need a firm, yet gentle hand. He's the … "

She chanced a look at his eyes, now swirling with emotion. She lowered her voice as she stared at him. "He's the guy that sneaks off to help build the manger for the church play. Or sends an anonymous donation he *thinks* I don't know about to the church when the heating unit went out." She chuckled when Jake raised his brow, obviously surprised by her level of intel.

She directed her attention to the VP and director and then took a deep breath. "You won't find a finer man than Jacob Ross, and I'm the luckiest woman in the world to be the mother of his child. You want someone to represent your family brand and he's perfect. Mark my words, Jake is going to be a wonderful father."

Jake smiled and squeezed her hand. "Do you see why I'm crazy about her?"

John gave them both a relieved smile and then leaned over to shake her hand. He hesitated, scanning her hand.

"Don't worry. This is the ink-free one." She smiled and held out her right hand.

"I'm sorry for misjudging you." He released her hand and offered a shake to Jake. "For misjudging both of you. I'll have to speak to our CEO and maybe even the board for final approval, but I think I should be able to convince them."

Jake nodded and gave him a smile. The brand director nodded his consent and focused on Gina. "Why don't you and I get together and brainstorm the new direction?"

Gina nodded pulled out a notepad. "I've got a few ideas already. I can meet now if you want?"

"Perfect. Jake and Charlotte? It's been a pleasure and congratulations."

They stood.

Jake cleared his throat. "Thank you for hearing us out." He shifted his attention to his agent. "Gina, I'll be in touch later."

Grabbing Charlotte's hand, he rushed them outside of the building.

Charlotte tilted her head up as they walked to the parking deck. "Do you think they'll keep you on?"

Jake smiled and nodded. "For a minute there, I didn't think they would. But you were so convincing." Clicking the button to his car alarm, he walked her to the passenger side and opened the door. Once he was settled into the driver's seat, she grabbed his hand and leaned in to whisper, "I meant every word."

Jake's strong, calloused hand gripped the back of her neck. His fingers lightly scraped her scalp, sending delicious tingles down her spine. "You and me, angel. We're a team, and we can handle anything life throws our way."

Chapter Seventeen

Charlotte pulled a variety of direct mailers, bills, and coupons from her mail cubby. A large, plain white envelope caught her attention. *Hmm … no address. Weird.* She opened it.

STAY AWAY FROM JAKE OR YOU AND YOUR BABY WILL DIE!

A chill wrapped itself around her spine. Her fingers shook as she held the note made from cut-out magazine letters.

Baby. Jake. Die? A white-hot ball of fear swelled in her chest and slithered up her throat. She glanced around. Who knew about her pregnancy?

The noises from the center faded away. She could only hear the desperate and shallow gasps of breath that far too quickly escaped her lungs. Her head swam. *Dizzy. Need to sit.* Instead of following her advice, she scanned the room from left to right, trying to figure out the culprit. Only teens and a few volunteers were scattered on the green turf, playing indoor soccer.

Self-preservation finally kicked in, and she stuffed the letter into the envelope. Rushing to her office, her first instincts were to call the police, but the pregnancy hadn't been announced to the world yet. She could still hide the baby bump.

Closing the door behind her, she tossed the letter on the desk and then grabbed her phone. Her trembling fingers pressed Jake's name.

"Pick up, please … pick up."

"Hey, angel." His deep-voiced greeting immediately lessened her erratic heartbeat.

"J-Jake," she whispered. "Someone knows about the baby. They sent a note with cut-out letters, you know, like the stuff in the movies where they cut out magazines to send messages, and I—"

"Slow down, baby. You aren't making sense."

She took a deep breath. "I'm in the office, at Refurbished Dreams. There was a plain white envelope in my mailbox. I opened it up, and it said …" She stared at the envelope and squeezed her eyes shut. "That I have to stay away from you, or they'll hurt our baby." She gasped for breath as an onslaught of emotions attacked her. She put a protective hand over her stomach. "They threatened Bean's life, Jake." She hiccupped and gulped down hot tears ripping their way up her throat.

"Go to Damien's office and wait there. Do not stop to speak to anyone. I'll be there in, shit, a half-hour if I can help it. Stay strong, baby. It'll be okay."

After hanging up, Charlotte rushed into Damien's office, stopping short after stumbling on him and Melanie in a passionate embrace.

"Charlotte?" Damien said over his wife's mop of curls.

Charlotte shook as she plopped into one of his visitor chairs. "Jake told me to come here. I … we're in trouble, and he doesn't want me to be alone." *I don't want to be alone.*

Wringing clammy hands in her lap, she continued. "I'm pregnant. Melanie and Tiana already know."

Damien furrowed a brow and swung his attention to Melanie, giving her a look that conveyed, "We'll be talking about this later."

"Don't be mad. I asked her not to tell you yet." Raising her head, Charlotte locked eyes with her boss. "But there's more." She recounted the entire story, minus the fake relationship—the pregnancy surprise, the high-risk danger for her and Baby Bean, and the Threx decision, and now, the threat.

Damien cracked his neck and folded his arms across his chest. "A stalker ... dammit. We'll take care of you, Charlotte. You aren't alone."

Of course, I'm not alone. I have Jake.

Melanie slid into the seat beside her and massaged her hand. "It's going to be okay."

Charlotte shifted her attention back to Damien, now pacing behind the desk. "We'll need to hire security."

"No, Damien." Charlotte shook her head. "We don't have it in the budget, and besides—"

"Not an option. I've been thinking of getting security anyway for our celebrity volunteers."

"But—"

"But nothing, Charlotte." Melanie squeezed her hand. "We need to keep you safe, and this is non-negotiable. Now, let's wait for your handsome boyfriend and come up with a plan."

"Handsome boyfriend?" Damien's eyebrows shot to his hairline. "You're not supposed to notice anyone but me."

"Sure I don't." Melanie rolled her eyes. "You're the only man who is attractive to me," she said in a dull, robotic voice.

Charlotte surprised herself with a giggle, and then her giggles turned into hysterical laughter. *I'm cracking up.*

Melanie's smile dropped. "We've got you. You'll be safe here. I'm sure we can figure out a solid plan for when you're at home."

"You're moving in with me." Jake's voice boomed from the doorway.

• • •

Charlotte shot out of her seat and ran into his arms. He breathed a sigh of relief, and the grip around his heart eased. Stroking her hair, he whispered, "You're okay. I won't let anything happen to you or Bean."

Nodding, she stepped back. "I know."

He sat in the vacant seat beside Melanie and pulled Charlotte onto his lap. "Thanks for looking after my girl."

"Of course. Charlotte is family," Damien replied gruffly. "I guess congratulations are in order." He gave Jake a pointed look, much like a scary dad who found out someone knocked up his little princess.

"Thanks." Jake's voice was flat and invited no further questions.

Damien apparently hadn't gotten the memo because he questioned further. "So what are your intentions with our Charlotte?"

Jake's temperature spiked. "Charlotte isn't *your* anything. She's mine. And I protect what's mine. But to give you peace of mind, because she cares about what you think, I intend on protecting her and our child."

Melanie, ever the peacemaker, smiled at them. "We know you'll take care of each other. We were just discussing security here, but the bigger issue is Charlotte's protection outside of work. Thank God the season just ended, but I'm sure you guys will start pitch practice soon.

"I'll change my schedule to train around Charlotte's work." He rubbed her thigh. "How about I pick you up here every day?"

She sighed.

He squeezed her hips. "I know this isn't ideal, but please do this for me. For Bean."

"You're right. It isn't ideal, but this isn't just about me. It's for the safety of Bean."

He kissed her cheek. "That's my girl."

She gave his hand a squeeze.

"I had to call Gina and Mark to let them know what was up."

Charlotte groaned. Ever since Gina's blowup about the pregnancy, Charlotte wasn't a fan of his agent.

"Sorry, baby, but it's important. We're gonna have to call the police. The news will leak soon, so I'll probably need to do a quickie press conference."

"I don't want to announce it just yet, Jake. Women already hate me, especially this stalker."

"I'm going to announce this by myself. You will be safely tucked away in our apartment with security detail."

"It's okay. We're a team. I'll go with you."

"No, you won't." He tucked a strand of hair behind her ear. "No more stress for you. We have to contain this as best as we can. I'll make the announcement and ask for privacy—"

"Which the paparazzi will totally ignore."

"Yes, but we'll keep you under the radar. Now let's call the cops."

• • •

Charlotte moaned as Jake massaged the soles of her feet. Nearly four hours and hundreds of questions later, she'd finally finished her statement to the police.

Tomorrow was going to be a long day, too. Jake would be announcing their pregnancy, and she would be working from home. He'd quickly hired a security detail based on Gina's recommendation. They'd be arriving bright and early at six a.m. to discuss procedures. Pressure built and settled in the middle of her forehead. *When did life get so crazy?* And now Jake wanted her to move in with him.

"Let's get you to bed. We've got a big day tomorrow."

Charlotte wiggled her toes when he stopped the massage. "No, *you've* got a big day. I'm just going to sit in your apartment surrounded by big dudes I don't know while the media slaughters you with uncomfortable questions."

Jake shrugged. "They aren't so bad. They've got a job to do. And to be honest, I'm more concerned about the stalker. Maybe the media following us isn't such a bad thing. That'll leave less opportunity for the stalker to get to you."

Charlotte shook her head. No matter what he said, she would never be a fan of the spotlight and downright rude questions. She pivoted the conversation instead of getting into a winless debate. "Have you heard back from Threx?"

"No final decision yet." He scooped her into his arms. "I'll leave that worry for another day. Right now, my focus is on you and Bean." He carried her to his room. "Let's get some sleep."

• • •

She was shacking up with a man. Charlotte stared at herself in the vanity mirror, waiting for lightning to strike. Big Mama rising from the grave to whoop her granddaughter's tail wasn't out of the question.

"I have no choice," she whispered before brushing her teeth. *Would Big Mama understand?* Charlotte wasn't so sure. Her grandmother had loved her dearly, but the God-fearing woman would've been disappointed to learn her granddaughter was "living in sin."

Pregnant, and now living with my lover. Shame seeped into her body, and her shoulders drooped. Big Mama's feelings should be the least of her worries. A stalker was on the loose. That and a now curious-and-determined media hounded her every move. Oh, not to mention heartbroken fans, both women and men, who predicted she would be Jake's downfall. Some commenter even compared her and Jake to Sampson and Delilah.

"I think your teeth are clean by now." Jake's panty-melting voice distracted her.

Leaning over, she turned on the faucet and rinsed out her mouth.

Jake stared at her in the mirror. "Everything okay?"

"Yeah," she lied and wiped her mouth. "Just got lost in thought."

Wrapping his arms around her waist, he pulled her against his bare chest. His chin rested on her head, and she grew warm from the intimacy. His cool eyes were still focused on her, inspecting her, trying to read her. "I know I'm not the best roommate. I promise to pick up after myself on the days my cleaning lady is off. I'm happy to split cooking duties. And I—"

"You're fine. The best roommate I've ever had."

Jake gave her a quick grin. "You're just saying that."

Charlotte twisted to face him. "Scout's honor. My first roommate in college, Nympho Nancy, had loud sex at all times of the day. Sophomore year, my roommate played acoustic guitar and practiced nonstop. I called her Coffeehouse Carly."

"And your junior and senior years?"

"Oh, I learned my lesson. I bit the bullet and stayed off campus by myself. I'm thinking," she stood on her tiptoes and kissed his chin, "that third time's a charm. Now I'm living with a sexy man who cooks and cleans. What's not to love?"

Jake grabbed her shoulders. "You don't have to fake it for me, angel. I know this has to be playing with your head. Living with a man before … you know."

"Marriage?" Charlotte lifted her eyebrows. *Jeez, he can't even say the word.*

He swallowed. "Yes, marriage. I want you to know that I'm not trying to jerk your chain. I care for you. *Deeply* care for you. And I'm happy and honored that we're starting a family together. I just don't want us to rush into marriage. I want us to get to know each other, and I never want you to regret spending the rest of your life with me."

Rejection replaced her earlier shame. Swallowing down the feeling, she grasped for scraps of pride. "Yes, and I know you don't want to regret being with me either." Her tone was sharp and bitter.

"No. I'll never have regrets when it comes to you. But I worry if you can handle being in the spotlight. You don't seem to like it. The media. The intense fans."

"I'm stronger than you think." She slammed her toothbrush into the holder, nearly toppling it.

Jake righted the holder. "I know you are. I just want to protect you." He leaned down to kiss her temple. "Is that so bad?"

"No, it's not. I love that about you. But trust me when I say that I'm not fragile. I know with Bean and my condition it would seem that way, but—"

"You're my Wonder Woman." His thumb stroked her chin. "I could never forget that. Which reminds me … I have a little something for you." He grabbed her hand and led her to the bedroom. On the bed were a pair of her favorite superhero's socks.

Rushing to the bed, she grabbed the Wonder Woman items. "Where did you get these?" she squealed. "I love them!" She ran into his arms and gave him a kiss.

"Those are a gift for both of us. Now you won't rub your cold feet against me when I'm sleeping."

She playfully hit his shoulder. "They are not cold."

"Woman, your feet feel like you went ice skating barefoot on an iceberg."

She giggled into his chest. "Ha-ha."

"But you're beautiful and you're mine, which is why I don't mind it so much." He lifted her into his arms, and she yelped. "Now, I'm going to make your favorite … chicken quesadillas."

"But—"

"No back talk. Bean needs his protein, and he isn't going to get it from those wimpy salads."

"Or she."

"Or she," he quickly conceded.

Charlotte leaned against his chest and inhaled. Maybe living with a man, especially a man like Jake, wouldn't be so bad.

Chapter Eighteen

"Slide the lock behind me," Jake yelled through the closed door.

"Got it."

"And activate the alarm."

"Aye, aye, captain." She was probably giving him a tired salute and backing away from the door.

He didn't move until he heard the lock click. Normally her cuteness would make him chuckle, but not today. Safety was top priority. He had an alarm-enabled app, an upgraded state-of-the-art alarm system, and a security detail for Charlotte that rivaled the Secret Service.

Because they hadn't heard from the stalker for a few weeks, she'd argued that it was time to let go of the security and had teased he was overreacting. Instead of letting them go, he'd compromised and had them move to the lobby.

What she didn't know was that the stalker had contacted him. Thank God security had intercepted and given the letter to Jake. Same style as the note to her, but mailed to his home— a plain white envelope and cut-out letters. The threat was clear. Direct and meant just for him.

DON'T MARRY HER OR ELSE.

Or else what? Raw and potent fear curdled like old milk in his stomach. He didn't want to find out.

After reporting the letter to the police and increasing security, he decided not to add to Charlotte's stress by telling her. No need to skyrocket her blood pressure. He would keep this to himself. Not that they were talking about marriage at this point, but he knew, deep in his bones, that she was the one.

He paused before opening the door to exit his building. *Damn. She's the one.* A four-hundred-pound sumo wrestler sat on his chest.

Just thinking of any harm coming her way or the pain she felt on a regular basis from the pregnancy drove him crazy, pressuring the possessive beast within him to take her to a deserted island and never let her out of his sight. *Fine time to have a revelation.* Nodding at the security officer in the lobby, he walked toward the parking garage.

He sighed, not at all looking forward to conditioning. Although the season was over, they were still required to work out. For the first time, he regretted his fame. Regretted being a household name and a highly sought-after celebrity. He couldn't help but feel all of this insanity was his fault. He'd told Charlotte as much, and of course, his angel disagreed.

As much as he loved and appreciated her loyalty, she was wrong. If he'd treated women with a little more respect and valued them more than for just a night in the sheets, the stalker wouldn't have reacted so strongly to Jake settling down. The detective handling the case had told Jake it was easy for someone, albeit a demented someone, to feel like he was hers if he never truly committed to one woman. Because in their mind, he simply hadn't found the right person.

But Jake *had* found the right person. And now she was in danger, and there wasn't a damn thing he could do about it.

• • •

Charlotte tilted her head back and let the sun warm her face. She was eleven weeks pregnant, and today was a pain-free day, so far. No fatigue or severe headaches, and no pain in the back. *A blessing.* She planned to take advantage of her good fortune.

Jake was the perfect partner. He cooked every day, gave her foot massages, and bought little gifts just to make her smile. And he did make her smile.

Every day, she looked forward to his surprises. The best one so far had been the autographed Black Panther poster, signed by the movie cast. He'd placed it in what he now called Charlotte's Corner—a cute nook he'd created for her desk and collectible items.

Despite her earlier reservations, she was falling harder and deeper for the man. And, she wanted to express her love physically. *Okay, so I need a release. Stupid pregnancy hormones.* When she wasn't in pain, she was horny. What a damn uncomfortable combination.

Because Charlotte was often fatigued, Jake had initiated a ban on sex. But during the last check up a few weeks ago, Charlotte had very deliberately, with blazing cheeks and stumbled speech, asked the doctor if they could have sex. Dr. Moira's eyes had sparkled, the only signal that showed her amusement, and she'd said yes.

Not that it did any good. Jake had it in his head that Charlotte was sick and needed protecting. *Apparently from his dick.* So not true. She was pretty sure the thing had magical healing properties.

Which was why she was on a mission. Well, she and Larry, her midday security guy, were on a mission. *Seduction.*

"This is the place." Charlotte pointed to the sign above Twisted Sister on the Lower East side of New York.

Larry cleared his throat. "Stay at the front of the store, near the register, while I do a quick sweep."

The stocky man who reminded her of a WWE wrestler disappeared. Less than a minute later, he returned. He pressed his index finger over the earpiece. "All clear."

Charlotte placed a hand on his large bicep. "Thanks for keeping me safe."

A flush of red crept up his thickly corded neck. "My job, ma'am."

Despite his few words, he was sweet and her favorite guard. He didn't treat her like she was a delicate flower, but a capable woman.

He listened to her gab about work or the baby. He would occasionally grunt, say a few words that were poignant, or squeeze her hand. The other guys, although efficient, were professional but distant.

"Okay. This should be quick. I special-ordered a costume, but I still need a sword and gold boots."

Larry lifted a brow and covered his mouth.

She elbowed him. "It's all about the boots." She leaned closer. "Trust me."

His lips twitched. "I have no doubt."

Browsing the store, she found the perfect metallic gold boots and a realistic-looking sword. After they checked out, Larry whisked her into the black Lincoln Navigator and back to Jake's condo.

Flashing his badge to the front-desk officer, the guard hurried Charlotte into the elevator and pressed the penthouse-level floor button. In seconds, the doors swung open to the apartment and a bag sitting on the floor. Jake had returned from his workout. "Okay. I can take it from here," she whispered in a giddy voice.

Larry shook his head, scanned the area, and quickly peeked into the bedroom. Jake must not have noticed because she could hear a steady stream of conversation from his end.

"All clear," the guard whispered. "*Now* you can take it from here."

Charlotte twisted the handle of the bag around her fingers. "Wish me good luck."

He shook his head again. "With those boots, you don't need it." Pressing the button to the elevator, he stepped backward. "Tomorrow, Ms. Jones."

• • •

Jake wanted to punch something. A wall, maybe. His agent's low and serious voice droned on, oblivious or uncaring to the chaotic tornado sucking him into an angry vortex.

"What the hell do you mean that they want us to get married?"

"Trust me, Jakey. I had a meeting and tried to push back. We yelled, screamed, and damn near threatened to expose them for their outdated, holier-than-thou attitude. Apparently, there's some old bird on the board that made a ruckus and turned the board and CEO against you."

"Damn."

"They wanted to drop you completely, but John fought them tooth and nail. He emphasized that you both were deeply in love and that it was only a matter of time before you two got married."

"Look. Sorry, Gina, but this is utter bullshit. Threx doesn't own me." *And I can't risk pissing off the stalker.* Giving into his fear and anger, Jake punched the wall with his free hand. The wall crumbled under his knuckles, leaving a deep basin shape in the surface. Thank God Charlotte was at work. He didn't want her to see him like this. He'd think up an excuse about the damage later.

"I agree, but the fact of the matter is you have seventy-million dollars riding on this deal. *Seventy million.* This isn't chump change, and I know you've already committed some of the monies to various charities and your family. You signed the contract fully knowing about the morality clause, because I sat there and explained it to you. *You* signed up for this, Jake."

He shook off the sting of pain and rubbed the white dust particles and paint from his knuckles. "I know, I know. But damn, they can't do this, can they?" He hadn't told Gina about the second stalker letter. He wanted to keep the information contained and his agent out of his personal life. The woman had been asking too many questions lately. *Is the stalker causing stress between you and Charlotte? Do you think you'll break up?*

"Sure, they can." Her voice turned soft, tired, and a bit melancholy. "I'm sorry I'm failing you, Jake. I want to fix this for you, but—"

"It's not your fault, Gina. You aren't the idiot that couldn't figure out the basics of birth control."

A shocked gasp behind him interrupted his pacing and ranting, and he spun around. Like a bucket of ice-cold water being dumped over his head, his anger was doused, and in its place now stood remorse.

Charlotte stood before him, dressed in a sexy maternity-style She-Ra costume. But she didn't look like a conqueror. No, she looked like her world had been destroyed. Her lips were clenched between her teeth, and her eyes reflected molten pools of pain.

"Gotta go, Gina. Something came up." He clicked off the phone before his agent demanded answers he didn't have. For her or Charlotte.

He reached out to touch Charlotte, but she flinched. "Baby, I—"

She raised a hand. "Stop. I'm not going to stomp away. I'm not going to cry." Her voice wavered, betraying the lie she told.

His look must've broadcasted his doubt because she gripped her fist by her sides. "I won't. Besides, I'm already dressed up in this ridiculous costume and I can't very well be She-Ra in twenty-degree weather with a baby bump." She waved to the bed. "Let's sit down and talk." Her tone was … off. She was calm and saying all the right things so far, but it was too impersonal, too cold, too formal. Nothing like his warm and caring girlfriend.

He remained standing, still trying to figure out the right words to say to fix his screw up.

Closing her eyes, she swallowed and then took a deep breath. "Please, Jake. Sit."

He nodded and followed her order.

"We seem to always catch each other in the middle of private conversations, don't we?"

Jake grabbed onto the peace offering in her soothing words and nodded. "Yes. I'm sorry you had to hear that. How much of the conversation did you catch?"

"That Threx wants us to get married. I'm sorry, Jake. I'm usually not much of an eavesdropper but … but when I heard you yell that from the guest bathroom … well, I came closer to the bedroom door and listened to the rest." She gripped the red cape into her hands. "It's clear to me that the thought of marrying me distresses you a lot, so I won't force your hand." Her brown eyes lifted from her lap to his face. "Ever. I want a man who doesn't doubt his feelings for me. And who loves me for me."

"Charlotte." He rubbed a hand over his face. "It's not the thought of marrying you that has me pissed. It's that they are forcing my hand. *Our* hands. They're tainting our relationship by waving money over our heads. I don't like to be told what to do. I like to be in control." *And I don't want to lose you.*

"Why is that?"

"Why is what?"

"Why do you have to always be in control?"

Jake shrugged his shoulders. "I told you I was the chubby and unpopular kid."

Charlotte nodded.

"Well, things changed for me when I took control of my life. I took control by sticking to a discipline. Eating well and exercising. And with focus and practice, I'm mastering the game. Not to sound arrogant, but a lot of people don't make it to the pros. I'm proud of what I've accomplished. But when someone comes in and tells me what I should or shouldn't do, basically dictating my life, I get pissed."

She nodded her head. "And you rebel because you don't like being told what to do."

"Yes. It's against my nature to be someone's 'yes man.' I feel like they're gripping me by the balls. And, with this latest demand that we get married, they're twisting them."

"So what do you want to do, Jake?"

"I don't want to get married," he lied. He did want to get married. Maybe a year or so from now, once the stalker got over this obsession with him.

Charlotte flinched at his bluntness. "Then we won't. But I won't lie, getting married is something I want to do one day. It's always been my dream to have a large family."

"Can I think about this? I need some fresh air."

"Of course." She scanned the room, avoiding his eyes. "I can crash somewhere else."

"No, baby, I need you here. Just give me a little time, all right?" He pulled her in, placing a kiss on her forehead. "I'll send someone from security up."

"I'd like some time by myself, too." She gulped and blinked. "Can you tell them to stay in the lobby? Or maybe by the door?"

He nodded as he grabbed his jacket. "I'll be back soon."

Chapter Nineteen

Charlotte doubled over in pain. Not from the baby, but from Jake. One thing was crystal clear: He didn't love her.

He cared for her, sure. But she wanted—no, she *needed*—his love. For the first time in her life, Charlotte wanted to go home and rest in the comfort of her mother's arms. She crawled into bed and laid her head on the pillow. Just before drifting off, she heard the sweetest voice whisper, *Go on home, baby.*

Her eyes fluttered open, and her heart rattled in her chest. "Big Mama?" Holding her breath, she listened for a response, but all she could hear was her thudding heartbeat. *I'm losing my mind.* But she couldn't shake the urge to call her mother.

Giving in to the impulse, she stretched for her phone on the nightstand and dialed.

Her mother picked up and answered, "Hey, Charlie baby. I was just thinking about you. I saw the cutest little hat and thought Baby Bean would be cute in it. Don't worry, green is a neutral color, right?"

"Mama?" she whispered, her voice hoarse with emotion. "I need to come home."

Dead silence echoed from the other end. Charlotte hadn't expected her mother to be so hesitant.

"Well, if it's too much trouble then—"

"Of course not, baby. You're always welcome. Now tell me what happened."

As Charlotte spilled her guts, a large boulder lifted from her shoulders.

"Charlie baby, may I give you some advice?"

"Of course, Mama."

"Now, I want you to listen to me entirely and with an open heart, okay?"

"Okay."

"I think you should come home, but not for the reason I think you want to."

Oh, goodness. Here we go. "What do you mean?"

"Charlie, sometimes … " Mama's voice was high and unsure. "Sometimes when the going gets tough, you get going."

The words stung, and Charlotte tried not to take offense. Tried and failed. "What do you mean?"

"Give me a minute or two, baby. You promised to listen."

"Fine," she snapped. "What else?"

Her mother exhaled into the earpiece. "You ran away to New York after graduating from college to get away from us. Didn't come home except for the holidays or when Big Mama asked you to come down. I understand that now, but I think if you would've told us how you felt back then, we could've worked out our misunderstandings. You rarely came back home to visit. Only a day or two, max. You're doing it again. You're running away, but this time from Jake. I want you to change your perspective. This entire time you've been talking about how *Jake* feels, what *he* wants to do. What about what you want?" She harrumphed. "You didn't get yourself pregnant."

Pacing the floor, Charlotte ran fingers through her hair. "I know. I just don't want to force him to marry me."

"And you shouldn't. But you need to evaluate your feelings, too. I want you to consider your future. Talk to that handsome boss of yours, take a few weeks off, and think about what you want to do. Do you want to stay with Jake? Move back home to

Florida? His family is nearby, so Bean can grow up knowing both sides of the family. The sky's the limit for you. Your life is just beginning."

She was twenty-six. Worked at a successful nonprofit and had a popular dance class. She could do this thing called life, with or without Jake. Charlotte slowed her steps and smiled. "You're right, Mama. I'll take a few weeks off. Damien won't mind."

"Or maybe more than a few weeks. You do most of your work on the computer, right? Other than your dance classes, you could work remotely."

Charlotte weighed her mother's words. Not a bad idea, plus she could get away from the media's prying eyes and Threx's subtle threats. "I'll ask Damien. Someone is already covering my classes, but the PR stuff I can do from anywhere."

"Great. I'll prepare your old room for you. Dad and I'll be sure to spoil you while you think things through."

"Sounds good, Mama. Let me talk to Jake when he returns, and then I'll talk to Damien at work on Monday."

"I'm excited, Charlie. Things will work out the way they are supposed to. You'll see."

• • •

Jake fingered the white and gray linen draping the black wood bassinet. The crib, shaped like a bean, had caught his attention. He didn't know how he'd ended up at the Pottery Barn, but the all-white nursery in the window spoke to him. Before his brain could react, his feet moved him into the store.

A tall, thin woman with a severe blond bun approached. "Can I help you, sir?" Her eyes flared when she recognized him. Immediately, she went into full salesperson mode, describing the soft, plush microsuede.

material, soft protective sides, and handcrafted basket.

Her voice droned on as he refocused on the bassinet. He wanted this—for Bean, for Charlotte. He closed his eyes and imagined little Bean sleeping safe and sound. That's all that mattered. *We're a family.* He smiled and then cleared his throat, getting the chatty woman's attention.

"I'll take it."

"It's a great choice, Mr. Ross. Can I show you some other necessities? A stroller or travel system? Or a lounger and bouncer?"

He shook his head. "No, I think my girl would kill me if I buy anything else without her." He focused on the bassinet. "She'll love this." *And she'll get a kick out of the shape.* "I'll pay now, and let's have this delivered tomorrow."

"Right away, Mr. Ross."

Jake paid and headed home, feeling optimistic. Buying Bean's first gift for their home brought everything into focus. He and Charlotte were a family and had something special. He wouldn't allow Threx or anyone else to taint it. When they were ready to marry, they would. And he wouldn't force her into some centuries-old arranged marriage contract and then a few months, or maybe years later, regret their actions.

He wouldn't sell his soul for a contract no matter how much money was involved. More endorsements were to come; he had a feeling this season would be record-breaking. He'd make damn sure Threx or any other brand who judged him for his past, would regret not picking him up as a spokesperson. He'd break records and win titles to prove he was the best.

Arriving at the penthouse, he released a relieved breath when he spotted Charlotte curled up on the couch. Her eyes were trained on the television. She was no longer in costume, but rather sported the Teenage Mutant Ninja Turtle flannel pajamas he'd gotten her.

Stretching her legs, she settled them on the floor. "How are you?"

Jake sat beside her, pulling her feet into his lap for a massage. She hummed in pleasure.

"I'm fine. How are you feeling?"

"I feel … " She wiggled her toes and lifted her eyes to look at him. "I feel like things are going to be fine." She gave him a small smile.

"I think so, too." He grinned, knowing what would make her smile grow wider. "I have a surprise for you and—"

"Jake, I … we need to talk. Again." She shrugged. "Sorry for all the serious conversations we've been having lately."

"No problem, angel. What's up?"

"I think I want to go home."

"Your apartment?" He wrinkled his brows. "I thought there were already new renters in your place."

"Not the apartment. I mean home, home." Her eyes bore into his as she whispered, "Pensacola."

His hands squeezed her fuzzy-socked feet as something else squeezed his heart. "I don't think that's a good idea, Charlotte. I need you here. Need to protect you. I … I don't understand. Why do you want to leave?"

She licked her lips. "I've been so focused on you." She waved toward him. "Your wants, your needs, your desires. And I've been so focused on making sure I'm taking care of Bean and dodging the paparazzi that I'm just tired. I need a reprieve, and I think going back home is just the answer."

"But you don't even like it there."

"Mom and I talk almost every day now. Prissy and I are getting along better, too. I think you were right in saying that I misjudged my family."

"What happened to us being a team?"

"We are a team, but right now I need a time-out."

"Charlotte, this is madness." He moved her legs from his lap and rose to stand. "Training camp is starting up in a few months, and I—"

"Won't be around anyway. How can you protect me then? When I go home, I'll see your parents and my parents. I have people to take care of me should an emergency happen."

"Are you trying to punish me?"

"No, Jake. Not at all. I just need to love myself a little bit more."

"You can't *love* yourself here?" Anger dragged his tone to the gutter.

"I need to go home, Jake. I'm not asking."

"What the hell, Charlotte? I'm sorry I'm not Prince Charming, but there's no need to throw away what we have."

Charlotte righted herself on the couch and gripped her knees. "I didn't ask you to be my prince anything. My moving down south isn't forever."

"Can you guarantee that? You and Bean will fall into a routine with the family. You said you wouldn't separate us, and now you're going back on your word."

She shook her head and stood. "I'm not, Jake. You will always have access to Bean. But for once, I'm prioritizing me, and I won't have you bully or emotionally blackmail me for feeling this way." Bowing her head, she seemed tired. Lost. He didn't want her to feel that way, but he needed her more. And with the stalker on the loose, he needed to protect his family.

"I'm leaving in a week." She opened her eyes, now burning with determination. "I'm sorry if you feel blindsided, but I need this. Can you please try to understand where I'm coming from? Besides, the stalker will be miles away from Bean and me. We probably won't even need security down there."

The anger that had heated his blood receded. Giving up the fight, he pulled her into a hug. She relaxed and sighed against his chest. The warmth of her breath gave him a fraction of comfort.

He'd do anything to ensure his family's safety. And much to his disappointment, it would be better for her to change locations. The stalker most likely had limited resources and couldn't follow her. And, best of all, the psycho would assume he and Charlotte had broken up. *Exactly what she wanted.* They were playing right into the stalker's hands. "Take a few weeks, but please ... *please* come back to me. Promise you won't leave me for long."

Charlotte didn't say anything, just tightened her arms around him.

Cracks and splinters crisscrossed his heart. Shoving away the pain, he focused on practicality. "You need to call me. Every day. Even if you think I'm working, leave me a voicemail. I need a daily report and pictures of your baby bump."

She nodded against his chest. "Okay, Jake."

He stroked her hair. Despite her soothing promise, he was losing ... losing big. He wanted to dig his heels into the floor and argue, but no. Charlotte needed a break, and he would give it to her. But that didn't mean he was giving up on their future together.

Chapter Twenty

Charlotte twirled in a circle, taking in her old childhood bedroom. The curtains had been spruced from a faded purple to pretty burnt orange, yellow, and white flowers. The pale yellow walls were the same, except instead of posters of her favorite movies and comic book heroes, they were bare. A vase of fresh flowers decorated a pretty chestnut brown desk sitting catty-corner near the window.

Surprisingly, her mother had supplied file and drawer organizers equipped with highlighters, pens, and pencils. The room was spacious with plenty of sunlight streaming through. Perfectly adequate for work, quiet time, and reflection. Deep thoughts like her career path … if she'd make a good mother … *Jake.* Coming home had been the right decision, but it still didn't stop the hurt that throbbed with every beat of her heart.

She smiled as she looked out the window and observed the quiet neighborhood. In her bones, she knew she would be a good mother. She wanted it all for Bean. A real family. A father who lived with them. Family dinners and busy Sunday mornings getting the kids ready for church. For a moment, she'd thought Jake could be that guy and she'd soared in the sky from elation. But like Icarus, she gotten too close to the sun and had plummeted down to Earth.

"Is the room okay, Charlie?"

She jumped at her mother's voice. Gathering her wits and scattered nerves, she smiled and sat on the wide windowsill. "Yes, Mama. Everything looks good."

Her mother nodded with a relieved smile of her own. "Good. We kept things minimal because we figured you'd want to add your personality to the room. And, if you decide to stay longer, we can make room for the baby, too."

"Oh, I … I'm not sure if I'll be here that long. Maybe a few weeks, no more than a month." She tapped her forehead. "Just enough time to get my head screwed on right."

Mama crossed the room, hesitated, and then gave Charlotte a tight squeeze. "I think you have a pretty good head on your shoulders already." Clearing her throat, she stepped back and tucked her hair behind her ears before clasping her hands behind her back. "You just need to evaluate your options, and there's no better way to do that than surrounding yourself with good country air." She waved her hands. "Take all the time you need, baby. Your father and I … and your sister and brother, too, are here for you and the baby."

Charlotte's body shook with emotion. "Thank you, Mama. This means a lot to me."

"And you mean a lot to us." She smiled. "Now, I'm going to cook your favorite. Pot roast with mashed potatoes and gravy and lima beans. And of course, my world-famous key lime pie."

"Key lime pie?" Charlotte repeated. Her mother hadn't made her favorite in years.

"Yes, ma'am, but it may taste a little funny. I'm experimenting with a recipe that has less sugar." She waved her hands in a defensive stance. "Not for losing weight, but for diabetes."

"It's okay, Mama. That's really sweet of you."

Her mother sighed, and her shoulders sagged in relief. "Anyway, dinner will be ready at seven-thirty, so you have all day to settle in. Prissy told me that she'd be over in a few hours to help you unpack, and I think she wants you guys to go shopping at some fancy maternity shop sometime this weekend. No pressure. Up to you. Dad will be around to hang up any pictures or your comic book covers, so don't try doing it yourself, young lady!" She waved her pointed finger.

"Yes, ma'am."

Mama nodded and moved toward the door, pausing before the doorway. "And Charlotte?"

"Yes, Mama?"

"Welcome home, baby."

• • •

Charlotte sat cross-legged on her bed, watching her father hammer in a nail for her framed posters as he chattered away about one of the new hires at the local plant he managed.

Am I in the Twilight Zone? Swinging her head, she scanned the room, looking for a camera, no doubt manned by bug-eyed green aliens with large antenna-like ears who'd swapped her father's personality or maybe took over his mind. But from what she could see, every nook and cranny was clear of any extraterrestrials.

Hammer in hand, Dad stepped back. "I swear that boy is gonna kill us."

That boy was actually a man named Joe, an eager beaver who'd nearly caused an explosion at the water treatment plant. Her father had mentioned something about ozone and organic chemicals. *All Greek to me.*

"Oh, he's probably just nervous. With you as his trainer, I'm sure he'll catch on quick."

Swiping another nail from the table, he snorted. "Shee-iit. That boy struts around like he's the second coming of Jesus, waving around his master's degree like we're supposed to bow down and kiss his feet. I told him there's a tree stump in a Louisiana swamp with a higher IQ."

Laughter bubbled from her chest. She doubled over and pressed her face into the pillow. She couldn't believe Vance Jones had cracked a joke. And a funny one, too. "Dad, tell me you did not say that to Joe!" Wiping tears that had formed in the corners of her eyes, she couldn't remember laughing so hard.

"Sure as hell did, excuse my language. The man nearly killed us all and had the audacity to say that it wasn't in his course studies. You can't teach common sense."

She laughed again, and he laughed along with her.

"Now, baby, where do you want this man in a cat suit?"

"Oh, Black Panther is front and center. You can put him on the wall over there." She pointed at the bare space opposite her bed. "Right in the middle."

"All right, then."

Charlotte's bedroom door swung open. "What's all this cackling goin' on in here?"

Prissy stepped in, dressed to the nines in a royal blue sweater dress and black leather knee-high boots.

"Hey, Priss." Charlotte waved from the bed. "Dad was just telling me about his near death experience a few days ago."

"What?" Her sister rushed into the room. "What happened and why was it so funny?"

"Tell her, Dad." Charlotte encouraged. After he'd recounted the story, Prissy told some more as she helped Charlotte unpack. Her sister was a paralegal at one of the biggest law firms in Mobile and had a lot of crazy clients and attorney stories. Pretty soon they were all laughing.

"Dinner's ready!" Her mother shouted from the kitchen.

"Right on time." Prissy hung up the last piece of clothing in the closet. "And sister of mine," she reached for Charlotte's hand and squeezed, "rest up tonight because you and I are going shopping for maternity clothes tomorrow."

Charlotte smiled, her heart warm as her family rallied around her. She rubbed her stomach. *We're going to be okay, Bean.*

• • •

"Get your head outta your ass, Ross!" Coach Conner yanked the cap off his bald head, slapped it against his knee, and then rushed to the pitcher's mound.

Jake wiped the sweat from his brow and sighed. He didn't need the pitching coach's shit today. Almost a month since Charlotte moved away, and it didn't seem like she was anywhere near making whatever fucking decision she needed to make. Anger and resentment seared his chest.

Coach wheezed as he neared the mound. "We're not repeating the shitty performance you did a few seasons ago. You're not some baby-faced rookie from nowhere Alabama anymore. You're a fucking Yankee!"

"Got it, coach," Jake growled, kicking up dust with his cleats.

"I don't think you do, Ross. J.J. just devoured your pitch like one of those fat fucks at a hot dog eating contest." He waved at the home plate. "Fucking J.J. bats two-seventy, and you're letting this mook get one over you?"

Jake squeezed the ball as he took in the coach's harsh words. The man was an asshole, but a talented asshole, and he was completely right. *I'm not focused.*

"It won't happen again, coach."

"You're damn right it won't. Hit the showers and get outta my sight." He jerked his thumb past his ear, pointing toward the stands. "You've been moping around like someone kicked your puppy. Whatever it is you've got going on, fix it before training camp starts."

Jake slid off his mitt and strode from the mound. Thank God the entire team hadn't witnessed his shitty pitching. For now, it was just Coach Conner, the five starting pitchers, and seven relief pitchers at practice.

Coach yelled from a distance. "Garcia, you're up, amigo! Fuck up, and you'll be hitting the showers like Ross."

After a quick rinse off, Jake sat on the locker room bench, contemplating his next move. Not in life, just the next hour in the day. He couldn't think too far ahead anymore, but he didn't want to return to his condo. To combat the emptiness, he took it a day at a time, step by step. If he thought too far ahead, he'd think about Charlotte and Bean.

My son. God, he'd learned over the phone they were having a boy. A fucking phone call. Would that be his role when Bean arrived? A phone dad? He wanted to jump on a plane and hold Charlotte, but he couldn't. She needed her *space.*

What widened the hole in his heart had been when his mother had called him. Her reasons had been two-fold: One, to argue with him about how good a woman Charlotte was and to marry her and, two, to schedule a date for the baby shower.

What can I do? Where can I go? One thing he knew for sure: *he* didn't want to return to the condo. It no longer felt like home. He tapped the fingers on the bench, thinking through his options.

I can call the center. Maybe step in and volunteer with something. He texted Damien to see if they could use a hand. The director quickly replied and let him know a few of the kids were bored and could use some entertainment. Slinging the duffel bag over his shoulder, Jake made his way to Refurbished Dreams.

Chapter Twenty-One

Jake bent over to pick up the sports equipment off the worn Astroturf, clearing the space after an impromptu game of indoor flag football with the kids. The white parallel lines were fading, and the former bright green color was just a shade or two from turning brown. The laughter and earnest questions about what it took to be a professional athlete had given him the distraction he'd needed.

But now that it was just him and Damien at the center, Charlotte and Bean edged back into Jake's thoughts. *Damn, I miss my angel.* He missed their Netflix and chill nights, their gym dates, their random arguments about superheroes and comic books. And somehow during their time together, she'd stolen his heart. And he didn't want it back. *After all this shit is done, I'm going to marry her.* He paused, mid-grab, elated and scared out of his ever loving mind. Elated because he'd found someone to share in his life, to take care and to love, scared out of his ever-loving mind because there was a stalker on the loose who thought themselves in love with him and couldn't conceive Jake being in a relationship because of his manwhore past.

But the stalker had gone silent, and Charlotte felt safe and free down south.

None of this is fair. His family seemed happy, and a few days ago, Grandma Etta had even begun calling him again. He wasn't the favorite grandson any longer, and he'd been written out of the will, which he imagined included knitting needles, pictures, and family recipes like the highly-guarded sweet tea. No problem. He didn't need the money, and he was pretty sure Grandma Etta would give the inheritance to someone in need.

"What are you up to these days, Ross?" Damien asked as he organized the flags.

Jake exhaled, happy to be pulled out of his thoughts. "Pitch practice. Gym. Not much else." He pointed to the ground. "I'm cutting Refurbished Dreams a check before I leave. We need to replace this turf."

Damien bobbed his head. "Appreciate it, man. It's been on the to-do list, but the damn heater going out put that on hold. "By the way, we're having a small get-together at our place this weekend. You should come."

Jake paused midway as he bent to pick up a mesh jersey. "I must look pretty damn pathetic if you're inviting me to your place."

Damien laughed and shook his head. "It wasn't me. Melanie."

"Ah, of course."

"And yeah, you have been looking pathetic lately, so I'm not taking no for an answer."

Jake nodded his head. "Melanie's doing again?"

"Nah. All me. And for God's sake, shave before you come."

• • •

"Jake!" Melanie rushed from the living room and into his arms. "Thanks for coming," she whispered into his ear. She stepped back, and her gaze roamed, peering at him like a weird specimen under a microscope.

He lifted the bottle of wine in his hand. "I come bearing gifts. And I shaved."

"Ummm … okay." She gave him a weird look.

"Per your husband's orders."

She snorted. "He had the audacity to tell *you* to shave?" She gave Jake a conspiratorial look. "Remind me to tell you the story when he was pining away for me."

"Woman, you can't tell all my secrets." Damien walked toward them and hugged her from behind. "Glad you could make it, Ross." He nodded toward the spread of food on a table near the kitchen. "Grab some grub. I think you know most people here."

Jake scanned the small crowd of eight, not including himself. Mostly couples. Tiana and Nathan. A few retired ball players and several people from Refurbished Dreams.

"Go," Melanie shooed. "Talk to people. We'll catch up later tonight."

She made good on her promise as the crowd eventually thinned. By the end of the night, the only people that remained besides the hosts were Tiana and Nathan.

Jake took another gulp of his whiskey sour. For once, he wasn't worried about how he would fill the loneliness the night would bring or how to go about the next day. He was blissfully buzzed.

Melanie sat on her husband's lap in the brown leather recliner, while Tiana stretched her long legs over Nathan's lap. Jealousy burned his stomach, hollowing out his insides.

He'd lost his girl. Lost her to a psycho and couldn't get her back without putting her and their son's life in danger. *Lost her because I thought I could play with women's hearts.*

"Let's talk, Ross." Damien's gruff voice cut into the spiraling thoughts.

Jake tilted his head back to the ceiling. "Ah, hell. Is this an intervention?"

"Maaybeee." Melanie's voice took on a higher pitch. "We just want you to be happy."

"And do right by Charlotte," Damien added.

"There goes my buzz," Jake mumbled under his breath. "Look, guys. I'm doing the best I can do in this situation. I have a stalker threatening the woman I love and a pissed-off agent. Coach is riding my ass because I can't get it together, and my biggest sponsor wants to force us to get married. But if we get married, the stalker has already told me she'd harm Charlotte and Bean." He rubbed his hands over his hair. "I'm at my wit's end. I don't know what to do, and the police don't have any leads."

"Whoa, whoa, whoa. Wait a minute!" Melanie waved her hands in the air. "You love Charlotte?"

Tilting her head to the side, Tiana scrunched her nose. "Umm … I think the most important thing from his rant is that someone has threatened Charlotte and the baby if they get married." She waved at Jake. "And that sponsor pressuring you guys to tie the knot is the cherry on top of his hot-mess sundae."

Nathan shook his head. "Damn, man. That *is* a lot."

"Yeah," Damien agreed. "We were going to give you shit about not visiting Charlotte, but I get it now." He narrowed his eyes. "I don't remember you or Charlotte mentioning the stalker's threat about getting married."

"I didn't tell her and neither will you." Jake gripped his hand around the stout glass. "She doesn't need the added stress."

"But she deserves to know," Tiana argued. "She needs to be aware that the stalker is still active."

"Her family, as well as mine, are on alert."

Melanie shook her head. "She deserves to know your side. Charlotte's in pain and not just from the pregnancy. She thinks you don't love her and that you don't want to marry her."

He swallowed a deep breath. "I'd give anything to marry that woman. I love her, but I'd rather she breathes easy for a while until we get this stalker situation under control."

"You're letting this person control your life, Jake. What if you never find out who the stalker is? Then you'll never be happy."

"If that what it takes to keep Charlotte and our baby safe, I'm willing to sacrifice."

"But—"

"Chill, Mel." Damien wrapped his arms around his wife. "I understand Ross and, hell, I'd do the same thing."

"So would I," Nathan agreed. "For what it's worth, I think the stalker will slip up. Keep your eyes open and stay alert. Trust no one."

"There has to be a way." Melanie twisted her hands in her lap. "I'm so sorry, Jake. I wish I could help you somehow. Maybe I could investigate, ask a few questions, and—"

"No," Jake cut her off.

"Hell, no!" Damien growled.

She lifted her hands. "Fine, fine."

Her husband turned her around to face him. "Promise me, Melly."

"Mmm hmm."

"I need the words."

"Sure, I promise."

"Repeat after me: Damien, I promise I will not go all Nancy Drew and stick my nose where it doesn't belong."

"Damien, I promise I will not stick my nose where it doesn't belong."

"Nope." He shook his head. "You forgot the Nancy Drew part."

She swung her head to face him, curls bouncing on her shoulders. She scrunched her nose in an adorable way that reminded Jake of Charlotte.

"Now you're just being insulting. I said I'd back off." The crossed fingers behind her back made Jake nearly choke on his drink.

Clueless to his wife's gesture, Damien sighed and relaxed his shoulders.

"I think it's time for us to head out." Tiana stood, and Nathan soon followed. "I'll give you a call tomorrow, Mel."

The hostess hopped up and gave her friend a hug.

Damien pointed at Jake. "Ross. You're crashing in the guest bedroom."

Jake nodded. After airing out all his demons, he wasn't in a rush to return to his empty home.

• • •

Charlotte dried the dishes she'd cleaned and placed them in the chestnut cabinets. After a month of staying here, she'd developed a routine. First, work on the assignments Damien sent, which took her three to four hours a day to complete. Next, email Tiana and Melanie, and then snap a pic of her growing belly to text to Jake.

Sometimes they'd talk on the phone, but lately it seemed like he was pulling away or punishing her for the decision she'd made. She missed him so badly her heart hurt thinking of him, but she had her pride. And she still wasn't any closer to figuring out what she wanted to do.

The phone she'd haphazardly stuffed in her back pocket dinged. "Probably a text from Jake." She glanced at the time on the stove. It was near time for her to send a picture of her belly. She clicked open the text.

ENJOY THE BASTARD CHILD WHILE YOU CAN. YOUR FAMILY CAN'T PROTECT YOU.

Clapping her mouth to stifle a scream, she tossed the phone onto the counter. In a haze, she stumbled, jarring her hip bone against the Formica counter.

They know where I am! Shoot. I need … "God, what do I do?" Her phone vibrated against the counter. This time she was unable to stifle her scream. The speed of her heart slowed down when she saw a familiar smiling face pop on her screen.

She clicked the answer button. "Melanie," she whispered. She hurried into her room, not wanting to alert her mother and freak out her family just yet.

"Hey, girl. How are you? Just checking on my godchild. I know you haven't officially made me a godparent, but I'm ready to make my case."

"Mel, I ... I need your help."

"What's wrong?" Melanie dropped her teasing tone.

"I got ... " Charlotte took a deep breath. "I got another message, a-a text message this time. This person, t-this maniac knows where I am. I ... I ... we ... we have no protection." Rushing over to her window, she closed the blinds.

"From who? The stalker? Oh, my gosh. What did the message say?"

"They threatened the baby, told me they knew where I am and my family can't protect me."

Oh my God! What if they go after my family? A large knot kicked her stomach, and it wasn't Bean.

"Deep breaths, Charlotte. I knew it ... I knew you should be here in New York. I knew Jake was ... "

Charlotte rubbed her sweaty palm against her pants. "Jake was what?"

"Nothing. I'm just being dumb."

"Melanie, I know you." She began pacing. "There's something in your voice. You know something, and I need to know what it is. Please don't leave me in the dark. I need all the info I can get."

"Okay, but before I tell you, you have to know that he's just worried about you. Jake thought he was protecting you and—"

"Just tell me, Mel. Please."

"I've been debating whether or not to. Heck, I even promised Damien I wouldn't tell. But I crossed my fingers, so it doesn't really count, does it? And now ... now things are different." She lowered her voice. "You need to know."

Charlotte remained quiet while her friend talked herself out of her guilt.

"But I just … I just have this feeling that I'm supposed to tell you. That the answer to the problem is within our reach if we just sit down and think. And I've been making a list of people in your and Jake's circle who would know about things, and then I—"

"Melanie, honey, you're rambling, and I don't understand what you're saying."

Her friend sighed into the receiver. "Right. Right. I need to slow down. Focus. Well, Damien, Tiana, Nathan, and I had a little sit-down with Jake. We wanted to help him pull his head out of his ass. To get him to see that you two were meant to be together, but he already knows."

Charlotte's heart stuttered, and she stopped walking. "He knows? Knows what?"

"He wants to marry you, Charlotte. He didn't tell you this, and you have to promise to keep quiet, but the stalker sent another message. This time to Jake. He or she told him *not* to marry you. And then right after, Threx flexed their muscles for you and Jake to get married, and he freaked out, rightfully so."

A vise squeezed Charlotte's lungs. She couldn't breathe. All this time she'd thought Jake didn't want her, when, in reality, he was protecting her and Bean. She sat on the bed.

"Wow, okay. That changes things. Maybe I should come back."

"No, you shouldn't. Call the local police to get them on board with this latest threat and then let Jake know before you do anything else."

"But I feel so helpless. I feel like we're letting them win."

"I agree," her friend quickly responded. "And if you don't mind, I want to check a few things out. I won't go full investigative mode, but I want to get a list of everyone, including family and your inner circle. I need a timeline of when you found out you were pregnant. Who you told and in what order. Figure out the dates you told them, if you can remember. And send me the number from the text message. It's probably a fake number, but I'd like to check it out."

"How can a number be fake?"

"You can use apps to create a fake number. But like I said, I want to check it out. I have a friend that can look into it."

Charlotte hopped from the bed and began pacing again. "I can do that. I'll check my phone logs to verify the dates and I'll have the list to you by tonight. We can't tell Jake about the list thing. He'll freak out if he knows I'm trying to go after the stalker."

"No. No, we can't. I think if we can narrow it down to one or two people, maybe I can investigate them and—"

"No, Melanie. You will not follow someone possibly dangerous around. If you do, I will pull the plug on this … this operation." She stopped pacing and giggled.

"Are you cracking up on me, Charlotte?" A hint of doubt tickled her friend's voice. "Maybe we shouldn't do this."

"No," Charlotte said between another giggle fit. "Okay, maybe a little bit. But that's not why I'm laughing. What's the name?"

"Name of what?"

"The operation?" Her friend always had a name for something serious she was involved in. Like when Melanie had planned to capture Damien's heart, it was Operation: I'm Gonna Make You Love Me. When Tiana moved from a toxic work environment in Atlanta, the name was Operation: Get the J-O-B in N-Y-C. Then, when Tiana realized her feelings for Nathan, the title was Operation: It's Been You.

"Okay, you got me. I'm in between either Operation: Hunt the Hunter or Operation: Get That Ever After."

Charlotte tapped her chin. "Hmmm … let's go with Get That Ever After."

"Sounds good. Okay, I'll look out for your list. Name the file 'party guests' just in case Damien gets suspicious. Same with the subject line for the email. Now," she took a breath, "tell your folks, Jake, and call the police."

"Okay, got it. I'm not getting you in trouble, am I?"

Melanie laughed. "No. Damien knew what he was getting into when he married me. I've been messaging Tiana on the computer. I've got her onboard, too."

"Really?" Charlotte was surprised that her more cautious friend would encourage the operation.

"Yeah, she's a mama bear when it comes to you. No one screws with our friends. You and Jake mean the world to us. "

"Thank you, Mel. You mean the world to me, too. And thank you for doing this."

"Of course. Stay alert at all times. We don't know what kind of resources the stalker has. Take your time with the list and try to be as accurate as possible with the timeline.

"Will do."

"Charlie, lunch is ready!" Mama yelled from the door.

"I gotta go. We'll talk soon, right?"

"Right. Take care, Charlotte. Love you, girl."

"I love you, too, my friend. Be safe."

Chapter Twenty-Two

Charlotte stared at her computer screen, as she had been for the past forty-five minutes. The cursor blinked on a blank excel sheet. She'd been so excited to take on the challenge of figuring out who could be the stalker. But now, a dull throb pulsed in her forehead and icicles wrapped themselves around her veins. She was frozen in fear.

Fear and hurt and anguish. Not for herself, but for the baby. Baby Bean was a blank slate. No sins committed. But the stalker didn't care. Charlotte had thought she was safer away from New York and without Jake, but she'd been wrong.

And, if Melanie's theory held true, someone she and Jake knew hated her so much that the psycho wanted to terrorize Charlotte's life. *And Bean's.*

The mama bear within her roared and cracked the icy fortress that held her captive. With renewed purpose, she wracked her brain. First, the timeline. She flexed her fingers and reclined in her chair. "Think, Charlotte. When you found out you were pregnant, who did you tell?"

Sitting up, she stretched her fingers to the keyboard and quickly typed it out: Mom, Jake, Melanie, and Tiana. She sighed. "Doubt any of them would be behind this. But what if my phone was bugged?"

She shook her head. *Keep it simple, Harriett the Spy.* "Okay, after I told my friends and family, Jake told his family and Shawn."

Jake had given his family specific instructions to keep the news to themselves. He'd even made his mom promise to keep it from her prayer circle.

Charlotte had also grilled her family this afternoon, asking if they had mentioned it to any friends or in public. They'd all vehemently denied spreading the news.

She then typed out notes to accompany each person. After Jake had told his family, he'd also called Gina.

Did she let the news leak? Charlotte shook her head. No, the agent was a little rough around the edges, but she was a consummate professional when it came to the media. Still, Charlotte added Gina's name and then Mark, Jake's publicist, to the list. *And Threx. The board and entire company could know.*

She stared at her screen until her eyes crossed. "Someone had to have told someone, whether or not they meant well." Saving the document, she then emailed it to Melanie per her friend's specific instructions.

Rubbing her belly, Charlotte looked out the window. "Now it's time to tell your grandparents about what's happening."

• • •

Charlotte had waited until after dinner to show the text.

Her mother jumped from the couch. "We have to give this to the police! Vance, you know the chief. Can you call him?"

"Of course, baby. We'll get this taken care of, you'll see." Her father grabbed his phone.

"I can't believe someone is scaring my baby." Mama's voice was shrill as she paced the living room. She pointed to Dad. "Where are the keys to the rifle?"

Charlotte's father cupped the receiver on the phone. "Not a good question to ask while I'm calling the sheriff, sweets."

"Fine, fine. You're right." Her mother moved to sit beside her. The cushions to the cream couch dipped slightly. "We'll take care of everything, baby. Just let me and Daddy handle it."

Nodding, Charlotte swallowed a hot ball of emotion, overwhelmed by the love and solidarity her parents were showing.

"Thank you, Mama. I'm sorry for bringing this to your doorstep. I don't want to put you and Dad in danger."

"Nonsense. Family sticks together, and it's our job to protect you."

"But I'm twenty-six."

"So what? You'll always be my baby, and nobody hurts my baby or my grandbaby." She nodded to Charlotte's stomach.

Charlotte's heart swelled so much and so quickly that she felt like she was floating. "I love you, Mama. I know I don't say it often, but I do." She squeezed her mother's hand.

"I know you do, baby. And we love you, too. Just sit tight and let us take care of you."

"Okay." The lie tasted like soot on her tongue. She hated to fib, but she was done sitting tight. And she missed Jake. She needed to see him. Each day she grew bigger and bigger. Bean needed his father, and Jake was all alone. She could tell from their conversations that he missed her. Her phone vibrated in a pocket. Grabbing it, she peered at the screen. *A text message from Jake.* She must have thought him up.

"Have you talked to Jake?" Her mother pointed to the phone in Charlotte's hand.

"No, not yet. Let's see what the sheriff says, and I'll catch him up."

The sheriff's office visit was surprisingly easy. Jake had already alerted the local authorities to what was going on and had asked them to occasionally drive by her parents' house.

Jake's thoughtfulness made her nose tingle and her eyes water. These days, it didn't take much to make her cry. Her dad had learned the hard way when they'd watched a Hallmark movie the other night. "Your daddy was looking out for us," she whispered to Bean.

After saying goodnight to her parents, she texted Jake to let him know she was sleepy and would talk to him tomorrow. No need to risk him hearing the worry in her voice.

Melanie knew about the latest threat, which meant Charlotte had to hurry to New York before her friend told Jake about it. She'd purchased a ticket and would fly out early in the morning. Soon, she'd be back home in New York, safe and sound in Jake's arms.

. . .

At six a.m., the morning was silent. Not even the birds were chirping, and the neighbor's dog Bruno—who Charlotte swore thought of himself as the unofficial neighborhood watch—wasn't barking. As she stuffed the last of her clothes into a rollaway bag, she felt like a twelve-year-old running away from home.

A pang of guilt seized her chest, freezing her quick and quiet movements. She didn't want to worry her parents so, like any good twelve-year-old runaway, she left a note to explain her actions. She couldn't stay here and risk the lives of her family.

Yesterday, she told her mother that she'd planned to meet Jake's mom and grandmother for breakfast so that Mama wouldn't be surprised by her absence. By the time her mother caught on, Charlotte would be halfway home. *I'll call Mama after I land.*

No turning back now. She would no longer put her family in danger. If the stalker could find her in Pensacola, she'd rather hide in plain sight with Jake's security around her. Hopefully, Melanie or the police would find the stalker sooner rather than later.

Charlotte had already scheduled a cab to pick her up since a car app service was unavailable in rural Florida this early in the morning. Creeping quietly out the door, she caught her ride and was headed to the airport.

. . .

Sweat beaded on Jake's forehead and poured from his temples. Taking the pocket square from his suit jacket, he wiped away the perspiration.

His brother D'Mario turned to say something, but Jake couldn't make out the words. D'Mario shook his head and then grabbed Jake's shoulders, pushing him out the door.

Now they were in a church. Everyone turned and whispered. But unlike most wedding days, no one smiled. Instead, they sneered, jabbed accusing fingers at him. Jake continued to walk down the aisle. Not that he had a choice with his brother pushing him like a warden escorting a prisoner to death row. At the altar, he turned to face the bloodthirsty crowd. With military precision, the congregation swung their attention to the bride. A fuzzy light surrounded her, and he couldn't see her face. She walked slowly toward him, but the closeness still did not make her image clear.

When she finally made it to Jake, his shaky fingers lifted her veil, and he released the breath he'd been holding. *My angel.* She was as beautiful as ever. Bending down, he gave her a kiss, and the suppleness of her skin peeled away, down to the bone.

Charlotte reached for him and screamed.

"Shit!" Jake's legs tangled in the sheets. He looked around his bedroom and sighed. "Just a nightmare." Nothing had been real, except for the sweat.

Pushing himself out of bed, he walked to the bathroom and started the shower. As the water heated, he stripped the sweat-soaked covers. He'd have his cleaning company change the sheets before tonight.

Returning to the shower, he stood under the stinging spray. The rain-head shower soothed his tense muscles. Closing his eyes, he relaxed against the tiled walls. He didn't need a psych degree to figure out his problem. *Stress.* Stressed and worried about Charlotte. The woman he loved was in danger from a psycho. All Jake could do was wait the stalker out and hope the creep outgrew her misguided feelings.

Yeah, right. He didn't take the stalker's silence as a good thing. Deep in his bones, he knew this was the calm before the storm.

Turning off the shower, he hurriedly dried himself. He was determined to hear Charlotte's voice and make sure she was doing well. It was seven in the morning, but he knew she'd be awake. Wrapping the towel around his waist, he picked up his cell and called.

"Hey, Jake." Her voice was chipper. "I was just thinking about you."

"Good thoughts, I hope."

"The best ... I miss you."

"You do?" Surprise and eagerness covered his voice. *Damn, I sound pathetic.*

"Of course, Jake." She sounded wounded with a note of surprise. "I do miss you. In fact, I want to come home soon."

Warmth his expensive shower couldn't provide invaded his body. "And I want you to come home soon, too, angel."

He thought of the skeletal-bride dream. Charlotte was safe and happy. In New York, she was still in danger. Despite his personal desires, she needed to stay put.

"But maybe it's a good thing you're down there, angel. You seem happy, and you and Bean are safe. My mom was talking my ear off about meeting your family for dinner last week."

"But what about you?"

"What about me?"

"Are you happy? You've mentioned me, Bean, your parents, and my family, but what about your happiness?"

He searched for the closest form of the truth he could muster. He was in a shit mood without her. If she knew just how much her leaving had ripped his heart out, she'd try to return. "I'm happy that you're safe. That's my top priority."

"But do you … " She cleared her throat, and her voice wobbled. "Do you miss me?"

Jake groaned. "Of course I do, angel, but I—"

"Doesn't seem like it." Her soft words pierced the white-knight armor he wasn't sure he was all that worthy to wear.

"Trust me, I miss you. Every damn second of every minute and every hour of the day. I miss your cold feet and the way you snuggle against me. The way you sigh when you find just the right spot on my chest to lay your head. The way you laugh and make me laugh. Trust me, baby, when I say that I miss you."

"Okay. I believe you."

He sighed. At least he could reassure her of one thing. "Good. I know sometimes I do and say things that don't match up, and it seems like I don't care, but I do. Never, ever doubt my feelings for you."

"I won't, Jake. Not ever."

"Good. I gotta get to pitching practice but I … take care, angel."

You can't tell her. Not yet.

Charlotte took a deep breath. "You too, Jake. See you soon." Her voice was soft and determined. A vow that made the hope in his heart soar.

Chapter Twenty-Three

The surround-sound speakers were jammed on full blast. After an hour of fruitless channel surfing, Jake selected a recording and caught up on his favorite ESPN show he'd miss while at practice.

He grimaced. The regular host was out on vacation and Dan Rudy was filling in. A few years ago, when Jake had gone through a pitching slump, Rudy's rhetoric fueled a movement to have Jake kicked out of the Yankees organization. He loathed the pot-bellied bastard, who still didn't have anything nice to say about him or the Yankees, and was itching to turn the TV off altogether.

The ringing phone, connected by Bluetooth to the speakers, interrupted the commentator's rant about a losing basketball team. Glancing at the screen, he saw his agent was calling yet again. He rolled his eyes and answered his phone.

"You can tell Threx to fuck off, Gina. I'm not getting married just to please their casting-the-first-stone-ass-crazy board members."

"I'm not calling about that." Her loud voice blasted from the speakers.

Wincing at the volume, he lowered it.

"I've already told them our position, and we're at a stalemate. John is trying to work his magic."

"Then why are you calling? Because I can't take another lecture from you about impregnating my girlfriend. I won't apologize for Bean."

A deep sigh played over the phone, followed by a string of Italian curse words. He'd learned quite a few being Gina's black-sheep client.

"I'm not here to give you shit, Jake. I know you're tired and stressed. And you're right, we don't need Threx. Something else will come along."

Some anger and stress seeped from his shoulders. "Glad we're on the same page."

"We are, Jakey. We are *so* on the same page, all right?" she cooed from the speakers. "I'm just checking on you to see how things are going? And to check on Charlotte and the baby."

Jake began to pace. "I'm fine. Charlotte's fine. The baby's fine." He was being short, but with Charlotte away, some of his basic manners had disappeared.

"Jakey. I'm on your side. No need to be rude, my goodness."

"Sorry. We're doing well. Charlotte is still down south with her parents, and I'm up here." *By myself.*

"I know it's tough, but it's good she's safe. Have you received any more threats?"

Jake stopped moving. He'd thought about telling Gina about his threat but decided against saying anything. *Knowing her, she'll get Mark to spin a sob story about me being a victim and right now the media is on a need-to-know basis.* "No. Nothing since the initial one."

She sighed. "Good. In the meantime, why don't you go out with some friends and blow off steam? I know I'm just your lowly agent, but if you need me, I'm here."

"Thanks, Gina. I'm glad you have my back. And I'm sorry if I'm a grumpy—"

The locks on the door twisted. "What in the hell?"

"What is it? Are you okay?" Gina asked.

Charlotte stepped through the doorway, roller tote in tow.

"Angel, what are you doing here?"

Pushing the bag to the side, she rushed into his arms. "I missed you. I missed you so much, and I don't want to be away from you anymore." She kissed his forehead, cheeks, nose, and lips.

He gripped his arms around her waist, still in shock that she was back in his arms.

"Baby, I thought you were home."

"I am home." She stepped away from his arms. Her eyes, now soft and shy, peered into his. "Wherever you are *is* home."

Her declaration sucked the air out of his lungs. *Fuck if this woman isn't trying to own me.*

"Call you back, Gina." Dropping his phone on the couch, he scooped Charlotte into his arms.

"Fine, Jake," blared through the speakers, followed by a click.

"I can't believe you're here."

"I had to see you. I love you," Charlotte murmured into his chest.

"Angel, you make it hard for a brotha to be strong."

She lifted her head to look at him. "What do you mean?"

He walked them to the couch and maneuvered her to sit on his lap. His hands spread across her stomach. The pictures she'd sent over the past month hadn't done her justice. She was round and glowing with his child.

He wanted to kneel and pray to thank God for the miracle that was Charlotte and his son. No way would he ever let them go again. She would forever be embedded in his soul. He stared into her eyes so she could see, so she could feel his truth. "I love you."

"Y-you love me?"

"Yes. I do. I want to be the man that wakes up to your sweetness every morning and not just because of Bean, but because I love you. I love you from the top of your head to the soles of your feet. And I've been scared, so damn scared, of placing you in danger. I ... I—"

"You ... what?"

"I hadn't realized the depth of my feelings for you until you left. You seemed so happy, and you were safe."

She cupped his face. "Jacob, I'm ... we're not all that safe."

Like an emergency brake, his heart slammed against his chest and froze in place. "No?"

"No, I … " She licked her lips. "I received another threat yesterday. That's why I left Pensacola. If I'm not safe anywhere, I want to be with you."

He placed her on the seat beside him. "I can't believe you're just telling me this." He rubbed a hand over his head. "Did you call the police? What did your parents say about you leaving? Hell, where are your parents?"

"My parents are home, and they know I'm here. I flew by myself."

By herself? He gathered his patience by taking a long, deep breath.

She rushed on to finish. "Yes, I called the police, and they were already circling the neighborhood because a little birdie told the sheriff about my troubles."

"You're damn right I told him. Not that it did any good." His blood pressure increased at their incompetency. "I'll be giving them a call." He grabbed his phone.

"Relax, Jake. I'm here safe and sound and in your arms. Let's just relax. We can watch a few episodes of *Daredevil*."

He sighed. "Fine. But tomorrow morning, bright and early, we are going to the police station."

Charlotte nodded. "Okay, Jacob."

He jumped from the couch. "Are you hungry?"

"Bean and I are starving!"

"Okay, I'll make some turkey burgers and sweet potato fries for lunch."

She stood and rubbed her belly. "Yum. And I think I'll take a shower."

• • •

Charlotte moaned under the shower spray, enjoying the soothing water and being home.

He loves me! Hearing that from the mouth of a supportive friend is one thing, but listening to it from the lips of the man you loved was another entirely.

"We're going to be okay, Bean. Promise."

"Yes, we are." A velvet-smooth voice from behind her did all kinds of damage to her girl parts.

"Jake," she moaned and moved away from the water. Hands covering her stomach, she tried to hide her baby bump, but he pushed her hands away.

"All of this," he touched her breast and then moved his calloused hands to her stomach and behind, "is mine. Don't hide from me, baby."

Wrapping her arms around his neck, she pulled him closer. "Jake ... " Her voice purred, nearly breathless. She wanted him with every fiber of her being. She lifted up onto her toes to kiss his lips. He was still at first, and her heart dropped. But then, he wrapped his arms around her waist and walked backward until he slammed into the tiled wall.

Cupping her neck, he lowered his mouth and devoured hers. Hard and wet and deep. He was out of control, and she was flying. *Soaring.* He broke the kiss, and his breath became erratic, like her heartbeat. He leaned down again and nibbled. From the grip on her hip and neck, she knew he wanted more, but restrained himself. She didn't want that. She'd fallen in love with the bad boy, and she wanted him to come out and play.

Reaching below his waist, she palmed and milked him. A low groan filled her ear, and his breath warmed her neck. She squeezed as she flicked her tongue to lick the column of his throat.

"Take me, Jacob."

Growling this time, he turned off the water. His eyes never left hers. Palms against the door, he opened the shower, carefully lifting and then lowering her onto the drying mat.

"I—"

He placed his finger over her lips. "No words. Not right now, baby. Otherwise, I might bend you over the tub," he jerked his head toward the corner, "and fuck you. So be a good girl. No talking and no touching." He licked his lips and then hers. "Yet." Grabbing a towel, he dried her off.

She shivered with need. Instead of verbalizing her desires, she took his silent signals when he wanted her to lift her arms and spread her legs to towel her down.

Still naked, he scooped her into his arms and marched into their room. Lowering them both on the bed, he positioned her above him so that she straddled his waist.

His eyes finally cleared. "Take control." He lifted her from his lap and swiftly entered her. She gasped at the onslaught of pleasure of being filled to the core.

"Take what you need." He jerked his hips and then pulled back. "You've got it all with me." His voice was strangled, and his face tensed. "We go at your pace."

Nothing was between them. Just his sex and a warm, ripped body against her skin. She flexed her inner muscles. His chest heaved.

She lowered her lips to his ear. "This is gonna be fun."

Pushing off his chest, she arched her back, creating a sexy rhythm that was familiar, yet the sensation seemed all so new.

"You're killing me, angel." His eyes burned her alive as she rode him.

She slowed down the pace, grinding against him, torturing herself with the speed. She wanted fast, but it'd been so long, and she wanted them to last. Sweat slicked their skin, and his muscles tensed as he continued to torch her with his gaze: hot, hungry, and passionate. Like a puppet master, he jerked her limbs to move at his will. Trying to regain control, she squeezed her eyes shut.

"Suck me." She leaned over so he could suckle her breast. He latched on, lapping and licking. She was close—*oh, so close*—so she pulled away.

Jake growled and, as quick as a flash but yet gentle, rolled them until she was flat on her back.

"But I thought I was in control." Her voice was breathless and ragged.

Still connected, he widened her legs and looked at her, eyes like a predator who'd just caught his prey. "I lied."

He pumped his hips uncontrollably, yet still artful. Hard but not rough.

"You know why I call you angel?" He grunted as he continued to move inside of her.

She shook her head. She couldn't speak, much less think.

"I knew that being inside of you would be the closest to heaven that I could be."

White-hot heat zinged from him and into her core. As he continued his release, he slammed his hips twice more before she toppled over the edge of abyss with him.

After a few minutes, she finally caught her breath. She puffed to move a string of hair that had fallen over her forehead, too lazy to use her hands to move it.

"That was … "

"Amazing. Didn't think we could get any better, but we did." He gathered her to rest on his chest.

She yawned as she struggled to keep her eyes open. "I wonder why?"

"Love, angel. Love."

• • •

Charlotte woke up alone, but her nose quickly solved the mystery to Jake's whereabouts. Putting on a shirt tossed on the sofa near the bed, she padded toward the kitchen.

Her man was shirtless. Taking a moment of silence, she admired his delicious muscles and broad shoulders as he faced the stove. "Mmm … everything smells good." She walked into the kitchen and wrapped her arms around his waist.

"Kick up your feet and relax. I know you have to be exhausted. From your *flight* and all. I can't believe your precious traveled by alone."

I knew he wouldn't let it go. "How else was I supposed to get here?" She shrugged. "And if I would've told you or my parents that I wanted to return here, ya'll would've talked me out of it." Rubbing his bunched shoulders, she kissed his back. "I called my parents after I landed. Let's not argue. I'm here, and I thought you were happy."

"I'm ecstatic, angel. Just … " He turned to faced her. With a finger, he tilted her chin. "Just promise to keep me in the loop. It wasn't a smart move for you to leave your family and travel by yourself, especially after receiving another message from the stalker."

She nodded. "I agree, and I'm sorry. I'll keep you in the loop, and you keep me in it, too."

"I will." He hugged her tight. "Now, go sit down, and I'll bring your food to you."

Following his bossy directions, she flopped onto the couch. A few minutes later, Jake followed with a food tray in hand. "Dig in, baby."

Charlotte bit into the hamburger and moaned. Lots of mustard, pickles, and just a hint of ketchup. *Just like I like it.*

Bean kicked up a storm. He was happy they were home, just like his mama.

Chapter Twenty-Four

"Get up, angel. We gotta go."

Charlotte mumbled against his chest and snuggled closer. She'd crashed after eating and midway through the show they'd been watching. No way was she getting up when the sun hadn't graced them with its presence yet.

"I've gotta hit morning practice." Softening his deep voice, he ran his fingers through her hair. "I'm not leaving you home, baby. You're coming with me."

She rolled off his chest and then rubbed her eyes. "Can't you call Larry from security?"

"I'll call them and sign the contract today after practice and after we meet with Detective Wen about the latest developments."

She lifted her head from the pillow. "Why didn't you keep Larry around for *your* personal safety? What if the stalker got impatient and tried to h-hurt you?"

"I'm fine, baby." He pulled her close again, and his beard lightly scraped her neck. "Just do me a favor and come along. I can't function if you aren't by my side."

Cupping the back of her neck, he kissed her. Bean fluttered in her stomach. Jake took her breath away. "Okay. I don't want to stress you out."

Jake gave her a warm smile and kissed her nose. "That's my girl."

"No fair," she whispered.

He tilted his head and smiled. "What did I do?"

"Your kisses are like the game Simon Says. Ask me anything after you kiss me, and I'll do it, no hesitation."

"Glad to know this relationship is somewhat balanced."

"Huh?" She scrunched her nose. "Of course it is. You know I've always had the hots for you. You didn't notice me until I bumped my head." She tried to soften her tone. But from the grin breaking across his face, she knew she'd sounded disgruntled instead.

"You taught classes every Monday, Wednesday, and Friday at noon and in the evenings at seven-thirty. I used to volunteer twice a month on Thursdays. One day, I had to shift to a Wednesday night and saw you. Then I permanently changed my schedule to Wednesdays and upped my volunteer hours to weekly during my off-season. Your favorite colors are red and blue and I get why … you love Wonder Woman. And, from your song selections, I know you're a card-carrying member of Beyoncé's beehive."

Charlotte laughed. She had probably played B's entire discography at least a dozen times during her tenure as the dance instructor.

"And one more thing: Shakira's hips don't lie, but baby, yours will get a brotha to tell the truth, the whole truth, and nothing but the truth."

Charlotte snorted and rolled over. "My baby bump isn't doing much for you or anyone these days."

"Did you not just ride me a few hours ago? And did I just not lose control and nearly break you in half?" He shook his head. "If you move your hips like you did the day you bumped your head, you'll give me a hard-on that'll last all day. I'll need to explain to coach why I can't come to practice."

Her breath toppled like dominoes. "We wouldn't want that, now would we?"

"Don't tempt me, angel. Get dressed and put on something not-sexy like a pillow case or a burlap sack."

"I'm seventeen weeks pregnant, Jake. That's the definition of *not sexy*."

"With *my* baby. That's sexy as hell."

"I'll just," she swung her feet on the floor and pushed off the bed, "wear a big shirt."

"Extra-extra-large," he said, still lounging in bed, arm slung over his forehead.

"Deal. Do you want breakfast?"

"Yes, but I'll make us something." He rolled up from his flat position and then moved from the bed. "An egg-white omelet sound good to you?"

Her stomach grumbled, and she blushed.

"I'll take that as a yes." He swept her into his arms for another deep kiss. "I can't believe you're here."

"Are you happy?"

"Happiest I've ever been."

• • •

Someone who wasn't happy was coach seeing Charlotte at a closed practice. The squat man had waddled over to Jake, looking very much like the Penguin from *Batman*. "No wives, girlfriends, or one-night stands at practice, Ross."

Jake folded his arms across his chest. "She stays, coach. You're well aware that her life is in danger, and she won't be leaving my sight."

"Hire a bodyguard."

"I will. After practice. Today, she stays."

Coach jerked off his hat and slapped it across his meaty thighs. "Jesus Christ on a popsicle stick, Ross!"

Lifting an eyebrow, he watched the man expend energy through a flurry of creative phrases and expletives. "You done?"

"Just get your ass on the diamond."

"You got it, coach."

After nearly an hour of practice, Jake was exhausted. Coach had ridden him hard, a silent punishment for bringing a woman to practice. The man swore women were bad luck, as if they were pirates on a ship.

Wiping sweat from his brow with one hand, he gripped the ball in his right, ready to toss another heater. He'd been on fire at practice today. *Thanks to my muse.*

Turning his attention from the batter to check on Charlotte, Jake nearly stumbled in his swing when he saw Gina there, too. They were deep in conversation. Two distractions, now. *Coach will skin me alive.*

He stopped his swing and reset again. "Sorry, Ethan," he told the batter. "One more time."

Charlotte turned his direction and gave him a shy smile and wave. His agent offered an impatient chin bob.

"Any time now, Lover Boy," Coach yelled.

Shaking his head, Jake leaned back on his right leg, lifted the left, and fired into the catcher's mitt. He gave coach a smug look and winked at his girl.

. . .

Charlotte watched as Jake delivered another scorcher to the batter.

"He's looking good, isn't he?" Gina nodded toward Jake.

"Yes, he is. But he always looks good to me." Smiling, she continued to watch him practice.

"He kinda lost his mojo after you left. And he's been a moody cow, which is why I'm here to check on him. Glad you're back to shake him out of his misery."

Charlotte turned to the woman and smiled. Jake's agent was a tough nut to crack, so Charlotte was honestly surprised by the compliment.

"Did *you* just give *me* a compliment?" She batted her eyes.

Gina tossed her hair and laughed. "Don't let it go to your head."

"I'll endeavor not to." Her cell phone vibrated in her jogging pants' pocket. Pulling it out, she glanced at the screen. *Mel.*

Can you talk? I have a theory I want to run by you.

Yes! Charlotte's heart ka-thumped in her chest, and her stomach knotted. The news she'd been waiting for. Fingers shaking, she quickly replied back.

Call you in a few minutes.

She needed to step away from practice to ensure Jake didn't know about the covert operation. Bean decided to make his daily appearance by playing hopscotch on her bladder. Her stomach clenched again.

Bathroom! Perfect excuse.

She turned to the agent. "I need to go to the ladies' room. Be right back."

Gina nodded. "I'll go with you. Jake wouldn't want you to be alone."

Charlotte's excitement deflated. "Oh, no, I'll be fine by myself. The restrooms are just around the corner.

"No." The persistent woman shook her head. "I'd feel more comfortable if we stayed together."

"Fine." Charlotte quickly conceded. *I'll just have to take my time and call Mel while I'm in the stall.* Charlotte stood and flagged down Jake, knowing he would worry if she suddenly disappeared. He was too far away to hear her, so she mimed going to the bathroom by squeezing her legs together and pointing toward the restrooms.

Jake shook his head no. Then Charlotte pointed to Gina and squeezed her legs together again. "C'mon Jake. I've really gotta go."

He tossed his hands in the air in resignation.

"I'll take that as a yes." The agent laughed. "Let's go."

• • •

Charlotte sighed and rolled her eyes when Gina knocked on the bathroom stall door for the third time. The woman was on Charlotte like she owed her rent money. *Now she wants to be nice.*

"I assure you, it's just a little stomachache. And I have a shy bladder. Can you step outside for a few minutes?"

"Are you sure? You haven't been able to go, and it's been like ten minutes."

Grabbing a toilet seat cover from the dispenser, she rustled it to sound busy. Tension coiled in her stomach. She swallowed down the rush of nerves. "I'm fine." She hated lying but was desperate to hear Mel's theory. "A few minutes, please. If I can't go soon, I'll return to the stands. Can you wait outside?"

"I … sure." Gina sighed. "But I'm right outside."

"Okay. Thanks!" Charlotte waited until she heard the door click shut. She quickly emptied her bladder, flushed the toilet, and stepped out of the stall. After washing and drying her hands, she called Melanie.

"Hey, girl! What took you so long?" Her friend answered on the first ring, sounding like she was on her fifteenth cup of coffee.

"Sorry. Someone felt the need to follow me to the bathroom."

"Awww, your family is just worried."

Charlotte didn't correct the assumption that she was still in Pensacola. "So? What's your theory? You have any leads? I don't have a lot of time."

"I have one hunch. It's a little wild, but I can explain why." Her friend took a deep breath. "I looked at the list you sent and reviewed your notes. You told family members you were pregnant, and the only friends you and Jake shared the news with were me,

Tiana, Damien, Nathan and Jake's friend, Shawn. From your notes, I don't think it's a situation like *The Bodyguard* with family or friends."

"What bodyguard?"

"You know the movie? Whitney Houston and Kevin Costner. The sister was jealous of Whitney's character, Rachel, and tried to kill her."

"Melanie … I need you to focus. I know it wasn't my sister or anyone else in my family. Prissy is a lot of things, but psychotic isn't one of them." Charlotte paced the floor. "Now, c'mon, Mel. I need you to tell me the rest. Quickly."

"All right. Well anyway, I scratched out obsessed fans. If the paps caught wind of your pregnancy, they would've descended on you like a pack of wolves. They didn't get involved until *after* Jake's announcement, and that was after the first threat. So after scratching them off the list, I have two hunches. You also told the staff at Threx, Mark, Jake's publicist, and Gina, his agent. It's got to be one of them."

Charlotte stopped pacing and turned toward the wall. Fear, tangy and bitter and sharp, shook her body. Her knees wobbled like a gelatin cake. "G-gina? You're kidding?"

Melanie's quick and hyper voice finally slowed to a normal pace. "Not so, my friend. Or someone from Threx or Mark. If you send me a list of names, I can do some investigating. In the meantime, sit tight and stay away from anyone on my suspect list."

"Melanie …" Charlotte's throat tightened. She couldn't force the words.

"Hey, calm down. I know it's a shocker. Maybe I should call Jake and let him know my theory. He needs to stay safe, too."

"No, Mel, I … I'm here in New York. I thought I would be just as safe here with Jake. And when you told me he actually wanted me, I-I … jumped the gun."

"Okay, that changes things." Melanie's voice dropped to a whisper. "Just stay away from—"

"I can't, Mel." Her voice shook. "Gina's here at practice in the stadium. And waiting for me outside of the restroom. I—"

"Knock, knock!" Gina rapped on the door and stepped in.

Phone still at her ear, Charlotte nearly snapped the device in half.

"Oh, hi!" Charlotte forced a light and chipper tone.

"Stay calm, girl," Melanie whispered. "Act normal and get back to practice ASAP."

"Okay, Mama. Everything is fine. Don't worry, I'm here with my friend Gina, and we're walking back to our seats. I've gotta go."

"No!" Melanie whispered-hissed. "Stay on the phone so I can hear everything. I'm using my app to record."

"Okay, I will. Bye, Mama." Charlotte pretended to end the call.

"You're looking a bit clammy." The agent's forehead scrunched. "You sure you're okay? I can go get Jake."

"Y-you would do that?" Charlotte couldn't tell if the woman was genuine. She didn't know what to believe.

The restroom door banging open made Charlotte jump. A man dressed in all black and a ski mask stormed in. Terror possessed her body, and Charlotte backpedaled until she hit a wall.

"Charlotte the Harlot." Gina smiled. "Now you're mine."

"You!" Charlotte clutched her stomach. A drum roll kicked in her belly. *Be strong for Bean.* Straightening her spine, she grabbed her fear by the throat and tossed it away. "You won't get away with this. Jake and the rest of the pitching team and staff saw you leave with me."

"Oh, I will get away with this. I'll be a hero. You see, Mr. Man here is going to kidnap and kill you. I … " She slapped her own face. "Will be the one who tried to save you from the madman, getting hurt in the process."

The madman himself stepped toward her. "Whatever she's paying, I can double it." Charlotte licked her lips. "Don't do this. Please. I—"

A crash interrupted her pleading. Gina had smashed her head into the mirror. *Oh my God, she's nuts!*

"What are you doing?" Charlotte screamed.

Blood trickled from the woman's forehead. She wrung her hands, her eyes wide with fear. "I-I tried so hard to try to save her, Jake. He was just too strong. He overpowered me and ... I just need someone tonight. Can you hold me?" She clapped her hands and cackled. "Been working on that for a while. You like?" Gina laughed and then shrugged when Charlotte didn't answer.

"Doesn't matter. You'll be gone and so will your bastard." Pointing to Charlotte's stomach, she turned to the masked man. "Get her out of here." She jerked her bloodied head toward Charlotte. "You know what to do."

He reached into his back pocket and pulled out a white cloth. Panic crawled up her throat. *They're going to drug me. I can't let him drug me.*

"No!" She screamed and pushed him away when he tried to put the cloth over her mouth. "Help! Somebody help me!" Her phone clattered to the floor in the struggle.

"Quiet!" the man's deep voice ordered.

"P-please. I'll be quiet. Just don't drug me. The baby."

"Get her out of here, Lorenzo."

When he tried to put the cloth over her mouth, Charlotte averted her face in the nick of time and pushed at his mask.

She gasped when she recognized his face. Those once-warm brown eyes were cold now. "L-larry? How? Why? I thought you were my friend."

"Dammit, Lorenzo!"

He shoved the cloth over her nose and mouth. Her eyes fluttered, and her head swam.

Larry's brown eyes filled her vision. She could've sworn she heard him whisper, "I'm sorry."

Chapter Twenty-Five

Jake glanced at the empty seats in the stands. *Something is not right.* They still hadn't returned after twenty minutes.

A phone rang in the dugout. A generic jingle. He couldn't tell if it was his or one of the other guys'.

"What did I say about turning cell phones off during practice?" Coach marched toward it and then grabbed the offending device from the seat. "Someone tell," he glanced at the screen, "Melanie Richards that now isn't a good time. Hell, I'll tell her." He tapped the screen.

Jake ran from the diamond. "Coach—"

"Melanie Richards? This better be life or death because— Shit, okay. Calm down woman. Ross!"

Jake had already reached the dugout and snatched his phone away. "What is it, Mel?"

"Charlotte's in danger. And Gina is the stalker. They're in the restroom, and some guy named Lorenzo or Larry or something just drugged her. Charlotte knew who he was. Gina hit herself and plans to pretend that she was attacked. I've called 9-1-1 and the medics."

Jake's blood ran cold. He dropped his phone, and coach grabbed his shoulder. "What is it, Ross?"

"My girl's in trouble. I gotta go!" He tried to rush past, but his coach grabbed him by the shoulder.

"Practice is over!" Coach yelled to the team. "I'm going with you, Ross."

"Me too," his teammates echoed.

No time to waste. He ran for the stands and then straight to the bathroom.

Fuck, which one is it? He eyed the signs and chose one that pointed right.

Rushing through the door, he found Gina curled up into a ball on the floor. His cooled blood heated to a hundred degrees. Players trickled in and rushed to help her stand. His friend Collins wet a paper towel and gently pressed it against her forehead.

"Where is she?" Jake roared.

She shivered in the corner.

"Calm down, Ross. Can't you see she's in shock?" Collins dabbed at the blood trickling from her head.

"She's the stalker." Jake marched toward her, shaking with rage. "It's all recorded. Melanie was on the phone with Charlotte. She heard everything."

Collins stepped away, dropping the bloodied napkin to the floor. "Guys, let's search around the stadium. Lopez, call security."

A few teammates filed out. Sirens filled the air.

Tears welled in Gina's eyes. "Jake, it's not what you think. I-I love you. From the moment I first saw you I knew you'd be mine, and I—"

"I do not need your shit right now. Where. Is. She!" He grabbed her shoulders and shook. "Where is Charlotte?"

Coach pulled him back. "Don't, Jake. You're better than this."

"Police!" Two uniformed cops and the detective Jake had been working with rushed into the bathroom. They immediately turned their attention to Gina.

"We heard the recording," Detective Wen addressed the shaking woman as the police officers cuffed her hands behind the back. "Ma'am, you're under arrest."

Her eyes narrowed, defiant and dangerous. "You'll never find her, and I'll never tell. She and that bastard won't survive the night." Her smile was slow and dangerous. "If I can't have you—"

"You have the right to remain silent," the detective interrupted her rant. While he recited the Miranda Rights, another officer cuffed Gina and steered her out of the bathroom.

"Ross." The detective's eyes softened with pity. "Our team will be looking at the stadium's security tapes. We'll get him."

Jake dropped to his knees, despair and pain filling his chest like a balloon ready to pop. *I couldn't keep her safe. I've failed her. Failed my family.*

• • •

She was drowning. That was the only explanation for the whooshing in her ears and the blurred vision. Opening her mouth, she forced air into her lungs as she struggled to breathe. Struggled to survive. *Jake. Practice. Gina.*

No, she wasn't drowning. *I was drugged.* She couldn't move and battled to fight off the sluggish haze warping her movements and her mind. Both her hands and feet had been bound together with sticky tape that cut deep into her skin. The van jumped over a pothole, and the rocking motion shifted a pillow cradling her stomach. Licking her dry lips and clearing her parched throat, she tried to speak.

"Larry ... " Her voice was but a whispered croak. She tried again. "Larry. Please don't do this."

"She gets what she wants," he muttered. "She always gets what she wants. I'm sorry."

He sounded sorry, but that wasn't enough. This was life or death. The van jumped again, and this time her body rolled over the lumpy pillow. *A pillow! Deep down he must care.*

She tried again. "Whatever she has over you, we can fix this. She's probably already been arrested. My friend had a hunch Gina was the stalker and called the police. I was talking to her in the bathroom and—"

The van stopped moving, and she stopped bargaining. *This is it.* Her blood pressure skyrocketed. Black dots, large and translucent, filled her vision. This was where she would die. She touched her stomach, and Bean moved.

We can't die. She counted her erratic breaths until the black dots disappeared.

When the door opened, a flood of light poured in. "Up, Charlotte."

She rolled over and sat, her legs straight in front of her and hands behind her back. Something pressed against her bottom. *The pepper spray!* She'd put it in her back pocket after Jake had pressed it into her hand and given her another rundown on how to use it.

Single hand … turn the tab … spray into the air.

Goosebumps formed along her forearm as she scooted out of the van. Puffs of short, rapid breaths revealed her fear. Rich and earthy smells assaulted her nose, and the rush of the river behind them matched the rush of blood in her veins—cold and deadly. Larry, no Lorenzo, pulled her along the worn path, facing her away from the river.

"Larry, I know I can't convince you not to … kill me, but can I have one last request?"

He nodded, but kept his eyes averted.

"Unbind my hands." When he looked up, eyes wide with disbelief, she shrugged. "I can't overpower you anyway, we both know that. I just want to … I want to touch Bean one last time. I don't want him to feel alone. I-I don't want to be alone."

He dipped his chin. "Just your hands.

A small victory. She nodded. *I can do this. I have to save Bean. Save myself. Save Jake.* He wouldn't survive if they didn't. Three fates were tied together.

She flinched when Larry flicked open a Swiss Army Knife. The blade moved closer, but instead of sinking into her flesh, he quickly cut through the gray masking tape. Charlotte rotated her wrists, flexed her fingers, and steadied her nerves. *No room for error.* He took three slow, measured steps back toward the van before reaching behind his back.

She widened her eyes. "Watch out!" She pointed into the distance, and Larry turned his head.

With the speed of a gunslinger, she yanked the pepper spray from her back pocket, slid the tab, and sprayed.

"Ahhh, dammit!" Larry stumbled, cupping his eyes, and the gun tumbled from his meaty hands. Feet still bound, she hopped three steps, grabbed the gun, and flicked off the safety.

"Larry." Calm, despite her frantic heartbeat, she focused. "Your gun is now pointed at your head and, trust me, I know how to use it."

He swung his arms wildly, nearly clipping her in the process. Firing, she shot his right foot.

"Shit! You shot me!"

"You were going to kill my baby and me. I have no sympathy for you. Now, toss your knife, keys, and phone on the ground. To your left."

Tears poured down his cheeks. *No mercy.* The man could be put under the jail for all she cared.

Grimacing in pain, he rubbed his eyes and then tossed his phone and knife.

"Keys?"

"In the van."

Gripping the pepper spray, she pressed the tab again.

"Ahh! Why'd ya do that?" He dropped to his knees and writhed on the ground. A gunshot to the foot *and* pepper spray to the eyes could not be a pleasant combination.

She hopped to retrieve the knife. Bending over, she used it to saw at the tape with one hand while pointing the gun with the other. Precious seconds later, she was free.

Grabbing the phone, she ran to the rusted white van and threw open the door. She slammed the door shut, pressed down the driver door locks, and then reached over to the passenger's side to do the same. Safe and secure, she then checked the ignition and nearly cried when she saw the keys. *Thank God he was telling the truth.*

Twisting the ignition, she revved the engine and drove to freedom. Despite the danger, she smiled, proud of herself. "I did it, Bean. We're going to be okay."

A blaring siren from an ambulance interrupted her self-congratulatory thoughts. She pulled over and clicked the blinkers. A half a dozen police cars sped past her. *Are they looking for me?* She leaned on her horn to grab someone's attention. A lone police car slowed and pulled up behind her.

A short female with red hair and a tall black officer stepped out the vehicle. She wanted to jump and wave, but was afraid of startling them. The male officer approached the driver's side.

"I'm Charlotte Jones. I was kidnapped but managed to escape."

The officer smiled. "We've been looking for you, Ms. Jones. Glad you're okay. Sheila, call it in."

• • •

Here they were. At the hospital. Again. Charlotte sighed as the nurse took her vitals. "I keep telling you I'm fine."

A strong hand squeezed hers. "Let them do their jobs, angel. We have to be sure you and Bean are okay."

Jake's plea and red-rimmed eyes silenced her protest. "I'm sorry. I'm just want to go home."

"I'm so sorry for introducing that psycho into your life. I practically handed you over on a silver platter."

"Stop it." She shook her head. "You aren't to blame."

"But—"

"Bean and I are alive. Don't trouble yourself with anything else."

He smiled, but the gesture was strained and tired, like his eyes.

"All done," her cheery nurse interrupted. "You're very lucky, Ms. Jones. You and the baby are doing well. Your blood pressure is stable, and the baby's heartbeat is strong. The discharge nurse will be here soon. You're good to go."

Charlotte wasn't lucky. She was blessed. The only explanation she was willing to accept. By the grace of God, she'd remained calm and thought quickly. She'd swallowed her sweet nature and had gone full-on Mama Bear.

She smiled at the nurse and then returned her attention to Jake. "Let's go home."

• • •

Two weeks since the abduction, and Jake still had nightmares. Charlotte, however, slept like the baby she was carrying, snoring lightly in his arms. Her feet, like always, were cold. But the rest of her was warm. *Alive.*

Eighty-seven minutes ... that's how long it had taken the police to find her. Gina hadn't cracked, but Melanie filled in the blanks.

She'd heard the name Larry, which Jake recognized. After connecting the dots, they realized he worked for the security company Jake hired based on Gina's recommendation. They'd tracked Lorenzo—aka Larry, Gina's half-brother—by his phone, which the police had later found in the getaway van's glove compartment. Luckily, his angel had escaped by then. So smart and brave. And soon, she would be the mother of his child and, if she was still willing, his wife. He itched to place the ring, nestled in the closet safe, on her finger.

The Yankees had given him a few weeks off to get his personal affairs in order, and he'd spent every single moment with

Charlotte. Not only because he was anxious after the kidnapping, but because he enjoyed her company. Enjoyed relaxing and lazing around at his condo. But now time was up, and tomorrow, he had to go to training.

He squeezed her tighter, kissing the back of her neck.

She wiggled and mumbled. "What time is it?"

He glanced at the clock on his stand. "Six." Too early for his surprise.

"Oh." Her stomach grumbled. "Too early for breakfast?"

He grinned against her neck. "It's never too early, baby. What do you want?"

"That low-fat berry cobbler you made?"

"Cobbler it is. Let me go warm it up."

"I'll come with you. I need to stretch my legs."

Getting out of bed, Jake walked toward the kitchen while Charlotte wobbled to the living room.

"My feet are cold."

"Where are your socks?" he asked over his shoulder.

"The bedroom. I'll grab them. Can we watch some TV?"

The woman could get him to do anything, including dancing in the middle of Times Square butt-naked.

"Of course, angel."

He plated the cobbler and turned on the living room light.

Charlotte squinted. "It's a little bright."

"Yeah, sorry. I couldn't see." His hands shook slightly as he placed the dessert and fork in front of her. He then rushed back to the kitchen and poured a glass of milk.

"So I was going to wait to show you, but I found a new comic book. It's a mixture between *Wonder Woman* and *The Invincible Iron Man* with Riri." Charlotte had been excited when Marvel had announced the new Iron Man would be a young black woman.

"Ohhh! Who is the creator?"

"Can't remember." Jake shrugged. "I'll go get it."

Running into the bedroom, Jake opened the door to his safe before returning to the living room with the pristine comic covered in plastic, and dropping it next to his angel.

"Ohh, fancy. I can smell the newness." Putting her plate down, she reached for the book. "Gimme!"

"*The Angel Jones Chronicles. Volume I.*"

"Oh, liking the connection already." She turned the page. The first scene was a young, curvy female surrounded by kids in a dance studio.

She looked up, wonderment shinning in her brown eyes. "Is this … is this me?"

"You tell me." He smiled. "Keep reading."

"This is the story of Angel Jones. By day, she melts the hearts of kids and parents alike at a nonprofit and teaches the community to dance. But don't let her breathtaking looks and warm heart fool you. Agent Angel Jones is one smart, courageous, and dangerous woman."

She turned the pages and smiled and laughed and cried. "I'm liking the love interest, Jax Ross." With a snort, Charlotte flipped more pages. "Nice. I'm telepathic, a healer, and I can control the elements. I am so kick-ass! I can't believe you remembered!" she yelled, referencing their earlier conversation about superpowers.

"You can do one more thing, too."

She turned the page. "I can fly!" She pumped her fist in the air.

"Of course you can. All angels can fly."

"And these are cool-looking wings. What are they made of?"

"Vibranium."

"Nice. From Wakanda? Like the Black Panther?"

"Only the best for you, baby."

She laughed as she turned the last page, then her smile dropped, and tears filled her eyes. Lifting the comic, she pointed to Jax Ross down on bended knee with a ring in hand. "Do you mean it?"

Jake knelt on the floor. "Angel. You are the smartest, kindest, and most resilient person I know. I wake up thankful you're in my arms. I love the life we are creating and, most of all, I love you. Would you please do me the honor," he reached into the pockets of his jogging pants, "of becoming my wife?"

Her mouth gaped open, but nothing came out. Fear curled his stomach. Too aggressive? Too quick in asking her to marry him?

I should've given her more time. He cleared his throat. "Or … or not."

"Not?" Her glazed-over eyes cleared. "No."

"No?"

She shook her head. "No, I mean yes! Of course, I'll marry you. I'd be crazy to say no!"

"Thank God. I was all out of moves." Releasing a breath, he slid the ring onto her finger. "I love you, angel. I'm crazy for you."

She grabbed his face and kissed him. "I'm crazy for you, too."

Epilogue

Six years later

The kids ran around outside the five-bedroom house in the Hamptons. Damien, Nathan, and Jake were on grill duty, while Melanie, Tiana, and Charlotte were on relaxing duty. Little Alexander, Jodie, Ramona, and Layla squealed as they chased each other around the yard.

Alexander—aka Alex, formerly Bean—was now five and a half years old and proudly boasted that fact to anyone who would listen. Pivoting on one foot, he nearly trampled Jodie, Tiana and Nathan's daughter.

"Be careful!" Charlotte yelled. "She's smaller than you. You can't be rough."

Jodie pushed Alex from behind. "I not small!" the four-year-old yelled.

"Stop it, stupid!" Alex yelled back, scrambling to his feet.

Melanie, who'd been telling the ladies a story, paused to gush at the kids. "Ah, true love!" Tiana and Charlotte nodded. All three women agreed that Jodie and Alex were meant to be.

Melanie and Damien's daughters, three-year-old Romana and two-year-old Layla, toddled behind the older pair.

"Finish up the story. Tell me you didn't invite the terrible duo to our cookout?" Tiana asked.

Melanie had run into her and Damien's former childhood best friend Terrance, Damien's former fiancée Vanessa, and their twin boys. They'd broken ties with the couple after Vanessa had cheated with Terrance.

"I was going to, but Damien clapped his hand over my mouth, told them I had the flu, and didn't want them to get sick." She rolled her eyes and shrugged. "It's been like eight years. I'm over it. And to be honest, they looked good together. They seemed like a normal, happy family." Mel bounced from her chair. "You ladies want a margarita? I think we waited a respectable two hours since we've arrived."

"Umm … I'm not really in the mood for a margarita." Charlotte's voice was high-pitched.

"I'm just going to keep my water for now," Tiana added and then sipped hard from the bottle.

Cocking her hip, Mel stared at both of them as if cross-examining a witness on the stand.

"Wait a minute. Since when have either of you turned down a margarita? Don't tell me you both are preggers."

Charlotte averted her eyes and pretended to watch the kids. Tiana looked at the sky.

"Both of you? At the same time? God help me. How many months?"

They both were silent. "C'mon, spill it."

"Ten weeks," Charlotte confessed, secretly thrilled to tell her friends. She'd wanted to wait a few more weeks, but Melanie had guessed it. After Alex was born, she'd gotten her blood glucose to a healthy range and now could have a normal pregnancy this time around.

"Fourteen weeks." Tiana sighed. "Nathan wanted us to tell you tonight. Act surprised, will you?"

Melanie's eyes went wide. "Why didn't you both tell me sooner? We could've coordinated our pregnancies. Now I'll be the lone unpregnant woman."

"You and Damien already popped out two. No offense, but you are the worst pregnant person ever."

"Am not!" she whined.

"Are, too," Tiana shot back. "You bellyached about your swollen feet, you demanded fresh fruit every morning, and you wanted shoulder rubs … from everyone!"

"Defamation!" Melanie raised a pointed finger into the air.

Tiana gave her a bored look. "Use it in a sentence, crazy lady. Otherwise, you won't get points for word of the day."

"I will sue you for defamation of character due to your malicious and unfounded lies."

"Ten points, Melanie." Charlotte joined in on the game. Melanie and Tiana had allowed her to join the word game a few years ago, with a lot of pomp and circumstance surrounding it. In other words, with copious amounts of nachos and margaritas.

"What are you going to do about the agency?" Charlotte asked Tiana. Tiana and Nathan had started their own marketing agency a few months ago.

"Oh, I'll still be involved up until I pop and we just hired a junior account manager to help with our workload. I can't let Nathan have all the fun!" She smirked.

Damien, Nathan, and Jake walked toward them in the front yard.

Jake bent over, lightly touched Charlotte's stomach, and then kissed her lips. "Food is ready." His deep voice sent delicious tingles up her spine. "Gotta feed the baby," he whispered.

Smiling, she grabbed his hand. "C'mon, Alex. We're moving the party to the backyard."

Alex rushed to his father, baseball cap on his head. "Daddy!" He hopped into Jake's arms.

Jake hugged him and gave him a noisy kiss on the cheek.

"Yuck, Daddy!" Alex giggled.

"Fine then. I'll just kiss Mommy. Mommy loves my kisses." Jake bent down and gave her a sensual kiss.

"Ewww ... yucky, Daddy!"

"Not yucky. Mommy is the yummiest thing I've ever tasted."

Melanie giggled from behind them. "And that's how Mommy and Daddy made another Bean!"

Acknowledgments

Wow! I can't believe this series has come to an end. I can't lie; this is bittersweet. Melanie and Damien, Tiana and Nathaniel, and Charlotte and Jacob have become my friends. I have real friends, I promise, but it's so hard to say good-bye. In fact, I'm listening to the Boyz II Men song right now.

The Crush On You series wouldn't exist without the help of others, and as I close out this series I have a lot of people to thank, so bear with me.

First and foremost, I'd like to give honor to God. Without his added strength, I would've given up on my dream of being published a long time ago. Thanks to the Crimson Romance family for giving me a chance. Jess, I'll miss your hilarious comments on tracked changes.

To my husband, Jason—thank you for believing in me. To my mother, who cultivated my love for reading and writing.

To my critique partners (I have a lot of them) Connie Gilliam, Ison Hill, Mary Marvella, and Pamela Varnado— thanks for making me a stronger writer. Thank you, Annie Oortman, for encouraging me to dig deeper.

To my cousin and number one beta reader, Charidee—thank you for being honest and making my stories better.

To my family, who harasses their coworkers and friends to buy my books. Special shout-out to my father and stepmother. And to my cousins, Shameka, Brittany, and Gia, and my aunts Wilma, Shirley, and Laine.

To all my family and friends who supported me through social media, word of mouth, or just checking in on me—I love and appreciate all of you.

And last, but certainly not least, thank you, dear reader. Your kind words, feedback, and reviews fuel me to keep going. I hope you were entertained!

About the Author

Rina Gray writes romance and women's fiction. She is also a digital marketing professional who explored her love of writing a few years ago. Writing has always been Rina's passion, though initially, she tried to deny it. In college she served as the copy editor for the entertainment magazine and newspaper. During her tenure, she had the opportunity to interview various talented entertainers. Rina has always been an avid reader, sneaking to read her mother's books she had no business reading, which sparked her love for horror. As a preteen, she received a load of romance novels from a family friend, and from that point, she devoured any book related to romance or horror.

Rina tweets about her writing journey and her unhealthy obsession with the NBA @rinagraywrites. Feel free to connect on Facebook: https://www.facebook.com/AuthorRinaGray. Her website is www.RinaGray.com.